# DEATH IN NORTH BEACH

# DEATH IN NORTH BEACH

A Carly Paladino and Noah Lang Mystery

## Ronald Tierney

This first world edition published 2009
in Great Britain and in 2010 the USA by
SEVERN HOUSE PUBLISHERS LTD of
9–15 High Street, Sutton, Surrey, England, SM1 1DF.
Trade paperback edition published
in Great Britain and the USA 2010 by
SEVERN HOUSE PUBLISHERS LTD

British Library Cataloguing in Publication Data

Tierney, Ronald
   Death in North Beach. – (A Paladino and Lang mystery)
   1. Novelists – Crimes against – Fiction. 2. Private
  investigators – California – San Francisco – Fiction.
   3. North Beach (San Francisco, Calif.) – Fiction.
   4. Detective and mystery stories.
   I. Title II. Series
   813.5'4-dc22


ISBN-13: 978-0-7278-6850-3   (cased)
ISBN-13: 978-1-84751-199-7   (trade paper)

*All Severn House titles are printed on acid-free paper.*

Severn House Publishers support The Forest Stewardship Council [FSC],
the leading international forest certification organisation. All our titles that
are printed on Greenpeace-approved FSC-certified paper carry the FSC logo.

**Mixed Sources**
Product group from well-managed
forests and other controlled sources
www.fsc.org Cert no. SA-COC-1565
© 1996 Forest Stewardship Council

Typeset by Palimpsest Book Production Ltd.,
Grangemouth, Stirlingshire, Scotland.
Printed and bound in Great Britain by
MPG Books Ltd., Bodmin, Cornwall.

*For Tao*

# Acknowledgements

Thanks to brothers Richard and Ryan and to David Anderson, Ray Ng, Jovanne Reilly and Karen Watt for their help.

San Francisco's North Beach isn't a beach. It once was. But a portion of the Bay was filled in to make room for more buildings. Now it is a low-rise village tucked in between Chinatown, the Financial District, Jackson Square, and the lofty neighborhoods of Russian Hill and Telegraph Hill.

North Beach is half tourist and half authentic San Francisco. The neighborhood wasn't made to look like an old Italian neighborhood. It is an old Italian neighborhood. True, modernity crept in as families died off. A hardware is gone. So are a few family-style restaurants. But the chain stores were kept at bay. There are no Olive Gardens or Starbucks. No Borders. No Banana Republics. No skyscraping office buildings or condominiums.

The Beat Generation was born here and so, perhaps, was the idea of Americans hanging around in coffee houses. It was and still is, in a sadly decreasing way, the neighborhood of poets, artists, writers, philosophers and strippers. Most of the Beats are very old or very dead now.

One of them, old and very recently dead, floats in a shallow pond on a small triangular island at the intersection of three streets. A few feet away from the pond, across one of those streets, was the victim's favorite watering hole, the Washington Square Bar and Grill. Lovingly called the 'Washbag' by its colorful and often celebrity clientele, the landmark has died and been reborn a few times. The cosmic jury is still out on Whitney Warfield.

# One

Inspector Vincente Gratelli, a man who looked older than his 60-some-odd years, didn't have to come far. He was awakened at five a.m. in his North Beach flat and told there was a body a few blocks away. By five twenty-five, the San Francisco police detective was there, standing within the confines of a waist-high wrought-iron fence that enclosed the strange little pond, a tree, a bush or two and some purple flowers. The body, suited, shiny and dark, looking like the wrinkled carcass of a walrus, had been pulled out. It rested on a bed of ivy.

Gratelli buttoned up his threadbare London Fog raincoat and tightened the scarf around his neck. The scarf wasn't there as a fashion statement. The air was damp and often cold even on September mornings and he had become prone to sore throats. He went about his business despite the grogginess of his brain. It was too early even for a cup of coffee. Caffe Trieste, his usual stop on the way to work, didn't open until six thirty. He'd been rousted from bed and missed his morning routine. He needn't have hurried. The dead, he reminded himself, were a patient lot.

Though he told no one, he guessed that the man was killed or placed at the scene around four a.m. It would be the time when the usually busy neighborhood would be the most quiet – after the bars closed and before the locals headed for work. The medical examiner and CSI had been called. A few early-risers had gathered and Gratelli had the benefit of a couple of uniforms to keep order. One of them called it in after a Chinese woman coming from the number 30 Stockton bus discovered the body.

Gratelli found the dead man's wallet. Aside from the credit cards, much of the wallet's contents were saturated. The driver's license, however, was laminated. Gratelli used a pocket flashlight to illuminate it. The name on it was Whitney Warfield.

Gratelli winced. Not usually excitable, the inspector realized what he had on his hands – a big, self-promoting curmudgeon of a novelist and an active political provocateur murdered in a sensational fashion. Gratelli looked around. A few more police cars had arrived and the intersection was lit like a carnival. Fortunately, because of the hour, it would be a while before the media arrived. But they would most certainly be there before the morning news.

Whitney Warfield, Gratelli knew, was a North Beach habitué. He lived just up on Russian Hill. He was a close friend of the North Beach board supervisor, one of eleven elected officials to advise and frustrate the mayor. He had legions of enemies; but they were usually journalists, novelists, the rich and the powerful, whom he held in contempt. None were likely to kill the author over his self-puffery and theatrical tirades — all designed to keep a writer who hadn't written anything of note in some time from fading from the limelight.

Gratelli verified the face against the photo on the license and allowed the thin, weak beam of light to traverse Warfield's body, discovering something long and cylindrical protruding from the side of Whitney Warfield's neck. It was a pen, a fountain pen. A Mont Blanc. An expensive weapon to leave behind. The killer had gone so far as to put the cap on the end.

Carly Paladino was afraid she'd be early. Her friend Anselmo was an angel of the night; an old angel, but an angel. He was an artist. Paladino, half of Paladino & Lang Investigations, was recently ensconced in a refurbished office and wanted one of Anselmo's paintings for the large wall behind her desk. She liked having familiar things around her, things that reminded her of people she cared about or times she could remember with fondness. Anselmo was part of that. A friend of her parents, his work was often featured in the restaurant they owned.

Anselmo lived in an alley not far from the heart of North Beach, a block from Washington Square and the imposing Saints Peter and Paul Church. The door to his place was open. The stairway that went up to his second floor space was before her. That door was open too. Perhaps Anselmo was expecting someone. He would be surprised to see her.

At the top of the steps she could see him in through the doorway of a room beyond the entry. He was face down on an oversized sofa, his huge body a range of rounded hills. As she moved closer, she worried that he might be dead.

'Anselmo,' she said, at first softly, then increasingly louder. 'Anselmo, Anselmo.'

His face was smashed against the corner of the pillow as if it had arrived there as a result of some terrible collision.

She leaned down, ear against his nose. He was breathing.

'Mo!' she said sharply, still thinking there might be something wrong.

The old man awakened with a start. Disoriented. Eyes darted for something familiar or solid. He looked at Carly. Still startled. For a moment, at least, Carly's face, like the rest of the universe, was undecipherable.

Wearing a black robe over some sort of black sleeping gown, the old man lurched to his feet, stumbled. Arms stretched out for a wall or a chair or a solid body, perhaps. His face was red, cheek creased, eyes settling now. He put his hand against the wall.

'Do you always get up this way?' Carly asked.

Anselmo took a deep breath. He looked around uncertainly.

'It is becoming more and more difficult to come back. Soon, maybe, I'll just stay.'

His eyes seemed to focus. He ran his hand down his full, silver beard.

'Did I tell you what happened last night?'

'How could you,' she asked. 'This is the first time I've seen you in months.'

'Ah, you never know about these things, Carly. Time is funny. You'll learn that some day.' His eyes softened. His face wrinkled in a smile. 'You are so beautiful, Carly. You've put this new day in a golden light. I've always had a crush on you, you know.'

'You have more crushes than a schoolgirl,' she said. He did. He wasn't fickle. He just loved – or hated – passionately, frequently.

Carly felt fortunate she could still charm him. She loved coming to the studio. She loved everything about the place. The smells especially. Oils and mineral spirits infiltrated by damp must. Anselmo had those scents about him, the smells of a painter's studio mixed with the smells of wine and tobacco.

'What brings you here?' he asked as she followed him to the kitchen, though the word kitchen might be too specific. All the rooms were rooms he worked in. He put a bent tea kettle on the stove and fired up the burner.

'I want to purchase a painting,' she said.

'You do?' He smiled.

'Yes. For my office.'

'Your stuffy old security firm?'

'No,' she said. 'I left Vogel Security. I'm out on my own.'

'Well, that's entirely wonderful,' he said, fumbling with a crumpled pack of cigarettes, eventually wrestling one loose. 'You're going to finally live a little, is that what you're saying?'

'Seems to be what's happening.'

'Tell you what, you model for me and you can go in the back room and have your pick of the paintings.'

'Model for you?'

'Yes. Nude. A celebration of your freedom.' He fumbled about and found an oversized matchbox.

'I'm not sure I'm that free, yet. And, Mo, I'm far from the nubile young women you usually paint.'

'You are beautiful. Look at you. You are slender where it counts. You have some flesh where it counts. Your dark hair and deep Italian eyes. My God, Carly. You are at that wonderful age when a woman is a woman. You are an inspiration.'

She smiled at his compliments. She didn't know what was so wonderful about her age.

He lit his cigarette. His eyes, rather than looking at her, looked beyond and behind her.

Carly turned to see a handsome man, dark hair with a little silver. He wore expensive clothes and wore them well.

'William,' Anselmo called out. 'Come in and meet Carly Paladino, the most beautiful woman in the world. Carly, say hello to Sweet William, the most charming man in the world. What a fine coincidence.'

William smiled, shook hands with Carly.

'Have you known this old poseur long?' William asked her.

'Since I was a little girl,' she said.

'Then there's no need to protect you,' he said. 'May I interrupt you two for just a moment? I have something urgent to discuss with Anselmo. For just a moment or two.'

'Certainly.'

'You know where I keep the masterpieces, Carly,' Anselmo said. 'Go pick one and I'll be with you shortly to discuss payment options.' He winked.

As Carly rummaged through the large paintings, all leaning against each other, she understood that she wasn't getting the right perspective. Anselmo painted as passionately as he lived. His work was achieved with broad, thick brushstrokes that created images in the abstract. She'd have to pull out the ones that she was drawn to and step back from them to fully appreciate them.

She slid one out carefully and brought it to the light. Closer to the other room, she heard what seemed to be William's desperate whispers and Anselmo's more controlled and audible voice saying, 'Calm down,' and 'I'm sure it's not as bad as you think.'

Carly was troubled by her impulse to listen more closely. But what could they expect, she thought, having a private investigator in the next room. Invading privacy was somewhere between a natural inclination and an undeniable urge.

'They heard us arguing,' said the whispering voice of the person the painter called 'Sweet William'.

'I haven't read the papers,' Anselmo said. 'What time was he killed?'

Carly couldn't make out the answer, but it was something about not being in the papers yet. She used to watch the morning news as she got ready to go to work at the security firm. Now that she was on her own, she was a little more casual about a lot of things. One of them was weaning herself from the morning shows. It was a depressing start to the day. The news was never good and the anchors tried to make up for it by an obscene amount of gushing goodwill.

This morning she had purposely avoided the news, taking her coffee and yogurt on her deck overlooking Mr Nakamura's garden belonging to the flat below. She had read a few chapters of Amy Tan's *Saving Fish From Drowning* before setting out for North Beach and her old friend, Anselmo. She wondered if she had missed something important because something important was going on in the next room. Carly was torn between listening to the sounds and looking at the paintings. She had pulled out two when Anselmo appeared.

'Oh,' he said, '"Fawn at Dawn" and "Salmon Moon".'

'That's what they are,' Carly said, not hiding the sarcasm. William had appeared in the doorway, pale but smiling.

'Why don't you give William your card, Carly?' He shrugged. 'Just in case.'

'Sure.' She retrieved a card from her bag, strewn in a corner. 'In whatever case,' she said, trying to tone down her sudden urge to flirt. William, she thought, belonged in a French film. She would even let him smoke a cigarette if he insisted.

William looked at the card. His smile seemed genuine though it didn't match his eyes. He was troubled.

'Thank you, Ms Paladino,' he said. 'Don't take offense, but I hope I don't need you.'

'Call me Carly. Though it's against my best interest, I hope you don't either.'

\*   \*   \*

Noah Lang, the other half of Paladino & Lang Investigations, watched as Carly struggled with the large canvas. He was standing in the little reception area of their newly expanded and revamped office. His dress was casual – worn jeans and a sweatshirt.

'A little help?' he asked.

'I got it,' she said. And she did, successfully maneuvering it through the office door.

It seemed to Lang that the look of her office had become a priority project. He knew she was trying as best she could to make the space her own, not to mention establish a little island of taste and dignity in an otherwise desolate environment.

Shortly after Carly moved in with Lang, they discovered the quarters were just a little too close. So when ageing PI Barry Brinkman, who had a neighboring office, told them he had to give up his space because he could no longer afford a place to nap and read the paper, the three of them worked out a deal and the landlord agreed. They knocked out a wall and connected the spaces.

Brinkman, who had his own PI agency for more years than he could count and who now came to work because he had nothing else to do, settled for a small, windowless room in the rear of Lang's office at token rent. Lang had his original office space back, defeating the purpose of subletting his space for additional income. Carly had her own space and Thanh could sit in the reception area or in Lang's office on those occasions when this mysterious and illusive being of alternating genders appeared. The three of them – Lang, Thanh and Brinkman – formed the little family in which Carly Paladino uneasily found herself, much to the amusement of Noah Lang.

He followed her into her office.

'You found a way to fit that into your little clown car?' he said, referring to her sporty little Mini Cooper

'It's only a clown car when you're in it,' she said, leaning the painting against the wall behind her desk. 'I tied it to the roof.'

'I'm surprised you didn't have lift-off.'

She ignored him. She took the large bag from her shoulder, tossed it on her desk. The *San Francisco Chronicle* spilled out. She turned back to stare at her new painting. He couldn't tell whether it was admiration or an appraisal. There were things about her he didn't quite understand. He liked that fact.

'What is it?' he asked.

'A fawn.'

'Oh.'

'At dawn,' she said. She looked at him, daring him to say something.

He wasn't sure how far he could go. They were still getting used to each other. Perhaps he had gone too far with the friendly jabs. But if that was a fawn, then Lang had a stain on his carpet that was the *Mona Lisa*.

'You don't like it?' she asked.

'I didn't say that.'

She looked at him. Expectation was on her face.

'Classy,' he said. 'Looks like we're movin' on up.'

He went back to his office, sat in the chair with the ripped seat, and put his hands on the wood desk, a piece of furniture out of the fifties with ring marks, dents, stains and scratches. The plant under the dusty window looked unhappy. The sofa was a green Naugahyde disaster. Its still shiny pillows floated precariously on a frame with broken springs. When the new office was annexed, the whole place got a coat of paint. Unfortunately, the contrast of old and new merely made his office look shabbier.

'Classy,' he said. He thought that most would think a man barely this side of middle age would have had a more mature environment in which to work. They, of course, would be mistaken.

'You busy?' Carly asked, waiting in the doorway.

'Just adding up all my assets. I just started. OK, I'm done.'

'I need a set of eyes.'

He followed her back into her office. She held up the painting, which was about as wide as she was tall. She lowered and raised it.

'There,' Lang said.

She moved it left and right.

'There.'

'Could you hold it here while I mark it?'

He did. She put two pencil marks and he put the painting down. She reached in her purse to get two sturdy nails and one tiny hammer.

'You borrow that from the Keebler elves?'

'I did. By the way, they don't like you.'

She pounded in the nails. It was slow going, but eventually she got the job done.

'Seems as if you live in a miniature world,' he said. She didn't answer.

Lang looked down at the newspaper. It was a late city edition, a rarity these days.

As Lang left Carly's office, his eye caught a photograph of San Francisco legend Whitney Warfield four columns wide and above the fold. The headline read: 'Warfield Dead in the Water'. Lang didn't know Warfield, but knew of him. Who didn't? The headline was a surprisingly playful reference to one of his books, *Dead in the Water*, one of the many books Lang hadn't read.

Lang was more of a movie guy. In fact, tonight, he was going to have crab cakes and beer and watch three of his favorites – *Blood Simple*, *Blood and Wine* and *Red Rock West* – all gritty little films about nasty people.

# Two

One could guess his age and be off ten years either way. Maybe more. On this sunny morning, Thanh wore a straw hat, a white silky shirt open two buttons at the neck, light, sharply creased slacks, and something of a cross between shoes and sandals. He – and Thanh was a 'he' today – looked a little pimpish or just maybe in the wrong town. This was fog city, not sin city. But it was also September. Essentially summer. That San Francisco is in California is a myth – except during the warm and sunny months of September and October.

Thanh stood just inside Lang's office this beautiful morning, not only wearing cool but being cool.

'There's a guy here looking for Carly.'

'Do I look like Carly?' Lang asked without looking up.

'No, I guess not. But maybe if we did something with your hair . . .'

When Lang looked up he got the full 'Thanh in the tropics' effect.

'You thinking about moving to Manila?' Lang asked him.

'You going out for a game of touch football?' Thanh said. 'You're one to talk. Look at you. You've worn the same sweatshirt for three days.'

'This week. All last week as well.'

'When was the last time you washed your jeans?'

'Oh, you're supposed to wash these things?'

'Now, take our guy waiting for Carly,' Thanh said. 'Good-looking guy. Expensive clothes. Sharp crease in his pants. Asked for her by name.'

'That's all very nice. I'm happy for him, but why are you telling me?'

'She isn't here.'

'Give him a magazine.'

Thanh sighed and left. One couldn't predict who Thanh would be tomorrow. It wasn't a game, this endless supply of identities. It was a way of life.

Lang looked at his watch. Carly was late. There were no posted hours, but during their relatively brief period as partners, she almost always beat him in.

He heard a door shut, conversation, introductions. All was well with the world. He went back to his computer, and his Netflix page. He was hungry for more of the kind of movies he watched last night. As he scanned a list of noir choices, he dialed up his iPod for 'Tony Bennett Sings Duke Ellington'. He would call around to see if he could dig up business, but he'd wait until ten. Meanwhile, he'd play. After all, he was his own boss and a very lenient one at that.

'Do I call you Sweet William?' Carly asked when they were seated in her office. To say she was aware of his green eyes would be an understatement.

'If you want to, but only Anselmo calls me that, a name he gave me years ago.'

He wore a blue blazer, a white shirt and Palomino-colored pants, all custom-made, Carly was sure. Loosely draped and elegant. If she had known he was visiting, she would have taken a little more care of her own appearance. However, at the moment, she was working on a more relaxed image.

'What can I do to help you?'

'I have some questions for you first. Do you mind?' William asked.

'No, it makes sense. What would you like to know?'

'What is your background?'

'I worked for more years than I care to mention at Vogel Security – one of the most prestigious investigation firms in the country.'

'And you went out on your own?' he asked.

'Yes. I hit the glass ceiling and the work was becoming routine,' Carly said.

'How big a firm is this?'

'We're small, just Noah Lang and I for the most part.'

'And Mr Lang?'

'He has been here for several years. He has tremendous experience in criminal defense work.' She waited to see if his expression changed. His blink, longer than usual, confirmed her feeling that he was here about Whitney Warfield. 'That can be helpful, right?' she asked.

William took a deep breath, looked around, started to talk, but stopped. He nodded toward the doorway.

'Thanh,' Carly called out.

'Yes.'

'Can you hear what we're saying?'

'It'd be better if you'd talk a little louder.'

William smiled, got up, peered around the doorway. 'Nothing personal,' he said, closing the door. He returned to his seat.

'You overheard us at Anselmo's.'

'I hoped you'd talk a little louder,' she said, smiling.

'The police came to my place early this morning,' he said.

'What did you tell them?'

'Nothing. I went out the back.'

'Not to drive business away, but maybe you need a lawyer not an investigator.'

'Look,' William said, standing, walking to the window. 'Here's my take on this. I was with Whitney late the night of his death. We were in a bar in North Beach. We were arguing. It got hot. He was drunk and unreasonable, though he doesn't have to be drunk to be unreasonable. He stumbled out. I followed. We argued on the street. Not good. Add to this,' he continued as he moved back toward her, 'most would not consider me a paragon of virtue. I'm a professional companion.' He waited. Carly remained quiet. 'There are other names.'

'There was a song,' she said.

He smiled.

'Once the police put my career and the argument together, they won't look anywhere else. And even if they can't prove I did it and don't, in fact, indict me, the suspicion alone is a career killer. What I need is for someone to find the killer. That's the only way I'm safe.'

'Were you drunk?'

'No. I never have more than two drinks in public.'

'What were you arguing about?'

'Are you working for me?'

It was clear to Carly he didn't want to say a whole lot more unless they had an agreement.

'Yes.' She explained rates and conditions, which included a retainer. 'I'll put it in writing.'

'I'll take you at your word. We were arguing over a book he was writing.'

'You were going to be in it, I bet.'

'I was, but that wasn't the worst part. I have had relationships with people to whom I promised absolute discretion. As smart as he is . . . was . . . discretion was not part of his vocabulary.'

'But if you didn't tell him anything . . .'

'He picked up a lot of gossip. Most of it was wrong. But if I corrected him, I was collaborating and going against my word. If I didn't correct him he was going to take it as a confirmation of his suspicions. And there were foolish people who confided in him as well as people who passed along confidences. He traded in such gossip.'

'Who are the people most likely to get hurt by the book?'

He gave the question a lot of thought.

'This is going to be absolutely essential. This is the suspect pool, William.'

He nodded, but stayed quiet.

'You've got to trust someone.'

He smiled. 'Not trusting has been the reason I've survived.'

'You mean that in a general sense,' she said.

'Yes.'

'I'm sorry. But in this case, silence is like going to the doctor and not telling her where you hurt.'

He nodded, but was still deliberating.

'I'm charging by the hour, William. And I'd think time isn't on your side.'

'Whitney knew that his life was coming to an end.'

'He knew someone wanted to kill him?'

'No. He was old and not in the best of health. It was a matter of time. And so far the end hadn't been kind to him. His books went out of print. The media didn't call him . . . about anything anymore. His old circle of friends and enemies were dying off. His whole story was losing relevance. He wanted to chronicle his time, with him as the star, of course. To build himself up, to make himself heroic, he had to drag down a few contemporaries, living and dead.'

'Somebody didn't want him to finish his book.'

'That seems the logical answer,' William said.

'Including you.'

'Precisely. The police would make that connection first. That, coupled with the events preceding his death, puts me right in the center of all this.'

'Did you and Whitney have an affair?'

'No. I can't tell you the number of very straight men who, after a certain age, flirt with the idea of playing around with a younger man. This is much more common than anyone admits. But Whitney had an overabundance of testosterone. He was definitely and wholly into women. But he was very interested in knowing the gritty details about those who liked to jump the fence now and then.'

'And you. Do you see women?'

He smiled. 'Yes. Most of my relationships are with women.'

'But?'

'Of course. I love people. I love money. I like the good life. I don't appear to have the same inhibitions as most people.'

'Different inhibitions. Like trust.'

'Yes.' He smiled. His green eyes bored through her.

She could see him on the arm of some middle-aged woman on opening night for the opera or symphony.

'Where are you living?'

He was considering a response, it appeared, not giving one.

'And your last name?' she added. 'Trust, remember.'

'Blake,' he said, smiling. 'You'll have to trust me on that. I travel some. But I live most of the time in a condo on Telegraph Hill.'

'You own it?'

'And you ask this because?'

'I guess I'm interested in how self-reliant you are financially,' she said.

'You want to be sure I can pay you?' he asked.

'That too. But I need to understand your motives. You've already admitted that you love money.'

'I don't own it. I house-sit for someone who comes to San Francisco for a month once a year.'

'He or she lets you stay there?'

'Yes.'

It was clear he wasn't ashamed of his life. Carly made no judgment either. Growing up in San Francisco, one learns quickly about how life is.

'Are you a native?' she asked.

'Yes. All my life. I come from a long line of companions,' he said, smiling again. Warm, flirting, funny. 'You?'

'I come from a restaurant family. Here all my life. I even live in the home I grew up in, near Lafayette Park. When my parents passed on, I inherited it. And as things seem to be going, I'll die there too.'

'Not too soon, I hope.'

'I plan to be around for a while.'

'I'd like to think I will too. I might need your help with that.'

'Beyond the police, do you think your life is in danger?'

'That's something I cannot know without knowing who killed Whitney. So, you see, I have very important reasons to find the murderer.'

'I need a list of all those people Whitney was writing about – that you know of. I need to know where he hangs out? What people he hangs out with? Friends, girlfriends. Can you do that?'

'Yes,' he said, sitting again. 'I can write them down now, if you like.'

'Good.'

She handed him a yellow legal tablet. He pulled out a black Mont Blanc pen from inside his jacket and began to jot down names.

'I'm going away,' William said without looking up.

'Where?'

'Just away.'

'For how long?'

'I don't know yet,' he said, looking up.

'It will make you look guilty. Running away.'

'I go away a lot,' he said. 'I don't tell people where I go. I could be in Europe for three months. No one would know. For all practical purposes, I'm not running. I simply have an engagement elsewhere.'

'How will I contact you?'

'I'll be in touch.' He reached in his breast pocket and pulled out a stack of banded bills. 'Retainer. I know you can't guarantee that you can investigate without getting noticed, especially the police, but I'd appreciate as much discretion as possible.'

He finished writing the list.

'I'm not sure the killer is on the list. But it's a start, I hope.'

'It is.'

'Thank you,' he said, nodding to her with a smile.

Paladino thought he didn't seem frightened. There was a confidence, or maybe aloofness, in his persona that suggested he was at home in the universe or, at best, had made peace with it. It was an attractive quality.

'William,' she said getting up and temporarily interrupting his departure.

'Yes.'

'This list,' she said, 'how do you know all this?'

'He told me. He was going to "slice and dice" them. That's how he said it. He told me who because he wanted what I knew about them.

Some of them I didn't even know. Some are dead. They aren't on the list.'

'So that's a complete list?'

'I can't guarantee that. Those are the people he said were on the list, the people he was going to get.'

Again he started toward the door. This time, he had it open.

'William.'

He paused, turned back slowly, waiting for her question.

'What were you arguing about?'

'What?' he asked.

It was a reflexive remark. He had heard her. He wanted time to think before answering.

'You and Mr Warfield.'

'What I told you. He was intentionally going to hurt other people.'

'Other people? Not you?'

'Me too, of course.' His smile let her know he was aware of having been caught.

'Why? How was he hurting you?'

'Some of these are people whose lives I've shared and because of caring for them I've been rewarded with kindness. We established that earlier, didn't we?'

'Wow,' Carly said. 'Did we dance around that one?'

'We did.' He smiled again. 'Let's do it next time with a little music.' He moved back toward her. 'Discretion is important. If you need more specific answers for your investigation, I'll be happy to share some deeply personal moments. But if this is for your . . . one's . . . personal curiosity, I'd prefer to leave this vague.'

'We'll see, William. I may need to know. I may need the details.'


# Three


'Let's go get lunch,' Lang said, looking up at Carly.

'Now?'

'It's early afternoon. While some folks may prefer lunch at midnight, I'm told many people often eat lunch this time of day,' he said.

'Some people . . .' She halted. Whatever she was going to say, she thought better of it. She took note of Lang's sandy good looks, rougher than William's smooth beauty. Interesting to compare men, she thought. Lang was a straight-on kind of guy. William seemed to cultivate mystery. Both were charming in their ways. Then there was Thanh. What was she to make of him? Or her?

'It'll take a while to find a parking place in North Beach,' Lang said. 'We can get a bite to eat, talk about your list and get the lay of the land.'

She nodded. It made sense, her expression seemed to say. She had been hesitant at first, but in the end she just blurted out her request for him to assist in the new case.

He understood why she needed help with the investigation. There were a dozen names on the list. And often, in these cases, one name led to another. It would take forever for one person to track them all down, interview them, follow up on leads they provided and put it all in perspective.

The wallet that Gratelli extracted from Warfield's soggy suit contained mushy bills, some unreadable notes on paper tucked in every little orifice, a check-cashing card, a charge card, a library card, and a San Francisco Museum of Modern Art membership card. A key ring and some change were found in his trousers. Inside the left front breast pocket of his suit jacket was a notebook. Also soggy. There was no pen. Gratelli thought that a writer, one who carried a notebook, would also have a pen. He concluded that the pen in Warfield's neck was the author's own.

Live by the pen, die by the pen. The pen is mightier . . . Gratelli let his thoughts trail off.

The lab worked on the notebook. It was far too delicate an operation for Gratelli to undertake the separation of the wet pages and the preservation of the writing on them. The notebook was back at his desk in the Homicide Detail office in hours and some names were legible. There were also a few phone numbers. Throughout the morning, Gratelli made the calls, looking up numbers for names without numbers and calling the numbers that were legible. He made half a dozen of these calls and two of them volunteered hearsay that Warfield had made a spectacle of himself again at Alighieri's, a bar just off Grant, and that he had argued with a man who one person identified as William. William was commonly thought a gigolo, said the man. By mid-morning Gratelli, through a series of additional calls and callbacks, used various sets of information to pull out other information. In hours, he had tracked

one William Blake to an expensive home on Telegraph Hill, a home
that he did not own. When police arrived, William Blake was either
not at home or he wasn't answering the door. Gratelli had the home
watched.

The widow, Mrs Elena Warfield, preferred coming to the office rather
than have the police at her home.

She was dark-haired, obviously Italian – still had a slight accent. He
would guess of peasant stock. He chided himself at the observation, but
forgave himself. Gratelli would boast of his own peasant stock – plain-
spoken people who worked the earth. It wasn't really a slight, though
he would not relate his observations to her.

Elena Warfield, a big woman with a hard to ignore ample bosom,
meant to be cooperative, but she was not helpful. She had no idea about
any book or why anyone would want to kill her husband. She often,
she said, didn't know where he went and just as often wasn't the least
bit curious. She had her friends. And he had his.

'And your son?' Gratelli asked.

She shook her head as if she had been beaten and stubbornly refused
to answer despite the torture.

'He's not mine.'

'Mickey Warfield?'

'I know his name,' she said.

'Thank you for coming to see me . . . on this day especially. I am
very sorry for your loss.'

'I can go?'

'Yes, ma'am.'

She stood, put on her coat.

'I won't have to talk to you again?'

'I don't know the answer to that.'

'There's nothing I can tell you.'

'If you think of something . . .'

'I won't,' she said, leaving at more than a casual speed.

The homicide inspector had put in a solid day's work and it was only
early afternoon. The key, he believed, was this William fellow, who might
be the last person who saw the old writer alive and, just as important,
had been engaged in a loud and angry argument with the victim only
hours before.

The inspector would do a little canvassing of the North Beach bars
tonight. He'd talk with the bartender and the regulars, which meant
he'd be out late in order to talk to the people who were out at the time

of the disturbance. He decided to get out of his office for a while, grab a cup of coffee, get a bite to eat.

Gratelli picked up a fish sandwich and a steaming cup of coffee from McDonald's. He sat outside at a picnic table. Not much of a view – a busy street, bail bond agencies and parking lots. But he needed a moment, just a moment, to gather his thoughts. He had a few minutes before meeting with the celebrated District Attorney. This was the second high-profile case he'd had this year – this on top of nearly a dozen other homicides he was working on. He concluded he was as ready as he'd ever be to tackle the forces at play now – politics, the media and the case itself.

The air was warm and the smell of boiling oil mingled with the scent of carbon dioxide. *Eau d'Urban*, he told himself.

The two of them – Carly and Lang – looked at the crime scene. A tiny, triangular park of sorts, fenced in, was formed by the intersection of three streets – Union Street going east and west, Powell going north and south, and North Beach's main street, Columbus Avenue, angling through them. The little park was more of a decorative median than a place to feed the squirrels.

There were six smallish trees that shaded an oval pond that Lang estimated was about twelve feet by ten feet. Around the pond were clumps of purple flowers. Inside, small goldfish darted about.

The area was still cordoned off by yellow crime scene tape.

'It would take some strength to get Warfield over the wrought-iron fence and into the pond unless he was chased there and his own adrenaline got him over,' Carly said.

'An unlikely place to escape unless he thought he could hide in there,' Lang said. There wasn't any real place to hide, Lang thought, but if it was night, maybe Warfield thought he couldn't be seen.

Lang looked around, trying to figure what direction he might have come from. The answer was multiple choice. Lang walked around the small triangular park, noting that the little purple flowers had been smashed on the Columbus side. If the bar was on Grant, Warfield might have come down beside or across Washington Square Park. He didn't know what good that kind of speculation was, but it was a start and stirred the juices.

Carly was making her own calculations.

'It's not a difficult fence to hop,' she said, 'but Warfield wasn't a spring chicken and if his murderer was one of his contemporaries, this looks pretty challenging. What do you think?'

'Lunch. I think lunch.'

Mario's Bohemian Cigar Store and Café was catty-corner from the deadly little triangle (Warfield's wasn't the first waterlogged body discovered there). The restaurant was small and was, as far as Carly could see, without cigars. There were eight tables and a dozen or so stools at the bar.

She knew the place. She knew her way around North Beach from the days her parents ran a restaurant there. She'd had coffee at the corner landmark many times and relished again hearing the cook and server talking Italian to each other just as her parents had done. The place had not changed. Mario's – she assumed they were his – bowling trophies were displayed above the bar.

Lang ordered the sausage polenta and a glass of Malbec. She ordered the chicken panini and a lemonade.

'I didn't take you for a wine guy.'

'No doubt other discoveries await you.'

She laughed. 'Now you're scaring me. Anyway, the list,' she said, shoving it across the small table.

There were a dozen or so names and a short note beside each one. He recognized a few of them from the news just as he had been familiar with Warfield. There were a couple of painters, a few writers and poets, a political activist, a newspaper editor, and a politician. Also noted were both Warfield's wife and his mistress.

She explained that Warfield was about to publish a book that told lurid tales about a number of the folks who traveled in his circle. Lang doubted there would be much national impact, but there had been a recent book chronicling the intertwining lives of some local rich and famous families, warts and all, by one of the sons. The book was a roaring success as far away as New York. Maybe Warfield thought he could pull this off or maybe he could resurrect his career the way Truman Capote promised in his largely imaginary tell-all, *Answered Prayers*.

'Who's on the case?' Lang asked.

'According to the newspaper, it's Gratelli.'

Lang was relieved. There were a couple on Homicide Detail Lang would like to avoid. Gratelli was a good cop.

'But you see the problem,' Carly said.

'I always try not to.'

'We're working on an active murder investigation. We haven't run this by the police. And we're working for someone who may turn out to be the prime suspect.'

Lang took a bite of sausage. He didn't have an answer.

'If we follow up on the names on this list, it will get back to Gratelli,' she continued. 'And, decent as the guy is, he's not going to be happy. We have licenses that can be lifted at will.'

'We lie.'

'Lie.' It wasn't a question for Carly, just a repetition to make sure he knew what he was saying.

'Redesign the assignment that your boy gave us.'

'First, he isn't a boy,' she said.

'OK, he's Cary Grant. Second?'

'What?'

'If you have a first, it means you have a second.'

'Second,' she gave in, 'second, his name is William Blake.'

Lang closed his eyes. The name bubbled up from his mind slowly. He put it in place.

'William Blake. The poet. *Thanatopsis*. The big death poem.'

'No, that was somebody else,' Carly said. 'But death was big with Blake too. So what is it we lie about and how will that keep us out of jail for interfering with a police investigation?'

'We redo Mr Blake's request. We alter it slightly. We are not hunting for the murderer.'

'We're not,' she said in a tone that suggested she was humoring him and was only playing along for the moment.

'We're looking for the book.'

'What book?' she asked.

'The book that Warfield was writing.'

'Do we even know if there is a book?' she asked.

'You are so literal. We believe there's a book.'

She was nodding.

'It gives us a reason to talk to all these people and if we find the book we find the murderer,' he continued.

'Well, that's a theory.'

'How do we divide up the list?' Lang asked.

She took the sheet of paper back, folded it roughly in half, creased it and then used the edge of the table to rip it cleanly. She handed him one of the halves.

'Very scientific,' Lang said. 'I can see a lot of thought was put into this.'

'You get six, I get six.'

'Twelve suspects right off the bat.'

'Zodiac,' she said, 'apostles.'

'Number of inches in a foot,' Lang said.


'Come with me,' Lang said after they finished lunch and paid the bill. He grabbed her hand and the two of them dodged traffic, jaywalking across the street to Washington Square Park.

'What are we doing?'

'We're going to sit a while in the park,' he said.

'Why?'

He didn't answer but took her across the expanse of grass to the north-east corner, where there was an unoccupied bench.

Trees lined the perimeter, but most of the park was open field, except for a grouping of cedars in the center. Most folks – homeless, jobless, lovers, nannies with strollers, and a smattering of tourists – sat on the shady edges. However, in one corner, a legion of Chinese women in baseball caps practiced t'ai chi, moving arms and legs in a kind of earth-bound synchronized swimming. In the sunlight there were sunbathers and dog walkers and people cutting across the park's expanse merely to get from one place to another.

'Noah,' she said, sitting on the bench, 'what are we doing here?'

'We're relaxing. We're contemplating the world.'

Not far away on another bench a young man played the accordion.

Carly laughed. Then she sang along with the tune, 'Let the devil take tomorrow . . .'

'Exactly,' Lang said.

'You are laid back,' she said. Then a little sternly, she added, 'We're working.'

'We're also living a life. Or haven't you noticed?'

Pigeons gathered in a loose formation and swooped from one corner of the park to the other, occasionally causing folks to duck. Then they quieted again.

Carly seemed to relax.

'I repeat. I think it's likely that Warfield came down from Grant,' he said, motioning behind him. 'He crossed the park and thought he could hide in that little island.'

'He was being chased?' she asked.

'Or followed and he became aware of it. He wasn't a young man. He couldn't run far. He probably felt like he couldn't make it home.'

She nodded. 'He would have had to run uphill.'

'He lived on Russian Hill, right?'

'Yes.'

'He wanted to rest, hide in the darkness. And it was dark in there, under the trees.'

'The only place that was completely dark,' she said.

There was at least five minutes of quiet. She looked out over the park. To her right and slightly behind her was the gigantic Saints Peter and Paul Church. She had been inside many times with her parents. Why didn't he go into the church, she wondered.

'The list,' Noah said. 'You should add your Mr William Blake.'

'That would make thirteen,' she said.

'The thirteenth apostle,' he said.

'Some feet are thirteen inches.'

'You're right.'

# Four

Carly didn't admit it to Noah Lang, but she knew he was right. She hadn't quite let go of her corporate weenyship. She left her safe and comfortable job as an executive investigator at Vogel Security because it was boring, stifling, and soul-killing. The same could be said about her relationship with Peter – safe, comfortable, boring, stifling and soul-killing. The difference was she quit Vogel Security. And Peter quit her. She was ready for change and leapt into it. There were times when she thought she wasn't quite over either one.

But the choice had been made. For better or worse, she was embarking on this new life when she stumbled upon Lang and his strange little family. And she had to give Lang his due. He was doing his best to keep her from sliding back to the way she lived before, which was, upon introspection, not exactly living. Carly was starting to like the guy she originally thought was just a little too 'street' for her. She was also, she'd have to admit, just a little smitten with William Blake.

'I'll be at home if you need me,' she told Lang, who had settled in behind his computer to get background on the folks on his list.

'Home?' He smiled.

'It's a beautiful day. I'm thinking my laptop, my big old sofa, and a glass of Pinot Grigio.'

She waited for Lang's reply. It never came. He simply waved.

She was still getting used to the lack of regimentation.

It was a good decision. The afternoon was sunny, warm with an occasional breeze. She opened the doors that led out to the back deck and opened the front window to let the breezes play through her flat. She picked out a selection of CDs that would enhance such a day. The first to click on was Astrud Gilberto. This was the right rhythm. Not too slow, but relaxed.

She plugged in her laptop and put it on the big, comfy sofa and opened a bottle of white wine.

'Go slow, now,' she warned herself about the wine. 'It's still afternoon.'

She looked at her list, the names and William Blake's brief notations.

Nathan Malone, Warfield's prime competitor, successful writer who occasionally focused on the Beat Generation writers and artists.

Lili D. Young, an artist. Warfield hated her. Not sure why.

Mickey Warfield, wanderer, Warfield's son.

Bart Brozynski, newspaper editor and publisher, visceral.

Samuel McFarland, SF Board of Supervisors, something personal.

Frank Wiley, photographer, portraits and North Beach environs, artistic differences.

The notations were helpful, but vague. What did 'visceral' mean in this case? Or 'something personal'? But this was a start. She'd begin with Google. Next, she would try to arrange a meeting. People who hate passionately – like people who love passionately – often enjoy talking about the object of their affection or disaffection. Of course, it was possible that not one of these people was involved in Warfield's death. But one had to start somewhere.

The wine was perfect, cool, its ability to quench a thirst probably less endearing to wine critics than it was to her at the moment.

The afternoon at her keyboard yielded quite a bit more in the way of biography for those on her list, except for Mickey Warfield, who didn't come up at all. Unfortunately, there was nothing on the surface that connected any of them to Whitney Warfield in any meaningful way, or helped to explain the various animosities. She found that she could reach Brozynski and McFarland by email through their websites. She could go through the galleries to connect with Wiley and Young. There were no phone listings for anyone and that meant young Mickey Warfield and Nathan Malone would be a little more difficult to locate.

Before the second glass of wine on an increasingly empty stomach mellowed her a little more than she anticipated, she had gotten phone numbers for the two artists and sent emails to the two who had published email addresses.

She decided that life was good after all as she prepared the scallops she had bought at the Marina Market. She lightly roasted some asparagus sprinkled with pecorino and sliced some tomatoes. She dined on the back deck as the sun declined, which it was doing earlier and earlier each day. The third glass of wine introduced a little melancholy. Why not, she said, giving in. Enjoy it all. She took a sip of wine and remembered she liked William Blake's sly smile. There was, though, at the edge of her mind, something dark that tugged at her newfound sunny disposition.

Gratelli napped. He had already put in a day's work and he was planning to canvas the North Beach bars this evening. There was a lot of pressure these days. On one hand citizens were complaining about too much police overtime. On the other, they were complaining not only about the rise in the murder rate but about how few murders were solved. Lab reports on DNA were taking months in some cases and there was bickering between the medical examiner and the police and the District Attorney.

He had just met with the chief and the DA. Because this was a high-profile case, Gratelli would have whatever resources he needed. His lab requests would be priority. He was paired again with Rose and Stern, two homicide inspectors who helped on an earlier case involving people who were just a little more important than the average citizen. The two cops could get on his nerves, but they were more than competent. Now he snored, feet up on the sofa, trying to store a little energy for a reluctant night on the town.

Lang tried to keep his work at work. Through the afternoon – and with Thanh's expert search skills – Lang worked his own list:

> Marshall Hawkes, artist. Warfield despised his effeteness.
> Agnes DeWitt, memoirist, wrote her own tell-all.
> Marlene Berensen, Warfield's mistress. In the will?
> Richard Sumaoang, poet/painter, publicly challenged Warfield's honesty.
> Elena Warfield, Warfield's wife and wronged woman.
> Ralph Chiu, developer, political activist, conservative, vilified by Warfield.

While Thanh pounded the Internet, Lang found a phone number in the White Pages for Richard Sumaoang, among the last, it appeared, to give up a landline. The guy proved amenable to a discussion of Whitney Warfield and a meeting was set up for the evening.

Thanh provided Lang with files of information gleaned from newspapers, websites, and other sources. One page was a photograph of Agnes DeWitt. She had to be eighty. There was a sense of spirit in her eyes, but she was quite likely incapable of chasing down Whitney Warfield, hopping a fence, and stabbing him in the neck. Even so, she was added to the list of people to talk to. The murderer, after all, might not be on the list.

The other thing that struck Lang was that not only was Agnes DeWitt too old to be chasing Warfield around North Beach in the middle of the night, Marshall Hawkes and Elena Warfield weren't exactly young gazelles.

A number of articles were written about Hawkes. He had endless mentions on Google, was listed in Wikipedia, and the stories about him were published in very reputable publications – *The New York Times, The Financial Times, Art World, Art Forum* to name a very few. His work had been auctioned at some of the prestigious auction houses – Sotheby's, Christie's and, locally, Bonhams & Butterfields.

Lang skimmed the articles and found a Q & A on how Hawkes fit in with the history of art. He was smug, condescending and funny. His comment about there being no great women artists in history set up a long discussion that fell victim to Lang's short attention span.

Thanh also included a sheath of documents on Warfield himself. Fascinating reading. No one, it seemed, really liked the guy personally, though he had admirers of his work and his 'take-no-prisoners' philosophy. He was among the early practitioners of fictionalizing fact or factualizing fiction. It was difficult to tell which was which sometimes. Warfield's language was colorful, strong, passionate and his characterizations often mean-spirited.

'Life is mean,' Warfield was fond of saying. 'It's a battle.' He was a fan of the rebelliousness of the Beats, of the truth-telling of the movement's artists and writers. They wrote about things that weren't necessarily pretty. They challenged the status quo. They didn't mind insulting what they considered the uptight middle-class masses with their words and actions. But for Warfield, there were those who simply abdicated responsibility, a kind of 'the-world-is-screwed-up, let's-dance' mentality. He didn't like them. He didn't like those who opted for some sort of humbling spirituality either.

He didn't like 'sissies'. He didn't mind 'queers', though. He said so. That's not what he meant when he used the word 'sissy'. He meant anyone who wouldn't fight – verbally or physically – for his or her beliefs. He disliked dissemblers. Stand up for what you believe. Call things as you see them.

'Let the chips fall where they may,' Lang said.

'Kill or be killed,' Thanh said, standing over Lang as he scanned the information about the victim. 'Ironic, isn't it?'

'Killed in the line of duty, maybe.'

Lang left at four, earlier than any ambitious businessman would. His approach to work was creative but not necessarily entrepreneurial. He locked the office. Carly was gone. Brinkman hadn't come in. And Thanh had run off to who knows where. Outside, Lang got into his banged up old Mercedes and drove to the Western Addition. Home, a former Chinese laundry, still looked like one from the outside. A Chinese name and characters, though scratched a bit, were painted on the windows. Inside, there was no trace of the former business. It was a big room. A skylight – two stories up – let in a bit of soft afternoon sun. Buddha, a brown, golden-eyed Burmese cat, waited at the door to welcome his human room-mate to *his* domain.

'You're on your own this evening,' Lang said to Buddha. He changed Buddha's water, filled in some dry food. 'You can meditate, contemplate your navel. Do cats have navels? Do bees have knees?'

Buddha walked away.

'I see. No sense of humor today.'

Buddha was his sister's cat and a reluctant adoptee. Shortly before she died she made Lang promise to watch over him. It was a situation neither he nor the cat wanted. But after a period of distrust, they bonded, and Lang was happy to have another living being nearby, especially one that, in the end, was far less demanding than one of his own species.

Lang watched part of an early Oakland Athletics game, then fixed dinner. It wasn't a demanding exercise. He opened a package of pot stickers he bought from King of Dumplings out on Noriega. They made them fresh. Three Chinese women sat around a table in the back rolling and pinching the product – and freezing them immediately. No MSG. No preservatives. He boiled a dozen of them for 10 minutes, then tossed them into a skillet with some peanut oil. He opened a beer and retrieved a bottle of Pearl River soy sauce from the cupboard.

Buddha sniffed the pot stickers on Lang's plate, but left, curiosity quickly quenched.

'You see, that's how you keep your slender figure.'

Lang felt a little disloyal preferring the Athletics to the Giants since he was living in San Francisco. But the Oakland team – and after all Oakland was just across the Bay – always seemed to have a little more spirit, had a little more fun playing the game, and they took some risks.

He had a few more hours to kill before meeting Richard Sumaoang at Alighieri's. It was to be a purposeful evening. He'd meet the poet and painter, have a little chat about Warfield and, when that was done, he'd quiz the bartender.

It had been a long time since Lang was in North Beach at night. His days hanging around bars were largely behind him. But when he first arrived in San Francisco, a couple of decades ago, he made the rounds of hotspots in the city. Many of them were in North Beach. In those days he frequented places that could be counted on to provide the kind of opportunities a young man appreciates – cheap beer, warm women and eight-ball. He was no longer that young or that interested – in eight-ball.

The North Beach he and Carly saw at noon wasn't the same as North Beach at night. Bars and restaurants, closed during the day, were open and busy. Neon glowing in the darkness gave the whole area a sense of mystery and adventure.

While the old, respected and authentic bars on Columbus – Tosca, Specs and Vesuvio – offered both locals and tourists pleasant spaces for friends to meet and talk, much of the action was on the oldest street in the city, Grant Avenue. Grant, which began near the upscale shopping district of Union Square, turned into the main tourist street of Chinatown, and eventually, as it crossed Broadway and Columbus, into the real heartbeat of the Italian village.

And it was in an alley off Grant that Alighieri's was inconspicuously located. The sign was small and blue. People who didn't know it was there would likely not find it. The result was that this was a special crowd, generally people who knew each other, and their guests. Being there meant, in a way, you had been vetted as a genuine San Franciscan, if not a genuine San Francisco character.

Inside, Alighieri's was a long, narrow room, with a long bar. There was enough space for a row of booths to line the wall opposite the bar.

Conspicuously missing was a pool table and jukebox. Tony Vale's mellow voice rose slightly above the chatter.

The bar was half full. Customers there had come solo. The evidence was that a stool or two separated the half dozen men at the bar. Maybe half the booths were occupied as well, with couples or threesomes. The low-backed stools were upholstered in black leather, the same leather that covered the seats in the booths. The tabletops were shiny black. The one he could see clearly was cracked. Halfway down the bar room, there was a break in the pattern of booths and a large poster hung on the wall. It was a large, old, framed illustration of a red devil and a bottle of booze. Lang could make out the words '*Anis Infernal*'.

The room was dark, the conversation low. From what Lang could see, the customers, mostly men, were middle-aged or older. They wore dark clothes, sported either beards or long hair or both. It was pretty clear none of them had day jobs in the financial district.

Lang looked around for someone who would fit the description of a Filipino artist and poet. No one. He looked at his watch. Nine. Lang found a stool that wouldn't disturb the protocol of keeping at least a stool away from the next guy and sat.

'Peroni,' Lang said, when the bartender came up. Seemed fitting to order an Italian beer. The bartender took no note. His look was neither welcoming nor discouraging.

'How's Mr Alighieri?' Lang asked when the beer arrived.

'Dead,' the bartender said.

'Sorry to hear that,' Lang said.

'About seven hundred years.'

'Has it been that long?' Lang asked. 'Time goes by so quickly.' He'd hoped he could get beyond the bartender's complete indifference, tap into a sense of humor. Not even a smile. That would make questions later a little more difficult.

Behind the bar was a wall of liquor bottles, the shelves interrupted in the middle by another large poster, this one showing a lithe and sly-looking green devil holding a bottle of spirits.

We've got a theme here, Lang thought. Drink and go to hell. Or, as he thought more about it, maybe they serve drinks in hell. He liked the idea.

Sumaoang appeared in that sudden way that Lang's cat Buddha appeared – one second nowhere to be seen, the next right beside him.

He was a slender man, short, fit, looking to be fifty maybe, though probably older. Jeans, a worn silk sport jacket over a dark shirt. Big eyes, soul patch just below his lower lip. A smile on his face.

'Noah?'

'Yeah. You picked me right out.'

'I know everybody else,' he said, slipping on to the stool beside Lang, and putting his iPhone on the bar. Tight clothes, Lang thought. Nowhere else to put it.

'Thank you for taking the time to meet with me,' Lang said.

'I come down here most nights,' Sumaoang said. It wasn't a warm smile he had on his face, but a cold smirk. 'Nothing special.'

Lang took the slap without showing he understood it. 'Buy you a drink?'

The bartender was there with a bottle of water.

'You must be a regular,' Lang said to the artist.

'Real regular. You want to know about Warfield?' Sumaoang asked.

# Five

After cleaning up the dishes, Carly brewed a cup of coffee and settled on the sofa with her laptop to follow up on the people on the list. Frank Wiley had several links on Google. She discovered his photographs were used in magazine and newspaper articles. They were included or featured in several exhibitions over the years. There was an out-of-print book on Amazon. His specialty was North Beach – the neighborhood, its characters, and its celebrities.

Some of the photographs she found were of the Beats, some of them about to make a name for themselves, the core group in their youngest San Francisco days. That meant Wiley was no spring chicken. Some of these photographs were taken in the fifties, late fifties probably, but still a long time ago. If he was twenty then, he'd be in his seventies at least. A murderer? Possibly, seventy is the new forty.

His work was currently being represented by Reed Fine Arts on Geary, according to a fairly recent posting on an art-oriented website. That meant the gallery would likely know where to find him. Tomorrow she could visit the gallery. It was in what could loosely be called the 'gallery district' – a small area near Union Square with a mixture of fine arts targeted to serious collectors and lesser ones targeting less knowledgeable tourists. Reed was one of the former. Perhaps she could also locate Lili D. Young through the galleries. There were casual mentions on the Internet. And eBay had one of her watercolors listed for $1,200. There was an old newspaper article that indicated that, at least at the time of that writing, she lived on Potrero Hill.

After the gallery visit, she'd check her email. If she hadn't heard from the newspaper editor Bart Brozynski or city Supervisor Samuel McFarland, she knew where to find them and she would hunt them down.

She felt as if she had put in enough time, even if half of it was in the comfort of her own home. She was beginning to like this new Carly Paladino, a little more laid-back, a little more spontaneous. Yes, it still made her a little nervous and she had twinges of guilt. But, she *was* getting the job done, wasn't she?

She poured herself a half glass of wine and stepped back out on to the deck. The cold had come in – good for sleep, but not so good for hanging out. She downed her wine, checked the locks on the doors, switched off the lights, undressed, and slipped naked into her luxurious bed.

As Lang talked with Sumaoang, he noticed something odd. As the night wore on, people came into the bar, walked past the two of them toward the back and didn't return. He thought, at first, they were going to the john. But it'd be quite a gathering in there by now.

Richard Sumaoang was talking about 'the scene' and it didn't take too much prompting to get him to talk. He said that when he came along, the old guard had either died or moved on. Allen Ginsberg, Gregory Corso, Jack Kerouac, Gary Snyder and many of the other core members of the 'Beats' were traveling the world, no longer just North Beach talent. But by the mid sixties, the energy these legends had supplied mutated. The center of the new culture moved from North Beach and the 'Beats' to Haight Ashbury and the 'Hippies'. With the media as an active accomplice there was dramatic, though philosophically slight, cultural shift. The Beats catered to a small, highly literate audience. The Hippies were mass-marketed. Jazz, the musical backdrop for the Beats, gave way to the Grateful Dead and Jefferson Airplane.

As Richard Sumaoang told the story, he preferred the Beats and remained camped out in North Beach, a neighborhood that was becoming rich in history, but drained of the spark that created such literary shake-ups as Allen Ginsberg's *Howl*, a book so threatening to the 'standards' of 'decent' Americans that some thought it was an exception to 'freedom of speech'. The case went to the Supreme Court.

Each of the names that Lang mentioned brought about a wistful smile and a little story. Marshall Hawkes hung around North Beach in the early days, but was never a part of it, according to Sumaoang.

'He was too materialistic, too practical,' Richard Sumaoang said. 'There was this great fight between Hawkes and a painter named Anselmo about art, but some say it was about love. Hawkes denied being queer, but most people thought he was and Anselmo was just a lustful creature. They're still fighting, I think.'

'What about Warfield?'

'He was a transplanted New Yorker,' Sumaoang said. 'That alone made him superior in his mind. He was never part of anything. He couldn't be. That would mean he would subsume his personality to something larger. A movement, for example.' Sumaoang smiled.

'What about Warfield's mistress?' Lang asked.

'Marlene? She'd have no reason to kill him. The theory was that whatever Warfield's estate was – and it was probably only the potential future income on the copyrights because he spent every penny he got – it would go to his wife, unless of course, the wife dies first.'

'You're saying if Marlene wanted someone dead it would be Mrs Warfield?'

'Yeah, I guess – if.'

'The wife then,' Lang said.

'What changed with his death?' Sumaoang asked. 'That'd be the question I would ask. Elena was his wife through several mistresses, all known to her. She delighted in it. She was Mrs Warfield. That made her a celebrity of sorts. And she enjoyed that. And she didn't have to put up with him, let alone sleep with him.'

Sumaoang laughed.

'Didn't she feel shame? Everyone knew.'

'Not a lot of shame being felt by anyone in that group.'

'There was a guy named Ralph Chiu. Also on Warfield's enemies list.'

'Pretty straightforward,' Sumaoang said. 'Chiu was a political conservative. Some used to say he was very powerful among the Republicans in the city. All twelve of them.'

'Just politics?'

'There is a rumor that despite all the Italian businesses in North Beach, the Chinese actually own all the buildings. I don't know the specifics but there was some sort of real estate issue between Warfield and Chiu.'

'What did Warfield have on Chiu?'

'I don't know the answer to that. But between politics and real estate, progressives and developers, there are some suspicious deals and lots of animosity. Could be that.'

'Chiu wasn't part of the North Beach people then?'

'Not in any movement sense. Just like the Italians weren't part of the movement.'

'I thought North Beach was all about the Italians.'

'Listen, the Italians, the people who had businesses here, didn't find the likes of us lovable. They were family people. Catholics. Hard workers. We didn't work. We hung around coffee shops and bars. We didn't dress right. We didn't play by the rules. The top Italians here were pretty conservative. In today's terms, they were very family values.'

'Can you handle another bottle of water?' Lang asked.

Sumaoang smiled.

'I'll pace myself,' he said.

Lang ordered a beer for himself and water for his witness.

'All right,' Lang said, after the drinks arrived, 'what did Warfield have on you?'

'I don't know,' Sumaoang said. 'I truly don't know. I came down here because you said Warfield was writing or had written a tell-all book and that I was supposed to be in it. I was hoping you'd tell me.'

'What have you got to hide?' Lang said.

'If I had something to hide, would I be telling you? Maybe you're the one writing the book.'

'Maybe a couple more bottles of water,' Lang said, 'and you'll become a little more compliant.'

'I've got to move on,' Sumaoang said. He slid off the stool, extended his hand.

Lang shook it.

'Tell me,' Lang said, 'all those people who walked by here. Where did they go?'

'What are you talking about?'

'Hey. Twenty people came in here while we were talking. They walked right by us. And they didn't come back.'

'Maybe out the rear door,' Sumaoang said.

'No, they just came and you're telling me they were just passing through?'

'It's private . . . for regulars.' Sumaoang looked around and turned back, saying softly, 'I'll leave it at that.' He nodded and went the way of the others. He stopped, came back halfway. He pointed his finger at Lang.

'Confidences should be honored,' he said with an edge of anger in his voice.

'Did you tell me any secrets?'

'No,' Sumaoang said.

'Then why are you telling me this?'

'Maybe you'll find out.'

Was that a threat or was he merely saying that this was what Lang should consider in his investigation?

It wasn't a bad night, Lang thought. Except for two things. The bartender was tight-lipped and a big guy kept Lang from going to the back room.

The poet/artist did fill in a few holes, but left a few unfilled. What did Warfield have on Sumaoang? Why was Sumaoang so willing to talk? The answer to the last question was that maybe he wanted to know what Lang knew? No slouch, he. Maybe Lang gave away more than he got. And maybe most of these folks would want the missing tell-all book, if there was one, to stay missing, wouldn't they? Lang laughed out loud in the increasingly cold and windy night. Maybe his bright idea was only so bright. He'd have to put the fear of a murder charge back into the conversation.

Now about Sumaoang. He was fit, lean and vital. He'd have no trouble handling an ageing chub like Warfield. Sumaoang would stay on the list.

Lang walked and tried to relax. But there was a little anger. He could feel it in his neck. What really bugged him was the back room at Alighieri's. It wouldn't have been so bad if it were merely locked. Unfortunately, someone committed the ultimate sin. They told him he couldn't go in. Now he had to.

Intense light came through the slats of the blinds and burrowed through her eyelids. She awoke somewhat startled at the sun's strength and the fact that it was a new day. She remembered climbing into bed last night and waking up as if time had not really passed. She got out of bed and was enveloped in the warmth of the room – a rare experience on a chilly San Francisco morning. It was nine a.m. Very late for her. But it would be fine. The art galleries didn't open until later in the morning. She still had time for a morning run.

She walked naked into the kitchen, put on some coffee, and then to the bathroom where she started the shower. As the water in the shower came up to temperature, she laid out her running clothes – the lighter Northface gear considering the day.

The shower felt good. Having a case felt good. She thought about calling the office, but that wasn't how it worked anymore. There were no expectations, except for those she had of herself. After her shower, she checked her cellphone in the event that she had slept through a call. No missed calls. No messages.

She dressed, took her coffee and her laptop out to the deck off the bedroom. Sprinklers were on and the wet greenery shined in the sunlight. Today she'd get through as much of the list as she could. Maybe she'd get a line on artist Lili D. Young and photographer Frank Wiley from the gallery people. They might know something about Nathan Malone as well.

After looking at news headlines and noting that no killer asteroids were heading toward earth, Carly checked her email. She had a message from the newspaper publisher Bart Brozynski and another from Supervisor Samuel McFarland's office. She read the publisher's email first. He was free at four in the afternoon – this afternoon. She would have to come to him. No additional information. McFarland's office wanted to set up an appointment weeks from now. That wouldn't do. She'd call when she got back from her run. But her day was filling up nicely.

This morning she ran with Louis Prima's 'Just A Gigolo' piped into her ears. It was a happy, bouncy tune. Up the hill toward Lafayette Park, around it and then through it, all the while thinking about William Blake. Had she picked that CD on purpose? The gigolo piece was paired with 'I Ain't Got Nobody'. She tried to repress a smile. She felt a little giddy and, she told herself, this wasn't something a woman of her age should feel. But what a charmer. She thought about Noah Lang's warning that Blake was playing her. Certainly, he possessed those skills. If he was as successful as he appeared to be as a 'professional companion', he'd have to have a good game. Lang was right. She'd have to be careful.

Second shower of the morning. The first was to wash away sleep, the second to cool off. Now in her robe, she poured herself a second cup of coffee, opened a small carton of yogurt to which she added fresh sliced peaches. As she prepared her breakfast snack, she thought about what she should wear downtown. What do you wear to high-quality art galleries? She had a light gray suit, but that seemed a little stuffy, especially so on a day that would grow warmer. She finished her yogurt and returned to the bedroom, where, staring deep into her closet, she was about to make the toughest decision of the day. Did she have anything elegant but fun? Arty?

\* \* \*

Lang had awakened early, traipsed down to the coffee shop at Hayes and Central and walked over to the Park between Oak and Fell streets. He sat on a bench near the bike path and watched as healthy, anti-global warmers and those who could not afford such luxuries as cars and gasoline, pedaled to work. Beyond the path were open fields and dog lovers were giving their charges a chance to answer nature's call and get in a little exercise before most of them would be left in the apartment for the day. The dogs were off their leashes and well behaved.

He liked dogs. He liked them better than humans. The lazy PI nibbled at the top of a muffin and sipped his coffee as he watched the goings on under the tall eucalyptus and the big blue sky. He had coffee at home but this, paper cup and all, was better and he enjoyed the fresh air. There were times when his place seemed a little claustrophobic.

Lang tossed the remainder of the muffin on the grass. Some creature would be rewarded. He opened the copy of the *Fog City Voice*, a weekly he picked up at the coffee shop. The paper focused on politics and entertainment, though in San Francisco the two were pretty much the same. Lang checked the masthead to see if the publisher was the one on Carly's list. He was. Also, among the contributors was Nathan Malone, another one on Carly's list.

Lang flipped through the movie listings, glanced at the masseuse ads and then checked out the first few pages of the paper to see what moral crusade they were on at the moment. There were several articles on a rumored new hotel in North Beach. The *Voice* was vehemently against it. He finished his coffee and walked back toward his place. Though it would be autumn officially in a few weeks, there was no hint of it in the air.

Two guys stood in front of his door. As Lang got closer, he saw who they were. Rose, a black guy and the smaller of the two, leaned back against the building, one foot up against the wall. He smiled. His partner, Stern, was a big white guy in his fifties, the strain of alcohol and general disdain etched on his face. He wasn't smiling. He stepped toward Lang as Lang approached.

'The party was last night,' Lang said. 'Next time.'

'You know, you're not as smart or as funny as you think you are,' Stern said. The guy's suit was two sizes too small.

'Of all the cops on the force why is it always you?'

'We miss you,' Rose said, coming forward to join the conversation. He had a casual attitude and a well-pressed look.

'No we don't,' Stern said.

'Stern doesn't appreciate sarcasm,' Rose said.

'He has a lovely childlike quality,' Lang said. 'I've long admired it.'

'What are you doing sniffing around the Warfield killing?' Stern asked.

'Who says I am?'

'Gratelli says so,' Rose said.

Lang thought that Gratelli must have come in the bar after he left. The bartender wasn't as tight-lipped with the homicide inspector as he was with Lang. And Lang had given the barkeep his card. In retrospect, maybe that wasn't a good idea.

'It's a murder investigation,' Stern said.

'I would think so,' Lang said.

'And you?' Stern moved closer to Lang. It was his way of intimidating people. That and 'the look'. The cop look.

'I have nothing to do with it. Hope you find out who did it,' Lang said. 'I leave it entirely in your capable hands.'

'That's very nice of you,' Rose said.

Lang looked at Stern. 'More sarcasm.' When Stern didn't respond, Lang said, 'You'll catch on.'

Stern sneered. Lang knew he shouldn't tease the bear. But he couldn't resist.

'You know about PIs and active murder investigations, right?' Rose said.

'Of course. Gumshoe 101.'

'Then what are you doing?' Unlike Stern's, Rose's tone was civil. Rose seemed the smarter of the two. But, having been partners for a couple of decades, they played games. When Stern was in a better mood, they would do a little comic routine.

'Just looking for a book,' Lang said.

'Then you should go to a library,' Stern said.

'You practicing your sarcasm?' Rose asked his partner.

'It's never too late to learn.'

'You want to answer the implicit question?' Rose asked.

'Won't be in a library. It's unpublished.'

'Let me guess. A book by Warfield.'

'God, you guys are good,' Lang said.

'You know there's a book out there?' Rose asked.

'No.'

'You're looking for a book you don't know exists?'

'Keeps me busy. I don't like crossword puzzles.'

'The book have something to do with the murder?' Rose asked, while Stern wandered off, stared down the street.

'I haven't read it yet.'

Rose smiled, shook his head. 'Don't piss him off too much,' he said softly, referring to his partner.

'Who is your client?' Stern said, coming back. There was anger in his voice, but there was almost always anger in his voice.

'I don't have a client.' Technically, William Blake was Carly's client.

'Then why are you looking for the book?'

'Because I don't know where it is.'

Stern's face reddened. 'I'm gonna beat the shit out of him,' he said.

'There's a right time and a right place,' Rose said, then turned to look at Lang. 'Maybe later.'

'You and your promises,' Stern said.

# Six

Reed Fine Arts was on the fifth floor of 69 Geary, an address where a number of respected firms had their galleries. Carly had settled on a loose-fitting knit sweater and slacks, a delicate gold necklace, and low-cut boots by Jimmy Choo she bought in a moment of weakness . . . or madness. But dressing right was important. She knew it was superficial, shallow. Sometimes she liked superficial and shallow.

She always remembered her grandmother taking her downtown to the City of Paris before it closed and telling her how important clothes were to the proper young woman. Maybe her grandmother made it true, but dressed like this Carly felt confident, and she was about to meet with people who were knowledgeable about a subject she knew little about. It was the philosophy that if everything is all right on the outside, the inside will adapt. It did.

There were two desks behind a rosewood wall on the right as she entered. At each was a young woman dressed in black, sitting in front of an Apple computer. They didn't look up as Carly passed by them. Beyond was where the exhibitions began. The first room showcased very large underwater photographs . . . brilliant blue-greens and ephemeral shapes in the water. The images didn't come from the ocean deep, but from swimming pools. There was something both ghostlike and cheery – a very difficult mood to embrace. Off to the left was a hallway, clearly a place for offices. But there was another opening, a smaller room where portrait photographs, maybe twenty-five of them, resided on white walls. They were all the same size and looked at first to be identical. In fact, they were portraits of just one person, each with a subtle difference.

Carly came back to the women who sat at the desks by the entrance. One of the women, a blonde of maybe thirty, looked up. Smiled and nodded. Eyebrows lifted, she was asking what Carly wanted without uttering a word.

'I'm trying to find Frank Wiley,' Carly said.

'The photographer?'

'Yes.'

'Just a moment,' the woman said, picking up the phone. After a brief conversation, she said, 'Mr Reed will be right with you.'

Carly moved into the room of swimming pool photographs and waited. A slender man in a pinstriped suit that made him look slenderer came in. He wore squarish horn-rimmed glasses. He was probably fifty. His hair was brushed back. There was a Fred Astaire kind of elegance, but his face was solemn.

'Yes?' He forced a smile from a face that seemed uncomfortable with the exercise.

'I'm trying to find Frank Wiley,' she said. 'I understand you carry his work.'

He put his fingers to his lips. Obviously, this required some thought.

'We did,' he said finally.

The conversation was held in hushed tones as if they were in a library or church.

'You don't anymore?'

'No. Mr Wiley, you might be interested to know, is holding his own retrospective. Probably his last. He wanted to do it here, but frankly . . . well, nothing.'

'His work has slipped.'

'No, it's just that his work is a bit . . . uh . . . historic now. He's a fine photographer. We've always been a little ahead of the times, you know.'

'I'm trying to find him. Do you know how I can contact him?'

'I'm not sure that would be appropriate,' Reed said.

'I'd like to see his new show,' she said.

'I'm sure there will be some notice in the papers,' Reed said. 'Anything else I can help you with?'

'Thank you for your time,' Carly said.

He stood for a moment, obviously waiting for her to depart. Instead she went back to the photographs. Reed gave up and disappeared into the hallway.

Carly stopped by the desk.

'I just got done talking with Mr Reed,' she said, misleading them with the truth, 'do you have a phone number or address for Frank Wiley?'

'Sure,' the blonde said. Her fingers tapped on the keyboard and when they stopped, she said, 'I'll write this down for you.'

Carly Paladino departed the gallery with the information on a Post-it note. She had a sudden thought and came back in.

'Do you have anything on an artist, Lili D. Young?'

The blonde looked at her then to her right where Mr Reed stood, more serious than one might think possible.

Carly smiled, waved. Noah Lang was rubbing off on her.

Lang stopped by the office. Carly arrived at the same time and they both took the stairs. The elevator was slow. A snail could make it up the steps faster than the clanging, groaning and notoriously unreliable lift. There, sitting in the reception area, was Thanh. He wore a blue blazer, a white shirt and Palomino-colored pants, all custom-made. The clothing was loosely draped and elegant. His hair was combed back, a touch of silver around the temples. There was an air of sophistication in the way he looked up at Carly, who was stunned for a moment.

'How is Carly Paladino today?' Thanh asked, barely suppressing a grin.

'You are a chameleon aren't you?' Carly asked.

He was an Asian version of William Blake, looking a little younger, a little slimmer, but catching that smooth, sleepy-eyed charmer completely.

Carly looked at Lang, who shrugged.

'You should see his Audrey Hepburn,' Lang said.

Carly thought that she shouldn't have been surprised at this act of impersonation. She'd seen Thanh in action before – as a glimmering goddess and then, of course, yesterday, when he looked like a slippery pimp from the tropics.

'Any calls?' Carly asked.

'One, but I just got here,' Thanh said, voice reverting to normal. 'You can ask Brinkman. He got here at seven this morning, said it was easier to sleep at the office.' He looked down at Carly's footwear. 'Jimmy Choo, cool.'

'Who's Jimmy Choo?' Lang asked as he headed for his office.

'Don't worry your pretty little head about Jimmy Choo,' Thanh said, smiling.

'That's a relief,' Lang said. 'I needed that room in my brain to figure out the meaning of life. Good to have the pressure off. And the call you took?'

'Marshall Hawkes,' Thanh said.

Lang stopped, turned back.

'He can see you today at noon.'

Lang looked at his watch. 'That makes it pretty much now,' he said.

It was a short walk to the address Lang was given for Hawkes. Even so, he was greeted with the usual South of Market population, ranging from the down and out and the up and coming. The architecture reflected the same arc of abandonment and resurrection. Empty, trashed buildings existed side by side with creatively remodeled spaces and shiny, new condominiums.

Inside one of those condo buildings, the artist, Marshall Hawkes, wore a silk kimono. The pinks and burgundy dominated an intricate abstract pattern in the silk that seemed more garish than it was because of Marshall's flaming red hair. The man was thin, sharp-featured, eyes narrow-set and a crisp, heartless blue.

Hawkes welcomed Noah with a thin smile and a dramatic gesture. The living room was very Japanese, very minimal. There wasn't the scent of oil or turpentine, just Marshall Hawkes's cologne. Off the living room was a terrace that overlooked the street.

'Yes,' Hawkes said, perching himself like a skinny bird on the edge of one of the two sofas, both upholstered in a fabric similar and complementary to the kimono.

'You know about the death of Whitney Warfield.'

'I know what's going on in the world,' Hawkes said. There was condescension in his voice.

'It seems . . .' Lang began, then with a nod asked if he could sit.

'By all means. You were saying?'

Lang sat on the opposite sofa. 'It seems as if Mr Warfield was writing a book . . .'

'That's what he does,' Hawkes said.

'. . . that was to chronicle the indiscretions of his friends,' Lang said, bumping up his tone and his vocabulary involuntarily. He couldn't help but smile at his own foolishness. He couldn't remember ever using the word 'indiscretions', let alone 'chronicle' as a verb in a sentence. 'And any other embarrassments. This means that people who have something to hide might also have a motive for his murder.'

Hawkes smiled. 'That's all very Agatha Christie, isn't it?'

Lang nodded.

'And what is it you want?' Hawkes asked.

'Just trying to get a feel for the people who traveled in his circles.'

'I don't travel in anyone's circle, Mr Lang. If there's any traveling done, they are traveling in mine.'

A fawn-colored greyhound peeked around a corner and retreated.

'Do you have any idea who might have hated or feared Mr Warfield enough to have killed him?'

'The buzz seems to be that a certain young man who sells his affections to the highest bidder had an argument with Whitney just before he was killed.'

'Word gets around,' Lang said.

'You know this fellow?'

'Never met him. You have a name?'

'William something. You could check with Anselmo Ruiz,' Hawkes said. 'They are very close. Other than having talked with Whitney, who was also curious about artists and writers in the city, I don't have much to add to the gossip. As I mentioned, I don't . . . what . . . don't *hang out* with the people who populate Whitney's world.'

'You, then,' Lang said. 'Did Warfield have something on you? Do you have something that you would prefer the world not to know?'

Hawkes laughed. 'Who doesn't? And I have absolutely no alibi. I live alone. However, Mr Lang, there's no way I would be out in the middle of the night in some wretched little park in North Beach. My idea of outdoors is a Martini by the pool.'

'How old are you, if you don't mind my asking?'

'I do mind,' Hawkes said. 'Why did you put me on your little list to question?'

'As I said on your answering machine, someone said that you were to be a main character in Mr Warfield's book.'

'And who gave my name?'

'A little birdie told me.'

Hawkes smiled. 'Your little birdie is an idiot. There are no tales out of school that would be embarrassing enough for me to kill.'

'You never know,' Lang said.

'I do know. Such motivation is rarely generated by indifference.'

'Could it be that you're gay?'

'Gay?' He looked almost puzzled.

'Some people think you're homosexual.'

'As long as they think it and don't say it. If they say it I'll sue them for libel.'

'Is it so terrible?'

'Terrible? I don't know and I don't care. It simply isn't the truth.'

'What's your dog's name?' Lang asked.

Hawkes looked puzzled for a moment, looked around.

'Pepe,' he said. His face softened. 'He was rescued. He ran his heart out for some gambling scum in Florida and when he lost a little of his speed on the track, they shipped him off to some death camp. Now, those folks I could eliminate without blinking.'

Hawkes stood. His look was one of dismissal. He had said all he wanted to say. His curiosity had been satisfied. He had no more use for Lang.

'So, it seems you are not totally indifferent, are you?' Lang said.

Hawkes ignored the question. 'If you choose to talk with Anselmo,' he continued as he walked toward the door, 'please, please do not give him my best.'

On his walk back to the office, Lang called Carly.

'Lunch?'

'It's on my desk, thanks,' Carly said. 'Anything?'

'I get the feeling I'm giving out more information than I'm getting. But I get a sense of these people.'

'Are either of them capable of killing Warfield . . . I mean physically?'

'Both. Richard Sumaoang is youngish. Looks pretty fit. Hawkes is maybe sixty, not particularly athletic, but it looks like he takes care of himself. Eats his broccoli. What about you?'

'I eat my broccoli,' she said.

'What's with your guys?'

'I'm still tracking some of them down. I'm visiting the *Fog City Voice* publisher this afternoon. Trying to connect with Supervisor McFarland. Frank Wiley isn't answering his phone. And I can't find Warfield's son.'

'Maybe he's with his mom, the widow . . .' Lang said. 'You see how this could come together?'

'I do.'

'You know, it occurred to me that if I murdered someone, it might be interesting to give someone a list of suspects that didn't include me.' Lang dodged a man pushing a grocery cart full of his life's belongings. He wondered why these guys got all materialistic. He'd seen some with two carts, slaving away moving them around, and no doubt worried about vandals.

'I'd agree with you, but he didn't have to come to us,' Carly said. 'He could have done that with the police.'

'So you're set for lunch?'

'Yes,' she said.

'OK, I'm going home, then I'll find somebody on that list to talk to. Thanh still there?'

'No. But Brinkman is. He's smoking on the fire escape again. From time to time he looks in through the window and smiles.'

'He never smiled at me.'

'And that makes you feel?'

'Happy.'

It was cool inside Lang's loft space. Buddha seemed puzzled at his room-mate's early afternoon return. No doubt Lang was disturbing Buddha's routine. But in moments, the golden-eyed cat adjusted. The two napped briefly on the sofa and Lang made a few calls – the ones to Elena Warfield and Ralph Chiu were fruitless. However, the mistress, Marlene Berensen, agreed to meet Lang in a public place. Eight in the bar at Enrico's.

Lang gave himself the rest of the afternoon off.


# Seven


Bart Brozynski was a big bear of an older man, probably heading toward 300 pounds and seventy, but at a plodding pace. He wore a somewhat bushy, wiry salt and pepper beard that added to an intimidating presence. He did not get up to greet Carly. It would have been difficult to do so because the circa 1930 wooden office chair fit him like a wedding ring on a swollen finger.

He nodded for Carly to sit in a side chair that was no doubt chosen for its lack of comfort. No one would hang around too long. She had to remove a couple of books to sit.

'You're here to talk about old Whitney. Is that right?' He talked slowly and deliberately.

'And you,' Carly said. She chose her tone carefully. She couldn't start the conversation as a supplicant.

Brozynski's eyes softened. A thin grin was barely perceptible beneath the facial hair.

He was as big as Anselmo. And both were bearded. But where Anselmo seemed harmless and moved about easily and fluidly once he woke up, Brozynski appeared as though he was repressing some sort of explosion and it took considerable effort to do so. Just turning his head seemed to be the result of a considered effort. This was not an impetuous person, she thought. He wore a sport coat that looked like it was made of canvas over a tee shirt that had some sort of faded graphics on its front.

'Go for it,' he said, his head falling back in a way that suggested he was determined to look down on her.

'What have you done in your life that is so incriminating that you would kill someone to keep it secret?'

He closed his eyes, pressed his lips together. He scratched his beard.

The room was full of old newspapers and books, all stacked against walls and on tables, threatening to tumble down if someone sneezed. His desk had messy piles of papers and a manual typewriter. Was it for show?

'I'd kill somebody for less than that if I thought I could get away with it.' He shook his head. 'I'll have to give that some thought. I've done many things. So this is your take on old Whitney's death. He was going to reveal deep dark secrets and someone strongly objected?'

'Seems so. We know he was writing a tell-all book . . .'

'His legacy.' His tone was derisive.

'And we have names of a few people whose stories were included in a very unflattering way.'

'There was no love lost between Whitney and me. None. He was a blowhard who didn't know when to call it a day. His first book, especially, covered some new ground and deserved the attention it got. But for a lot of writers, unfortunately, there is really only one story. And if you keep writing you simply tell it over and over again. That was Whitney. People grew tired of it. Yet, he demanded attention, demanded to be treated like a star. He was pissed that the paper wouldn't give him the attention he wanted. In fact, he submitted articles. And we rejected them.'

'We?' Carly asked.

'Me,' he said. 'Me. I rejected them. I called him personally. I loved to get his goat, get him all riled up. I'd tell him I had an intern position open if he wanted it. I liked getting him all blustering and spitting.'

'You do that with many people,' Carly said.

'I do. It is my *raison d'être*.' He smiled. 'Now that's a phrase Whitney would have used.

'What did he have on you?' Carly asked.

'Personally, I live a pretty boring life these days. I regret to admit there is nothing scandalous here. My obsessions are public. You can read them every week in the paper.' He halted, took a deep breath. 'I haven't killed anyone. I haven't had sex with a goat, but even if I did, no big deal. You know, if there's something really embarrassing to be revealed about me, I'm as interested as anyone else.'

He said all of this in a casual manner, halting frequently to choose his words.

'What do you know about Frank Wiley?' she asked.

'Excellent photographer, but caught up in the romance of the Beats. Kind of limited his appeal.'

'He's on the list. Why?'

'This list, where did you get it?'

Carly smiled. 'An anonymous source close to the investigation.'

'We don't use anonymous sources in our publication,' he said. 'Unlike the mainstream press, we are journalists.' He grinned. Perhaps he wasn't so tough, Carly thought. 'I don't know what,' the publisher said, 'if anything, Frank Wiley would have to hide.'

'Agnes DeWitt?'

'She wrote her own tell-all and had some nasty things to say about Whitney. She's not quite capable of killing anyone. She's almost blind and nearing death, herself.'

Carly realized that Brozynski was enjoying the conversation. As a journalist, he was about to find out, if Carly continued, everyone who was on the list. Maybe it wasn't wise to continue. If she did it would be in next week's *Fog City Voice*. Maybe that was good. Maybe not.

'Who do you think might want Mr Warfield dead?' Carly asked.

'Shifting gears, I see,' he said. He was enjoying himself.

'Who?'

'Who might want him dead and who might be willing to do it are two different things. Warfield's son hated his father. We don't know why. Maybe just being in the man's shadow was enough to piss off young Warfield. Maybe it was that Whitney cheated on his mother. Whatever it is, his intense dislike of his father was known around town.'

'Who else?'

'Who else do you have on the list?' he asked.

If it were going to be tit for tat, she would offer up one.

'Samuel McFarland.'

Brozynski thought a moment. Nodded. 'Sure.'

'Why?'

'A host of reasons. McFarland was for the new North Beach hotel. He and Chiu.' Brozynski thought for a long time and Carly was happy that she got a second on the Chiu inclusion. 'But McFarland was trying to lay low in public on the issue. It was one of those deals that would piss off half his constituency. If he came out against it, he'd piss off the other half. The money half. It opened up the whole debate about North Beach as a thriving viable neighborhood versus honoring its history and leaving it as part of authentic San Francisco. Whitney was opposed to anything that would change things in North Beach. North Beach was a shrine. He bled at each change. He snarled at tourists too. He was vocal. And he had some pull.'

Brozynski seemed to tire after navigating his last answer. His eyes lost focus. He was either drifting off to his own thoughts or was bored. He excused himself, though he didn't get up. It was clear, Carly was expected to leave.

She got up to leave.

'By the way, I've been on many lists,' Brozynski said. 'Better ones than Warfield's – mayors, bikers, hospitals, corporate executives. I was probably on Nixon's.'

Carly met her friend Nadia at Delfina's on 18th Street near Valencia. The two of them got together at least once a week for a little light chatter. And Nadia's office – she ran a non-profit organization that helped artists – was in the Mission, where many of the younger, struggling artists congregated. Low rents. But that was changing, as it always did, and part of the Mission was no longer low rent. Trendy restaurants, like Delfina's, popped up all over on Valencia and Guerrero. Eventually, the Mission, like all San Francisco neighborhoods, would be gentrified.

Carly found Nadia sitting at an outside table at the restaurant's recently added Pizzeria – a more casual and less expensive place than the highly recommended dining room. Two glasses of wine were on the table.

Nadia smiled.

'I took the liberty of ordering you the cheap wine,' she said.

'You know me too well,' Carly said, settling into the chair and looking at all the young and mostly hip folks seated at sidewalk tables or walking by. 'What's up?'

'Putting together a show. I've rented a gallery for three weeks and we're pressing on new work in all media.'

An attractive woman came out to take their orders. They ordered Monterey Bay Sardines and a Margherita pizza. They would share. With Nadia, one always shared, which meant that any time they dined together, it would be a negotiation worthy of ambassadors and international trade.

'Sounds exciting,' Carly said after the server left, 'the show.'

'It is. I can't tell you how energizing it is to work with all this young talent.'

'Just working?' Carly asked, an edge in her voice. Nadia was often more than a little taken with her discoveries.

'Just work.' She smiled. 'Just work.' But the way she cocked her head suggested that the situation was fluid. 'And you? How's your partner?'

'Fine. We're working together.'

Nadia smiled. 'You come to terms about how you feel about him?'

Carly shrugged. 'We're *working* together. I think that's a wise way to keep things.'

'What are you working on?'

Carly explained. Nadia was fascinated, as Carly knew she would be, with William Blake. Why not? The good looks, the notoriety, the secrecy.

'And he's disappeared?' Nadia asked.

'For the moment.'

'And came to you because? You have such a reputation on the street? Because of your extraordinary beauty?'

'You might remember Anselmo Ruiz.'

'Yes, the old pervert.'

'I was at his studio picking out a painting for my office . . .'

'You went to him? You know I have access to some of the finest emerging artists anywhere. You could have a great bargain with all sorts of investment opportunities. Anselmo, bless his obese heart, is where he's going to be.'

'I like his work. I like him. And it reminds me of another time, with my parents, those days.'

'Sentiment. You're getting soft in your . . .'

'Old age?'

'. . . post adolescence, I was going to say.'

'I got it, Nadia. The cheap sentiment of an old woman.'

Nadia nodded. 'If you like.' She smiled as she shook her head. 'Yes. OK.'

'So I have a list of folks to find out about, some of them artists.

Can you fill me in?' Carly asked about Hawkes and Sumaoang even though they were on Lang's list. And about Lili D. Young and Frank Wiley.

Nadia did. Lili Young was a huge black woman who did watercolors of flowers. They were wonderful and in demand internationally. Her clients, Nadia explained with a touch of disdain, were interior designers not gallery owners. But she did well. She had no idea what Warfield might have had on her.

'I hear she is a tough, passionate woman,' Nadia said. 'She scares some folks.'

'OK, Richard Sumaoang,' Carly said.

'No, can't picture him. There are many folks out there putting oil on a canvas and hanging on.'

'Marshall Hawkes.'

Nadia raised her eyebrows. She grinned, then took a sip of the Multipulciano.

'A hateful little man,' Nadia said. 'But he is one of the most respected artists on the West Coast. His work isn't in the hundred thousand dollar bracket, but it's getting there. He is respected. Worshipped by those who favor his approach and his paintings are in all the right collections.'

'His secret?'

'He's a flaming queen,' Nadia said.

'Come on. That's nothing anymore. Certainly not in this town and I can't imagine it making any difference at all in the art world.'

'Exactly. But he tries to convince people he's straight and he's sued at least two publications for suggesting otherwise.'

'I don't get it,' Carly said.

'Neither does anyone else.'

'Why would Warfield dislike him?'

'I didn't follow Warfield. I mean, I knew he was some sort of legend in his own mind, but his life didn't in any way intersect mine.'

'OK, last one. Frank Wiley.'

She nodded. 'Now we're notching back down again. I only know about him because he belongs to some photographers' group. His work is, as far as I'm concerned, archival. Not that it's bad. He's very, very competent. But aside from a few portraits that found their way into *Time* and *Newsweek* back when North Beach was the center of the universe, he's pretty much of a nobody.'

Nadia continued to talk about other San Francisco artists, not realizing Carly had drifted off a bit.

'Are you seeing anyone?' Carly asked to change the subject.

'I'm seeing everyone,' Nadia said. 'And you, my little precious?'

'No.'

'Peter hasn't called again?'

'No.'

The rest of lunch was light gossip centering around Nadia and her young artists and about a planned trip to a hill town in Mexico where she would hook up with the best artists designing silver jewelry.

At home, Carly dodged the sprinklers Mr Nakamura had on a timer for the dry summer. It hadn't rained since February. Not really. In less than two months though, the rains would begin, and they would seem never to stop. That's how it was in San Francisco most years.

# Eight

As Carly left Delfina's in the Mission, Lang was across town, waiting at a table just inside the broad opening at the front of Enrico's in North Beach. He was waiting for Whitney Warfield's mistress. The restaurant was one of Lang's favorites and for a short time was doomed to the dustbin. Some said the assaults and killings in the neighborhood – most of them late at night on the same stretch of bawdy Broadway as Enrico's – might have dampened the enthusiasm of the restaurant's clientele.

But it was back, a little whitewash on the walls, some great jazz, and good food. Marlene Berensen was only twenty minutes late. She didn't apologize. Noah Lang could have forgiven her several more sins. She stepped out of a forties movie, a standard mistress. She might have been fifty. Then again, if she was, she was a pretty spectacular fifty. She and her clothes had attitude, a kind of casual attitude, the knowing, ready-for-anything look on her face complemented by something expensive she slipped on without thinking too much about it.

'Mr Lang?'

'Noah. And you are Marlene Berensen.'

'If not I've been living a lie,' she said, her smoky voice sounding like the crunch of dry leaves.

'You know Humphrey Bogart?' he asked.

She sat down. She got it. She didn't like it. The waiter came over immediately.

'Should I bring you a Scotch?'

She nodded.

Not a big surprise. It was her idea to meet there. But it was all playing too cool. In the real world and considering the number of years they were together, Lang thought, Warfield's mistress should look like Aunt Bee. She didn't.

'You wanted to talk about Whitney?'

She looked like she wanted a cigarette.

'I do. I'm trying to locate a manuscript he was writing,' Lang said.

'And if he was writing something, how do you figure you are entitled to it?'

'We think it might lead to his murderer,' Lang said, giving up the ruse since it didn't make a whole lot of sense after Marlene's question.

'And who is we?' she asked.

Here we go again, Lang thought.

'I've got this problem. I keep losing control of the interrogation. You'll help me out, won't you?'

'No.'

'Did you kill him?' Lang asked. If subtle conversation failed, maybe sudden rudeness would work.

She laughed. 'Where's my Scotch?' she asked the universe. The universe answered.

'Here, Ms Berensen,' the waiter said.

'You don't look devastated by his death.'

'I'm sorry. But I'm not devastated. Every night we slept together, I prepared myself to wake up to a corpse in the morning. He was overweight, ate and drank too much, never exercised, and had high blood pressure. Type A personality, full of anger and frustration. I'm surprised he lived as long as he did.'

'With all those qualities, no wonder you were attracted to him,' Lang said.

'He was also sweet, generous, frightened, creative and he loved me unconditionally.'

'Qualities he was careful to hide.'

'All men are babies,' she said. 'These silverback apes yell and beat their chests, but when they're alone at night, all by themselves, they need someone to help them through their nightmares.'

Just as he'd seen her before in countless movies, he'd heard the 'big baby' line before. Was that because it was true? Or was it that she was playing a role?

'I always thought that we are the people we were in the third grade,' Lang said. 'That's my theory anyway. If you remember who you were and how you acted in the third grade, that's you.'

She didn't respond.

'What kind of girl were you?'

'The kind of girl who stayed away from class clowns.'

Ouch. She wasn't far off.

'You weren't after the money, were you?' Noah sipped his beer.

'He didn't have that much. So where are we going here, Mr Lang?'

'The person who killed Whitney Warfield is likely someone who didn't want the book published. I'm told he was planning a tell-all and you were on the list of people who might object to that.'

'The theory is that the other woman is supposed to be a secret and that as that other woman I would be upset that our affair would become public. Everyone in Whitney's life knows about me – including his wife. I like Elena. We get along. We are polite to each other and the only consideration we do for the public is that we aren't in the same place at the same time with Whitney. I have no other shame. And Whitney would never do anything to hurt me.'

'You have any idea who wanted to kill him?'

'I came to meet you out of curiosity,' she said, getting up, grabbing her coat and bag. 'I'm leaving you out of boredom.'

'Who gets his royalties?' Lang asked.

She stopped. 'His family.'

'Don't you want his killer found?'

She didn't look back.

Musicians were setting up inside. He was either going to commit to a night of jazz and alcohol – and maybe, just maybe meet a beautiful girl – or head home to spend some quality time with Buddha.

'Boring?' he asked, as he stood and put enough dollars on the table to cover the drinks and a tip. 'Me?'

Frank Wiley's place wasn't all that far from Anselmo's. Nor was it all that different on the outside. Unremarkable exteriors on unremarkable streets. She found Wiley's dilapidated stairway halfway down the half block that dead-ended at another wooden structure.

She had to feel for each step as she climbed up to his door. The light that came from a naked bulb above his door did little more than cast indistinct shadows on the steps. Most of the light was absorbed by the blanket of night.

There was light inside. She knocked, waited, and knocked again. If he was there, she was determined to get him to the door.

She heard some muffled grumbling before the door opened.

Frank Wiley stood there, all bones and pale flesh. He had a skinny mustache and wisps of hair combed as if he had a full head of it. He wore a sleeveless white shirt and gray work pants and sandals with white socks. He also wore big, horn-rimmed glasses. Carly thought he looked like a bug. A nice bug. A harmless bug. His initial smile gave way to a look of befuddlement.

'I'm Carly Paladino. I'm an investigator looking into the affairs of Whitney Warfield.' Nice and succinct, she thought

His eyes, already magnified, widened. His face went dark.

'That's no affair of mine,' Wiley said. His tone was dismissive. He didn't quite close the door, but he had narrowed the gap.

'I'd really like to talk to you,' Carly said. 'I'd appreciate it very much. We're just trying to make sense of his death.'

'Why does that include me?'

'I'm afraid there is an indication that you and he had a falling out.'

'And you are not police,' he said. Though it was not a question, it seemed to demand confirmation.

'No.

'And if we talk?'

'I'm just trying to track down some nasty rumors,' Carly said.

'Involving me?'

'Perhaps.'

'Come in,' he said, stepping aside.

The room she stepped into was, in fact, set up as a small gallery. Aside from the sixteen large, flat cartons leaning against the far wall, the place was neat and clean, ready for visitors. Even the cartons were neat, stacked in groups of four, probably containing frames for large photographs or the photographs themselves. Black and white photographs were on the wall. She recognized a photograph of the old hungry i, an old hardware on Grant she remembered from her childhood, the Condor Club when Carol Doda was its headliner, and a place called the Black Cat.

'Where is the Black Cat?'

'Nowhere now,' he said. 'Closed in the early sixties. One of my first shots. Queer place, but everybody went there. It was over on Montgomery near Columbus.'

She noticed photographs of places she knew – Caffe Trieste, City Lights Bookstore, Vesuvio, Tosca, the Savoy Tivoli, Caffe Roma long before it was refurbished. There were photographs of restaurants, many of them still there. But she was reminded how many had gone. She looked around for a photograph of her parents' place. Didn't see it.

'Did you ever photograph Paladino's?' she asked.

'You that girl who used to fill up the water glasses?'

She nodded.

He seemed to soften. 'I'll find that photograph for you when we're done. Have a seat.'

There were three mismatched chairs. She chose one.

'What would you like to know?' he asked.

'Who hated him so much?'

'He was not a likable guy,' Wiley said. 'It's kind of a cliché, but he was a complex person. I think he hated individual people but loved mankind. He was constantly disappointed with every cause he ever pursued and in every person he came to trust. They couldn't help but betray him in some way. Yet, he had this ability to attract people at the same time. The one thing he never lost was his passion for telling the truth.'

'As he saw it,' Carly said.

Wiley nodded. 'Of course.'

'What was your relationship with him?'

'We remained friends, I think, mostly because I didn't talk much. I listened. I took "pictures", as he used to say. He'd love it when I photographed him. He used to tell me that I was the only one who told the truth.'

'Is that right?'

'I let the camera talk.'

'No portraits up there. I read you photographed some of the greats from the Beat era.'

'I did.'

'You don't have any up on the walls.'

'I don't have a lot up on the walls.'

'I understand you have a big show coming up.'

For a moment, his stare was cold. 'Who told you that?'

'The people at Reed Fine Arts.'

'Yeah, well. I do, I guess.'

'New work?'

'Never before seen,' he said. He was uncomfortable.

'Are those for the show?' she asked, pointing to the sixteen cartons against the wall.

Wiley looked nervous. 'What is it you want?' he asked.

'Can I get a sneak preview?'

'No.'

'Mrs Wiley, who might be either angry enough to kill him or so ashamed of something they'd kill him to keep him quiet?'

'I don't like the question.'

'You're not going to answer it?'

'Not my business,' he said.

'Police may want to talk to you,' she said. It was not so veiled a threat, but Wiley had thought through it.

'Can't do anything about that, I guess.'

She got very little else. Wiley only had nice and very general comments about the folks on the list, except for two, and he chose to say nothing about them. Marlene Berensen and Mickey Warfield.

*Inspector Vincente Gratelli requests the honor of your presence at the Thomas*
*J. Cahill Hall of Justice, San Francisco Police Department, Homicide Detail,*
*850 Bryant Street, Room 563, at 9 a.m. tomorrow.*
  *Your loving and devoted inspectors,*
  *Rose & Stern*

The note was tacked to Lang's door.

Room 563 had maybe a dozen desks. Along one wall was a row of smaller rooms with windows that opened to the larger room. Gratelli, in a gray, slightly wrinkled suit, was talking with Noah Lang when Carly arrived.

'You got the invitation,' Lang said to her.

She looked puzzled.

'I got a call last night at home,' she said.

'Well, I got a formal invitation. Not quite engraved, but the intention was noble.'

The two of them followed Gratelli into one of the interrogation rooms.

'This is pretty scary,' Lang said, grinning. 'Should we call a lawyer?'

'We're short of conference rooms,' Gratelli said. The two private investigators sat on the far side, where suspects usually sat. Gratelli sat across from them, hands folded on the table, a look of troubled patience on his woeful, ageing face. 'We have two ways of doing this,' he said without menace. His tone was almost always sane and drama-free. 'One, we can make your lives miserable because you are interfering in a police investigation . . .' He waited.

'Or?' Lang said.

'Or we can work together. One problem we always have as civil servants is that we are understaffed. Now, officially, we aren't sanctioning private investigation, but we can all go about our business in a friendly way by including the others in what we find out.'

Carly looked at Lang. Lang nodded.

'We can do that,' she said.

'All right, let's start with this: Who is your client?'

Both Lang and Carly smiled and in the same not-on-your-life way.

'We'll give you a list of names,' Carly said. Lang winced. 'These are people we are told who have at least one major reason to keep Warfield from publishing his book.'

Gratelli nodded.

'What can you give us?' Carly asked.

'I can tell you what the medical examiners said.'

'What was that?' Lang asked.

'He was killed by a Mont Blanc fountain pen.' Gratelli gave them a long look. 'I'm telling you this, but I'm not releasing that information to the media or to the public in any way. You understand?'

Lang nodded.

'And what did you find at the crime scene that would be helpful?' Carly leaned forward.

'Nothing. No fingerprints. Nothing left behind in the crime scene. No footprints. Nothing.'

'Insurance? Wills?' Carly asked.

'Too early.'

'Well, you're coming up short,' Lang said. 'Not exactly a fair trade.'

Gratelli unfolded and refolded his hands.

'One of the most important things we can do in a murder investigation is to understand what we don't know.'

'This is a known unknown or is that an unknown known?' Lang asked and then responded to Gratelli's raised eyebrows. 'The great poet Rumsfeld. Rummy as he is often called with very little affection.'

'Known unknown,' Gratelli said. 'You see, you're catching on.'

'Thing is, you have nothing,' Carly said.

'We have a body. Actually we do know what he had for dinner, that he was on high blood pressure medicine, that his liver would have done him in pretty soon. We also know you've talked with Richard Sumaoang and Mrs Berensen and that Ms Paladino raised the ire of Mr Reed and Reed Fine Arts and amused the publisher of the *Fog City Voice* who wanted to send out a reporter to interview me for a story. Your investigation hasn't been particularly subtle.'

'It wasn't meant to be,' Lang said, defensively. 'And we're just looking for a book, remember?'

'You might be surprised to know there is some validity to your claim,' Gratelli said. 'Warfield's hard drive was stolen and if he had downloaded any material on disks or thumb drives, they're gone too.'

'Broke into his house?' Carly said.

'His studio,' Gratelli said. 'A small place in back of his house where he apparently went to write or escape the family.'

'And he'd want to do that because?' Carly continued.

'The Warfields are not the Nelsons.'

'You have any thoughts on any of those folks on your list?' Gratelli asked.

'No one admits to having a motive, but so far everyone seems to agree that he had enemies.'

'We'll keep in touch,' Carly said, getting up. Lang followed her lead. 'So you keep in touch.'

Gratelli nodded, but didn't move.

Lang turned back. 'Do your friends Rose and Stern know we're all one big happy family?'

Gratelli's look suggested that Lang already knew the answer.

'They know.'

'But?' Lang asked.

'Yeah, but what am I gonna do?'

# Nine

Lang ran into Brinkman on the first floor.

'We can walk faster,' Lang told Brinkman as he stood in front of the elevator doors.

'But I'd have to move my legs,' Brinkman said.

'Yes. There are disadvantages.' They stepped in the elevator and it slowly began to clunk upward. 'Incidentally, your fly is open.'

Brinkman looked down, zipped up, looked at Lang.

'Why in the hell are you looking down there? Jesus.' He zipped up angrily.

'If you think for one minute that I'm interested in an ill-tempered, sloppily dressed old male carcass, you are mistaken.'

'Ah . . .' Brinkman said, shaking his finger at Lang, 'your lips speak but your eyes say different.'

After a brief eternity, the doors opened in front of Lang's office. Lang stopped to respond to the strange look on Thanh's face. Brinkman went on.

'There are a couple of guys in your office,' Thanh said to Lang in the reception area. He made a grim face. The hard, tough look was especially strange because Thanh was a kind of androgynous creature this mid-morning. Dark hair swept back in what used to be called a page boy, a loose-fitting, expensive tee shirt that dipped unusually low from the neck, and a gold bracelet, also loose-fitting, on his left wrist. However, what make-up, if any, Thanh had applied, was invisible. Lang doubted anyone could be sure whether this mysterious being was male or female.

'Stop over when you're done,' Carly said to Lang. She took a long look at Thanh. Her eyes smiled even if her lips didn't.'

'Rose and Stern?'

Thanh shook his head, spoke in a whisper. 'Not cops. Not accountants either. The big guy, a gun under his left arm.'

'A gun?' Lang asked softly.

'Or his lunch. But it's something.'

Lang nodded, took a deep breath, walked into his office.

The big guy allegedly carrying a weapon was looking out of the window. He turned to face the room. He could have been Stern's brother, a big white guy who, like Stern, wore a suit he grew out of five years ago. The other guy, seated on Lang's tacky sofa, was at least six foot, but he was all bone, almost lost in his suit. Eyes recessed in their dark sockets, he had a feral, hungry look.

It was the big guy who spoke first. He came away from the window, took a few steps and stopped. He pulled on his nose, perhaps, Lang thought, to show how bored and unintimidated he was with his task, which began to unfold immediately.

'Lang, nobody likes violence,' the man said.

'Nobody,' the feral man agreed.

'You should tell the film industry,' Lang said. 'Body parts flying everywhere.'

'So you like violence?' the man asked as if it was an objective inquiry.

'I'm not committed to it.'

'You have any idea why we're here?' The big man walked over to Lang, who remained by the door.

'Apparently to register your personal opinion on the nature of the world, but I'm not collecting or keeping track of opinions. You might want to talk to the Gallup people.'

The big man smiled. Maybe he was going to get to enjoy his work.

'But sometimes violence is the only answer,' the man said, 'don't you think?' He maintained a cool, conversational tone.

'Depends on the question,' Lang said.

'Exactly,' the feral man said.

'Yes,' the big man said, 'he seems to be bright enough to understand.'

Lang waited.

'The question is: Will you drop your little adventure regarding Whitney Warfield?'

Thanh came into the room. He brought with him a 35 mm camera. He smiled at the gentlemen.

'Could you two move closer together, so I can get you both in?'

The big man looked shocked. The feral man started to obey.

'Get the fuck outta here, whatever in the hell you are,' the big man said.

'Solo portraits are good enough, I guess,' Thanh said.

He brought the camera up to his eye and the flash went off once. Thanh pivoted and caught the feral guy as the man started toward Thanh.

Lang tripped him.

'We have a collection of thug photos,' Thanh said, as the big guy reached for his pistol.

'It's a lovely album,' Lang said. 'You are perfect specimens.'

'My boss loves people like you,' Thanh said, 'His album is titled "Thugs I have Known".'

'And loved,' Lang added.

The feral man climbed to his feet, pulling out a 9 mm.

'You are one sorry bitch,' he said to Thanh.

From the back room came Barry Brinkman, a lit cigarette between his lips, and a shotgun in his hands.

'You're not supposed to smoke in here,' Lang said.

The two intruders turned back. From the look on their faces, they didn't know whether to laugh or run.

'You guys are spoiling my nap,' Brinkman said.

'Get back in your cage, you old fart,' the feral man said.

The sound of the shotgun firing shook the office and created a steaming hole in front of the big man.

'Now I got one barrel left. Who wants it?'

Thanh took more photographs. The lights were flashing as Carly rushed in. She stopped abruptly.

'What's going on?'

'Brinkman's smoking again,' Lang said. 'The only way to trust him is to keep your eyes on him.' He looked at the big guy. 'You see what I have to put up with? You guys want some coffee or anything?'

'Way too cute,' the big guy said.

'Too cute to live,' the feral guy said. It was obvious the situation for them was awkward and embarrassing.

'Take out your guns carefully,' Brinkman said.

'Don't have one,' the big guy said.

'Yes you do,' Thanh said. 'Or a major growth you might want to have a doctor look at.'

'Put it on the floor,' Brinkman said, aiming the shotgun at him.

The man did as he was asked and when Brinkman pointed the shotgun at the feral man, he too put his weapon on the floor.

They left, backing out to the outer office, then turning and moving quickly. Lang nodded toward Thanh. Thanh nodded back.

'You had to actually fire the damn thing?' Lang said to Brinkman after everyone left the room. Carly had been the last to go, smiling and shaking her head in disbelief.

'Didn't mean to. I farted, startled myself so bad my finger flinched. Reflex.'

Fortunately concrete separated the floors, Lang thought.

'Let's take the ammunition out, remove the firing pins and drop the guns down the trash chute,' he told Brinkman.


Carly and Lang went to the trendy little neighborhood of Hayes Valley for lunch. They picked out some miniature sandwiches at the new Boulangerie, some bottled lemonade and, because the bakery was crowded, took their treasure to a narrow park – a wide median, between north- and south-flowing traffic ending at Hayes Street.

'I used to live in a little studio apartment at the Estrella,' he said, pointing east to a thirties brick building, 'when I first arrived. This area was basically Needle Park. I saw more fights at the laundromat than in most redneck bars. Now, its all shoe stores and restaurants.'

'And slender, fashionably dressed young people,' Carly said with a sigh.

'And you are slender and fashionably dressed,' Lang said.

'Two out of three, huh?' She'd see if she could get by with 'slender'. It wasn't likely she could get by with 'young'.

'Young is relative,' Lang said, taking a bite of chicken and Brie down-sized baguette. 'This is why the rest of the country hates us.'

'Chicken or Brie or tiny sandwiches?'

'Brie mostly. I didn't eat Brie until I was thirty-five.'

'You eat it often now?' Carly asked.

'Usually with beef jerky, some pork rinds and a PBR. You?'

She repressed a grin. 'I do. I began eating Brie shortly after I was born.'

'Mmmmh, I hadn't thought about that. You don't need teeth. We should bring some back for Brinkman.'

'That's cruel.'

'Have you listened to his graphic lectures on the horrors of growing old? That's cruel. It's heartless. It's best to make that journey in blissful ignorance . . .'

She laughed, but caught herself.

'They came to see *you*,' she said, trying to introduce the business at hand.

'That means it's someone on my half of the list.'

'Somehow. Directly or indirectly.'

'Somehow,' he agreed. 'I talked with Richard Sumaoang, Marshall Hawkes and Marlene Berensen. So these two Mensa candidates were bought by someone who knew how to find them. I don't see it.'

'People talk,' Carly said. 'One of your guys talked to someone who talked to someone who became worried.'

'Doesn't give us much.'

'Thanh is following them,' Lang said. 'He'll find out something, maybe only where they live or work. We can go from there.'

'What do you think of the people you talked to?'

'As I told you earlier, Marlene is well preserved, doesn't seem too broken up. Richard gave me nothing. He's in great shape. Physically he'd have no problem killing his prey. Marshall Hawkes doesn't seem like a physical kind of guy, but using the pen as a weapon has a certain bit of poetry about it and Marshall seems to appreciate that sort of thing. What about your people?'

'The publisher. I'm not sure he's agile enough to catch Warfield. Frank Wiley seemed so content to be on the outside looking in, I'm not sure what he'd have to lose if some secret came out, unless it could get him arrested.'

'That could be enough. Pedophile kind of taboo.'

She sipped her lemonade from the bottle and looked at her watch.

'I have Nathan Malone at one thirty and Lili D. Young at four,' she said.

Behind Carly, a teen girl with a bare midriff twirled a hula hoop, entertaining a small audience, the most avid of which was a golden retriever. The park served its purpose, providing a brief respite to office workers on lunch break and a soft landing for a couple of homeless people who parked their shopping carts for a little while.

'Mr Chiu is always unavailable, Mrs Warfield is still grieving,' Lang said. 'But I'll try to get in to see ancient Agnes. Maybe she knows somebody who knows somebody.'

They talked about movies, finished their lunches and went their separate ways. On the way to Lang's beat-up Mercedes, Thanh called. He had some information.

# Ten

Carly thought about Lang's comments on Hayes Valley – how it had changed from derelict and dangerous to stylish and expensive. Where else would you find a liquor store that sold only sake? San Francisco had changed. She'd heard the complaint many times. With each passing generation, the older one bemoans the changes brought about by the younger ones. The Castro area she was driving through was a prime example. At one point it was an Irish neighborhood, then it became the most famous or infamous gay neighborhood in the world. Young guys with mustaches wore Levi's jeans and plaid shirts and posed as Marlboro men not that many decades ago. Today, young heterosexual couples with their baby strollers were coming over the hill from Noe Valley to mix with the gay couples and their baby strollers. Just as there were no more pirates on the Barbary Coast and the Chinese were finally permitted to leave Chinatown, the entire city was both better and worse for changing times. Prejudice had indeed gone down. The cost of living had indeed gone up. San Francisco had one of the highest median incomes of any city in the country.

She turned left on Hill Street and entered a quiet little hilltop neighborhood with handsome, well-kept homes; many, she guessed, with remarkable views. To the north one was likely to look down a long way as homes stretched out to the Bay. Nathan Malone lived on the other side of the street.

Mrs Malone, as she introduced herself, was a silver-haired, spirited woman in a yellow pantsuit, who was carrying what appeared to be a drink. There was a twist of lime, an inch of clear liquid and some ice. She was in her late sixties or early seventies, Carly guessed as the woman guided her to the back of the house. They went through an arch and into a room where a wall of windows looked out over a deck and an expanse of homes that climbed up another distant hill. The walls on either side of the window were lined with bookcases. Malone was at the computer and hadn't looked up, perhaps finishing a sentence before engaging the visitor.

Carly noticed that the top row of the bookcase behind his desk contained books Malone had authored. Non-fiction mostly. Some biographies. Some seemed to reference history. But there were a couple, she recognized from her background check, that were novels.

Nathan Malone got up from his desk. He was as striking and as energetic-looking as his wife and probably very nearly the same age. His hair, and it appeared he had all of it, was a mix of silver and blond in tousled curls. He came from around the desk to shake hands.

'Can I get you anything?' Mrs Malone asked.

'No, thank you. Just had lunch.'

Malone answered his wife with a subtle shake of his head and a frown. His gaze was directed at his wife's drink. She didn't notice. He raised his eyebrows. His expression seemed to be one of total submission to the forces around him. As his wife retreated, he nodded toward a big, high-backed chair upholstered in brown leather, he sat in a matching chair separated by a small table. On the table were two magazines – *The New Yorker* and *Publishers Weekly*.

'You're from New York, right?' Carly asked.

'I am. In terms of career, moving out here may have been a major mistake. In those days and for many years thereafter, serious writers were supposed to live in New York.' He paused, shook his head. 'But you wouldn't necessarily be interested in all that. You wanted to inquire about Whitney Warfield, you said on the phone.'

'Yes, thank you for taking the time. We believe he was writing a major tell-all book that might have caused his death. Your name was given to us by someone who said that some of what he had to say would embarrass you.'

Malone smiled. 'I'm sure he could embarrass me. We had quite a few moments together, especially in our youth, that wouldn't be flattering, but not worth killing over.'

Malone seemed in general good humor.

'I'm very sorry he's dead,' he went on. 'I think we had a few wonderfully embarrassing moments ahead of us.'

'Maybe you could just tell me a little about the man.'

'Whitney always considered himself a major writer. If he had been a politician he wouldn't have been satisfied until his countenance was on Mount Rushmore. So he felt slighted that the world hadn't acknowledged that he was the voice of his generation at least. No Nobels, no Pulitzers, no National Book Awards.'

'Were you too much competition, perhaps?' Carly asked.

Malone laughed. 'Of course. He loved the competition and often regarded his competitors as noble opponents. As life dealt him serious blows to his ego, his competitors seemed to lose their nobility.'

'You haven't had contact with him?'

'No. But I doubt if his character has changed much. He was really, at heart, a noble warrior. He believed in truth and honor and loyalty.'

'This is a man who cheated on his wife and was about to tell on his friends,' Carly said.

'If you have the scent of the killer, it could hardly have led you here, but for those of us who know and love Whitney, this is not in any way contradictory. What you have to understand is that when you are Whitney you are God, judge and jury. He is allowed his foibles because of how much he suffers . . . suffered for his art. It's an ego not uncommon with writers. They create their own universes. And most, foolishly, mirror this one.'

'You liked him?'

'Sure. We were very close friends.'

'You wrote a book together.'

'Not really. We both contributed to a photography book. Frank Wiley's. It was Wiley's book, really.'

'What happened to you two?'

'I don't know what you mean. We stopped hanging out with each other primarily because I settled down. I no longer wanted to engage in drinking contests. I wanted to be with one woman. I wanted to go to bed early. I'm afraid I dwindled in Whitney's esteem, but he didn't hate me. And I didn't hate him.'

'He knew no damning secret about you?' Carly smiled. She had received a thorough looking over when she arrived. He may have wanted to be with one woman as he said, she thought, but he wasn't done looking. It was also clear that he was debating something. There was a long, long pause. Carly waited it out.

Malone got up.

'Once, when we had been drinking, which we both did to excess at the drop of a metaphor, we were talking about what it meant to be a man. And in order to be a man, one had to be willing to fight, physically, whenever it was called for. Honor, loyalty, etc. One wasn't much of a man if he never seriously considered killing himself, never spent a night in jail, never planted a tree, never fathered a child, never slept with a whore, never . . . I forget. There was quite a list. And so we were being honest with each other.'

'Trying to out-macho the other guy.'

Malone grinned. 'Well, yeah. Otherwise what was the point? That was part of being a man. You know, lifting more weight, throwing the ball farther, having more foul words at your command . . .'

'You outdid him?'

'Foolishly, I told him something. When you're drinking and the conversation and the competition escalates and the inhibitions fall by the wayside . . .'

'And?' Carly asked, trying to drag him back from thoughts to words.

'After tales of bar fights and injuries, I told him something.'

He walked to the glass doors and stepped out on the deck.

Carly followed. He was still debating whether to tell her. She knew it. He wasn't trying to talk himself out of saying any more.

'It's the "something" I'm interested in,' she said.

The wind blew. There was a light arctic chill just behind the warm breeze. The sky was pure blue – no clouds, no smog.

'Tell me.'

'I regretted telling him. Very much. Now he's dead. It's not out there anymore.' He seemed to be talking to himself. 'Why would I want it to be?'

'It might be in a book.'

He turned to her. There was a smile on his face, but his eyes looked sad.

'I killed a man.'

He said it. Now he was questioning himself. Why had he said it? She could see that on his face.

'In war?'

'No.'

'Accidentally?'

'No.'

'Murder.'

'A court might think so,' he said. He laughed, but it wasn't jovial. 'I guess I had to make sure someone knew. Better a stranger now. You know I can deny it.'

'What happened?' she asked.

'I'm not going to tell you. I need to withhold the facts. You can see why. I don't want you looking into it.'

'What happened when you told him?' she asked.

'What I expected, humiliation.'

'Jealous that he hadn't killed anyone?'

'Partially.' Though expression on the lips had been suppressed, there was a grin behind Malone's eyes at the moment. 'It's not just a man thing . . . it was a writer thing too – at least for those of us in that generation. We needed to understand the human race in order to tell our stories. Understanding with the added benefit of suffering, or maybe just experience of any kind, yields a broader, richer insight into the human condition.'

'So he was going to tell the world you killed someone?'

'Would he, if he could? I've no idea. But he knew everything. Who, when, why, how, where.'

'And you could be brought up for murder.'

'I could.'

'Why did you tell me?'

'God knows,' he said then, without looking at her.

'Thank you,' she said.

He stared at her for a moment, though she wasn't sure he was looking at her. He swallowed hard and his eyes flickered in recognition as if he'd just come out of a coma.

'You can find your way out. If you run into Meg, tell her to bring me a Scotch.' He turned to her and smiled. 'If you find the book, make me a copy. I want to see if the old loony still had it in him.'

According to Thanh, the car he tailed on his bike parked on Geary and the two thugs went into a neighborhood bar called McKinney's. The big guy was in there maybe an hour and then came out. Thanh continued to follow the big guy because he was the one who appeared to be in charge and he was still moving. The man drove to Leavenworth and Post and went into an apartment building. Thanh didn't follow him inside. He waited outside, used his phone to photograph the apartment directory, and when the guy came out – ten minutes later – he drove to a parking garage on Polk Street. Thanh waited until the man emerged on foot. He went to a Chinese restaurant. In a few minutes the guy came out, pink plastic bag in hand, walked a few blocks and entered a building. That's when, at Lang's request, Thanh ended his tail.

Lang found the two-story brick building on Polk Street. Retail below, offices above. The door to the office space was unlocked. Lang went in. The stairway was carpeted, clean but a little musty. Upstairs was a hallway, two doors on each side. Two accountants, an attorney, and a door with a plastic sign on it that said:

SCOTTY MARKHAM
Personal Security
Confidential Investigations

Given the earlier clumsiness Lang was doubtful the guy had many cases that involved any real discretion – more likely bail skips and repos. Not that Lang could turn up his nose at those kinds of jobs without insulting himself. Markham probably specialized as a bodyguard when it required more muscle than brains and had colleagues of equal intelligence – the feral guy for example – he could pick up for a couple of bucks.

Scotty Markham was eating out of the white to-go container he held in one hand while diving in with a plastic fork with the other. A newspaper was open, sprawled out on top of the desk. At the edges were half a dozen fortune cookies, a stack of napkins and a can of Coke.

'You should have read your fortune before you showed up today,' Lang said.

Markham looked up. He wasn't surprised. He wasn't happy.

Lang came over, scooped up a couple of cookies.

'I see, you don't like one fortune you keep breaking them open until you find one you like.'

'Not lookin' to be entertained and you're not gettin' the name of my client, which is why you're here.'

'Pretty dumb, what you did,' Lang said. It wasn't meant to antagonize and it didn't.

'Yep.'

'You didn't think that a couple of guys making threats would change anything?'

'Nope.'

Lang stood, waiting for an explanation. He looked down at the floor. Black and green asphalt tiles. The walls were hardware versions of wood paneling, once shiny, now not so much. There were two metal chairs with green vinyl cushions. The guy was living in a parallel universe to Lang.

Markham looked up again. 'You still here?'

'Just trying to make sense of it all,' Lang said.

'Look, a guy hires me. Tells me what to do. I tell him it is foolish. He says, do I want the money? His dime, Lang. That's how I make a living. Tell me how you do it.'

'Not that far off.'

'I didn't think so. Listen, I'm not lookin' for buddies. You got something else to say?'

'No. I'll let the guy know he should have listened to you,' Lang said.

Markham made eye contact, smiled, nodded. 'You do that.'

# Eleven

Carly found herself on another hilltop, this one Potrero Hill. From its main street one had a dramatic view of the city's skyline. Quaint restaurants, a coffee shop, a grocer or two lined what could be the business street of any small town. She thought the place should have its own mayor and its own sheriff. But it was just another San Francisco neighborhood. She found her street, turned right and finding her address she discovered a parking spot not too far away.

No one answered the door. Carly looked around and found a narrow brick walkway between the artist's home and her neighbor's. There was sun at the other end. In the sun was a large and attractive black woman in a big straw hat and a leafy print dress seated beside a pond, one foot in the water. Around her were small glass dishes, each with a different colored mixture of paint and water. And near her was a sheet of thick paper on which she painted exotic flowers.

'Lili?' Carly asked.

The woman turned around, gave Carly a warm, welcoming smile.

'Come sit by me while I finish this,' she said.

'Sorry to interrupt your work,' Carly said.

'Have to if you want to talk with me. All I do is work. I put the brush down, I go to bed. I get up, I pick up the brush.' She smiled broadly and, it appeared to Carly, with honest joy. 'It is my life.'

'Pretty tough schedule.'

She grinned again.

'Of course, I do put in some time eating, as you can guess, so don't go feeling too sorry for me.'

According to the various stories on the web about Lili D. Young, the artist had become more of an illustrator than painter. Her watercolors could be found on greeting cards and on menus and signs. She was successful enough to have a nice house, probably bought years ago when Potrero Hill was considered a less desirable neighborhood.

Carly sat on the ground, giving Lili the space she needed for her work. It was pleasant. Carp cruised and darted around Lili's submerged foot and beneath half a dozen lily pads.

'You come to talk to me about Whitney?'

'Yes. You knew him?'

'A long, long time ago. He used to come down to this big old building where all the artists hung out. He had artist friends and he was welcome. I was young and skinny and sexy and I had the agility of a gymnast. And I think old Whitney – he seemed old even then though he couldn't have been – picked me out of the herd.'

She smiled.

'I know what I'm saying. That's the way he was. Of course, I have to say, that's the way a lot of them were. And I didn't always dislike being picked out. Different days then . . . um . . . what's your name again?'

'Carly.'

'Those days were so different, Carly, I can't tell you. Seems like human beings figured out that sex was . . . well, you remember . . . no, you don't remember all that much, but people said "whatever gets you through the night". And people slept with each other because there was no damn good reason not to. It wasn't about making a family. It was about love. Love with a small "l". The other love would come later if it came.'

'Did it come for you?' Carly asked, instantly regretting she did.

'You don't want to go there, sweetheart. You don't have the time and I don't have the inclination.'

The face was kind but the eyes weren't.

Lili continued to apply color to the paper, dipping her brush in the pond water to dilute a color. Carly noticed that Lili, unless she had help, and judging by the lush growth of ferns and palms and exotic flowers, had to have done a fair amount of digging, pruning, fertilizing, watering and whatever else was necessary to have a little Eden on the hill.

'You live here by yourself?'

'Just me and the ghosts,' Lili said.

'The ghosts?'

Lili smiled broadly.

'All of us have ghosts,' she said.

'You and Mr Warfield have ghosts in common?'

'This is about him getting killed,' Lili said.

'Yes, and about a book that allegedly reveals secrets about some people.'

'And I'm one of them?'

'That's what we hear.'

She put the brush down. Her face lost its sense of joy.

'Are you OK?' Carly asked.

'Sure, sweetheart. I'm fine. Just thinking about secrets. We were talking about ghosts, weren't we? You want to forget so bad and you can for periods of time. But they sneak back from the basement to the front room of your mind like a sly child. And they make you take notice and make you feel what you felt then all over again.'

Lili pulled her leg from the water and stood up. She left her brushes and the little dishes of paint. She picked up her unfinished painting and started toward the house.

'Hope you won't mind too much, Carly, but I'm exhausted.'

Carly got to her feet.

'Maybe . . .' Carly managed to get out.

'Maybe we can, sweetheart,' Lili said, turning back briefly. 'Some other time. Maybe there's more to talk about. Maybe there isn't.'

It took a little longer than it should have, Carly thought as she walked the narrow walk back to the street, for her to realize she had become the ghost bearer. She would have felt better if she'd left her interviewees angry, but she was making them dredge up old feelings they wanted to keep buried. Except for Bart Brozynski, who seemed amused, Carly was bringing only pain, no cure.

Maybe one of these people killed Whitney Warfield, she thought. If that was the case, it might mean eleven of them didn't. But they'd have to suffer some anyway.

\*　　\*　　\*

Agnes DeWitt was a pale, delicate woman, tiny spider web cracks in her porcelain face, Lang thought. Research put her at ninety, not eighty. She met him at the door of her apartment just off Van Ness near the Civic Center.

'I don't know what I can tell you,' she said after cordially inviting him in. She wore jeans, a white blouse and a sweater, though it had to be about eighty degrees in her apartment. 'May I get you some tea or a glass of water?'

Her living room was not one of an elderly spinster. It was full of books, art and bright colors. Lang was sure that the huge painting over the sofa was done by the same artist as the painting Carly just brought into the office.

Agnes DeWitt saw him stare at it.

'Anselmo Ruiz,' she said. 'An old friend.'

He did want a glass of water and followed her to the kitchen, all the while trying to imagine this slow-walking brittle woman chasing down Whitney Warfield at three in the morning and stabbing him with a pen.

'We can sit here, if you like,' she said. 'It's cheerier than the living room.'

'I appreciate your taking the time to speak to me,' Lang said, sitting down.

She laughed. It was a little girl's laugh. She opened the refrigerator and pulled out a pitcher of water that had a filter system. She poured into a clear, unadorned glass. Her hand and arm shook slightly.

'I'm going to put some tea on for myself,' she said, turning on the fire underneath an ancient tea kettle. 'Are you sure you wouldn't like to have some tea as well?'

'This is perfect,' Lang said. 'Are you working on anything these days?'

'I have thoughts. Mostly, that is what I have. Thoughts.'

He watched as she prepared the tea. She brought a napkin, a teacup and saucer to the table. She moved with precision. Was that her nature? Or was it a necessity?

'Did you know Ginsberg and Kerouac and the other North Beach legends?'

'Oh, yes. Poor Jack. He was such a sloppy writer. I wanted to take him under my wing and teach him it was not a crime to edit one's own words. They are not sacred.'

'Were you a prim and proper young lady?' Lang dared to ask.

She turned to look at him. Her eyes came to life.

'Whatever made you think that?' She was amused at the question.

'There's a lovely formality about you.'

'I think that is very nice of you to say. The use of the word "formal" is probably apt. I believe that is the person I seem to project. But we are not always who we appear to be. We're not being dishonest. Sometimes the outside betrays the inside.'

'Did you know Whitney Warfield?'

The tea kettle hissed. She poured a little hot water into a small teapot – "hotting the pot", she explained – then poured it out. She put some tea in the pot and followed it with more hot water. She brought the pot to the table and sat.

'Yes. I knew him quite well. I was one of the older ones in a loose-knit group. It wasn't official, you see. People who had similar philosophies and similar goals seemed to find the same bar or coffee shop. Whitney was part of the second wave of these people, the first being Allen and Jack and a dozen or so others. Whitney really wasn't in the same league.'

'He wasn't a good writer?'

'On the contrary, he was an excellent writer; a little too blustery for my taste, but others could have learned from him. What I mean to suggest is that real genius creates new ways of thinking and creating. Allen's *Howl* and Jack's *On the Road* launched a movement and those who were around at the time were taking similar risks. They weren't always completely successful, but they were legends, not necessarily because of their talent, but because they were first.'

'That bothered Warfield?'

'He refused to accept his station in literary history. I wrote about that in one of my books and Whitney was livid.'

'You know he was writing a book. I gather it is a book of revenge, revealing secrets about people who may have done him wrong.'

'That wouldn't surprise me, Mr Lang.'

'You have secrets, Ms DeWitt?'

'Would life have been worth living if we hadn't done something we wish to hide? And I suspect the world is allowed only so many saints.'

She poured tea into her cup, barely able to hold the pot steady. Even as she raised her cup to her lips to delicately blow on the surface, her hand trembled slightly.

Lang wondered if he'd get to that point where he found lifting a cup of tea a strenuous task.

'What do you think of his death?' Lang asked. He wanted to get more from her, some perspective that may have escaped his own, uninformed analysis.

'He was a man who started many wars, personal wars. He was, in his way, a violent man. His words were full of violence. His death fits into the context of his life.'

'You have any idea who might have killed him?'

'It seems evident, doesn't it? Not who – I don't know – but why,' she said. 'One doesn't kill over general dislike or disapproval. It has to be more personal.'

'Yes, to prevent the publication of a deep, dark secret.'

She smiled.

'Did you want to kill him?' Lang asked.

'Do you want to know my whereabouts at the time of his death?'

She gave 'whereabouts' a special emphasis, smiling as she said it. 'Whitney never gave up, never gave in. He never knew when the party was over.'

'You knew,' Lang said.

'I did. I believe I did. I knew when it was time to move on. And I did, perhaps until now. Now, I'm digging in my heels.' She smiled. Her eyes were very much alive. She was engaged and enjoying it. 'I do live in the past, I admit. There's so much more of it. Still, inside this body of vanishing flesh, diminishing muscle and worn organs, there is a girl of eighteen.'

'I believe it,' Lang said. He almost said 'a very beautiful girl', but caught himself. She was beautiful now. 'I didn't know you when you were younger,' he said, 'but you couldn't have been more beautiful than you are now.'

'And all I gave you was a glass of water,' she said, still smiling. 'You are much too easy, Mr Lang.'


# Twelve


Unlike cities and towns in the Midwest and most of the West, San Francisco's neighborhoods have buildings that open directly to the street or very near it. Whatever outdoors is connected to the home, business or apartment house is usually behind the structure and relatively private. Without alleys, a square block of backyards – some with exquisite gardens and others neglected – butt up against each other. Those with flats or apartments on the second or third floors can look out over an entire square block of backyards.

Lang, sitting in back of the former Chinese laundry in the Western Addition – in the darkness – could see various windows lit. He didn't have Jimmy Stewart's voyeuristic view in *Rear Window*, but he could imagine in this incredibly diverse city all sorts of families and relationships existed behind these windows. He could imagine how each created its own cultural enclave – Spanish, Chinese and English coming from the television sets, curry, ginger, chilies coming from the stoves.

And there he was, sitting on a rickety chair on a slab of concrete in the night, thinking about his part in all this; thinking about the day and his conversations with Carly. He sipped his Cabernet and smiled at what many of his old friends, miles to the east, would think of him. They would think of the horrible things San Francisco does to a real, beer-drinking, hotdog-eating, football-watching, Ford truck-driving man, turning him into a wine-tasting, Brie-eating, opera-listening, cat-loving, Volvo-driving, sometimes life-experimenting, self-reflecting alien. The horror of it all.

The thing was, Noah Lang liked the fact he was no longer the Noah Lang of ten or twenty years ago – a lousy husband with an angry, fenced-in mind and a hardened soul. Since then he had yielded to the universe a bit, following the cosmic joke school of philosophy, modified only by loyalty to friends and a willingness to do what is necessary for his and his friends' survival.

The night was clear enough to see the stars. The sound of a saxophone came lightly from the stereo inside. For some reason he remembered his sister. Her lovely life was too short. Death plucks you from earth when it will. Sometimes you see it coming; sometimes you don't. Lang had come to terms with mortality, or perhaps just with the idea of mortality. Buddha traversed a narrow swatch of light that escaped from inside, his dark body blending with the darkness and Lang ended all thoughts that might lead to personal enlightenment.

The very old and very elegant Agnes DeWitt was off the list of suspects. In addition to the obvious factors for elimination, she had already won in any competition with Whitney Warfield. That left everyone else on his list – artist and poet Richard Sumaoang, the widow Elena Warfield, the prissy artist Marshall Hawkes, the mistress Marlene Berensen, the real estate developer Ralph Chiu and Lang's own contribution – the charming gigolo himself, William Blake.

In the morning he would see what he could do with the other list, the one Thanh compiled from the directory of the apartment building the bumbling gumshoe had visited before returning to his office.

*        *        *

Carly Paladino had ended her work day that afternoon by stopping by City Hall, a building bigger and grander than most statehouses, and topped by a gilt dome that seemed to symbolize former Mayor Willie Brown's imperial reign. The visit might have been a wasted effort. Supervisor Samuel McFarland was not to be found and his staff was not to be bothered.

Carly smiled at the bored male receptionist, dropping a card on the desk. 'Tell him it's about murder and scandal. Perhaps his.'

She turned, suddenly in a good mood. What she had said was true, but this was not her usual approach. Her partner Noah Lang seemed to be rubbing off on her? So be it, she told herself.

She picked up her dry cleaning and stopped at Whole Foods where she created her usual at the salad bar and selected two slices of pizza from the deli. The evening was planned. A load of laundry, a shower, one – and only one – glass of wine with her dinner, maybe a movie or a book and then to bed. Tomorrow morning was a running morning. That meant getting up early after a night of real sleep.

Her cell rang just as she got inside her flat. She dropped the dry cleaning on the sofa, freeing one hand to get the phone as she continued toward the kitchen with her dinner.

'Hello, Paladino speaking,' she said, flipping the phone open, jarred a bit by a light on in the kitchen.

'McFarland,' came a harsh voice. 'What is this crap you're peddling to my staff?'

She was about to answer when she reached the kitchen area. William Blake stood by the sink. He lifted a bottle of white wine and two glasses, a happy and expectant look on his face.

It was hard for her to get her bearings. It was only a minor problem being screamed at by the caller. It was a major problem having her home invaded by a man – handsome, yes, but still a relative stranger – who appeared to have some sort of celebration in mind.

'Mr McFarland. I've emailed and I've called. Again and again,' she said, glaring at Blake. 'You haven't given me the courtesy of a reply. At the moment, we have word that you and something very embarrassing about you may be revealed through a manuscript written by the late Whitney Warfield. We need to talk. I'm free at ten a.m. tomorrow morning. Your office?'

'Let's meet somewhere else. There's a coffee house on Church, near Market. Across from Aardvark Books. You know it?'

'I do. Ten.'

He disconnected.

'On the job,' Blake said. 'I'm impressed.'

'I'm not impressed,' Carly said.

'It's rude, I know. Calling you I run the risk of being overheard. Waiting outside for you to come home was too risky. I ran out of options.'

'I thought you'd be on some exotic island by now.'

He removed the cork from the bottle, 'You'll have some with me, won't you?'

She nodded. She might come across as petulant and petty if she didn't agree.

'I'll fill you in on what we have, though it isn't much. Too early.'

He poured the wine and handed her a glass. 'It's especially good for a white Bordeaux. Surprisingly smooth.'

'No fingerprints. The police have no clues. You are high on their suspect list. Our suspect list isn't thinning by much. The highly dangerous ninety-year-old Agnes DeWitt has been crossed off, I'm told.'

Blake nodded, obviously humoring her sarcasm.

'And I have trouble imagining the rather large artist Lili D. Young chasing Warfield down, hopping a fence and plunging a Mont Blanc pen in his neck.'

'A Mont Blanc?'

'Maybe like yours.'

He took a sip of wine, hopped up on the counter. 'I still have mine and wouldn't have left something so expensive behind.' He wore what appeared to be a light, cashmere blue-green V-neck sweater and tan slacks.

'You stay remarkably well dressed for a man on the run,' she said.

'I've never put all my eggs in one closet.'

'Warfield's computer seems to be missing and there are no discs or CDs to be found. No fingerprints found there either. Someone was very smart.'

'You see. There *is* a book then?'

She put her pizza and salad in the refrigerator.

'Dinner?' he asked. 'Would you like some dinner?'

'I wouldn't think you'd want to go out?'

'I know of a spectacular delivery service – duck confit, lobster, a Porterhouse, some exotic ravioli – whatever you want.' He smiled, slid down to the floor and moved to her. 'What about it?' He was close now, eyes looking into hers. 'I organize dinner here and maybe lay claim to your sofa just for tonight?'

Her mind went where she did not want it to go. Pheromones? What in the hell was going on? She tried to bring it all back to reality, but one thing was very clear. She had absolutely no interest in doing a load of laundry.

The silence awoke him. Gratelli closed his eyes again because everything seemed as if it were viewed through a fog. He blinked several times. Slowly the room came into focus. The music was gone. He had missed half of the opera, at least consciously, but it had been the score for pleasant visions. He and his wife had walked the beach in Hawaii in fragrant breezes, a gentle sun warming them. Memory, if that's what it was, hadn't faded the colors. They were intense and the time seemed more real than this moment.

He looked at the clock on the fireplace mantel. Eleven twenty-seven. He had slept past his bedtime. He stood, bones aching, and made his way to the kitchen where he ground some coffee and prepared the coffee maker for the morning. All he would have to do was push a button. He filled a glass with water and put it by the bed. In the bathroom he set the pills out for the morning and put them where he would see them. He checked the locks on the doors.

Gratelli undressed, put on his pajamas, climbed into bed and picked up the book on the bedside table. He made every effort to pick up where he left off. But he couldn't make it through the first sentence. He knew what it was. The decision to work with the two private investigators was nagging at him. He didn't usually second-guess himself, but this one might turn around and bite him in the butt.

He reminded himself that he needed the help. Even with Rose and Stern helping out part time – they had a load of cases they had yet to clear unrelated to the Warfield murder – Gratelli did not have enough time to do all that he needed to do. And where was this new partner he was supposed to get? How long was that going to take?

Nothing he could do. He made his bed, he thought, now he would lie in it. If only he could go to sleep in it.

She couldn't sleep. It was torment. She wanted to forget that William Blake was in the other room, so close. It was frighteningly intimate even if she could suppress the thoughts that made her uncomfortable. She wished she didn't have the conflicting feeling of wanting and not wanting.

'I'll do nothing to encourage it,' she told herself, turning again in bed, sheet and blanket askew. 'But if . . .' her mind continued, '. . . why would I stop it?'

Carly could feel a change. Air pressure perhaps. The room was quiet, but she knew. She did not hear him, but felt his presence.

'You need to get some rest,' he whispered as his body slid next to hers. Her back was to him. She didn't know whether to turn toward him or not. His lips touched her ear. 'I'm sorry. I didn't mean to make you anxious.'

She could hear herself swallow. He put his arm around her shoulders.

'We're going to sleep,' he said softly. 'That's all we're going to do.'

Even with the disappointment she could relax. She remembered little else until she awoke in the morning. There was a note on the kitchen counter.

'Thank you. Talk to you later.'

No signature. Beside the note was an envelope filled with large bills.

All he could remember of his dreams was running. He ran and ran last night, up hills, across sandy beaches, urban streets and long stretches of soft grass. He ran effortlessly, not knowing or apparently caring what it was he was running toward or from. Whatever the meaning, he had apparently worked up an appetite.

He dressed quickly, foregoing coffee at home, scratched Buddha behind the ears and walked down to Eddie's Cafe on Divisadero. He settled for the counter and scrambled eggs and hash browns. This was fuel. Only fuel. Home for a quick shower and the morning news. It sounded like yesterday's news and the day before.

Thanh was in jeans and a sweatshirt, looking young mannish. It took Lang a moment to see that Thanh had dressed like him.

'You have a rough night?' Lang asked him.

'It could have been rougher.' Thanh smiled.

'I don't want to know.'

'I don't want to tell.'

'Why are you dressed like me?'

'I'm not. You don't see any wine stains on my shirt do you?'

'Oh.' Lang looked down, lifted the bottom of his sweatshirt, shook his head. 'I dressed in the dark.'

'I don't want to know.'

'Is there any reason at all why I came in today?' Lang asked.

'No one called. No one came in. Carly will be in after her ten a.m.

meeting. I'll be in and out. You have a confirmed meeting with Ralph Chiu at three.'

'I thought no one called.'

'No one did. I called Mr Chiu and told him that you wanted to discuss something he might find embarrassing. And that he should see you.'

'Thanks.'

Thanh handed Lang a piece of notepaper bearing the name 'Chiu Realty'. The address was on Geary. The thug accompanying the PI was dropped at a bar on Geary, Lang remembered. But then again, there were a lot of small bars, offices and shops on Geary. It was the business district for many unremarkable enterprises.

On Lang's desk was another piece of paper from Thanh. This one was the list of about twenty names from the directory of the apartment house Scotty Markham visited before returning to his office. None matched any suspects on his or Carly's list. He'd keep it handy.

'Could you look up a PI named Scotty Markham?' he asked Thanh. 'Maybe Scott Markham. Scotty may be a nickname, so do your best.'

The place was called Thorough Bread and Pastry. It was a little before ten and she saw no one in the front who looked old enough to be a seasoned city supervisor. She had Googled him, knew what he looked like – a San Francisco businessman. That is, in the photo he had a suit and tie, but the look wouldn't play in the Financial District. His hair was just a little too long for most executives. He was playing down the middle. Maybe forty-five. White guy. Not a given in San Francisco. Of the eleven supervisors, roots could be traced to Africa, Asia, Mexico and Persia. Gay was OK too.

The little cafe was pleasant, offering what they promised, pastries, some prepared sandwiches, and coffee. The walls were shelves filled with fine wines. Straight ahead, past a few tables, was a three-step rise to the outside.

Carly guiltily ordered a latte – she'd flaked out on her planned morning run – and headed toward the outdoors, her feet crunching on the gravel once she got there. It was a shady, cool place, under surprisingly tall trees.

She sat so she could see back through the opening to the front door. In the next few moments she reviewed her strange night. She had not only allowed a strange man with questionable occupation to stay over but climb in her bed. If that wasn't some indication she was slipping out of control, then the fact that this man could himself be the killer was. Yet . . . yet, she thought, he was, after all, a powerfully calming force. She didn't understand it, or herself at this moment.

Promptly at ten, Mr McFarland appeared to rescue her from the unending loops of worry. He wore a tan raincoat, though rain was not in the forecast, showing a cautious personality and an awareness of the weather prognosticators' justifiable inability to get forecasts right. He also seemed nervous, all hunched into himself and looking around warily.

Carly stood and motioned. He saw her, paid for his coffee, and carried it carefully toward her, up the steps and to the table.

'Thank you for coming,' she said.

'I wasn't aware I had a choice.' He started to take off his coat, looked up and decided against it. There was an odd fussiness about him as he settled into a seat.

'You didn't return my calls.'

'I was out of the country.'

'I'm sorry. Your staff said you were unavailable.'

'Vacation. My staff is protective. I got in last night and then I got this message today. What's this all about?'

He was seated now, seemed to settle in.

'How long were you gone?' Carly asked.

'Why are you asking me all this?'

'Whitney Warfield was murdered. The story is that he has written a book in which he names names and couples them with embarrassing anecdotes. You were on that list. You are, some say, running for mayor. You don't want scandal.'

'What do you want?' he asked. 'Or should I put it this way: how much do you want?'

'No, no, Mr McFarland. I've been retained to find the manuscript. We think it has been stolen. It's out there somewhere. We want to find it.'

'And the person who stole the manuscript is the same person who killed him?'

'Did you know he was dead?'

'Yes. We got a call. We were told.'

'Where were you vacationing?'

'Costa Rica.'

'How long were you gone?' Carly asked.

'We were gone a week.' He took a deep breath, smiled. 'Well, I couldn't have done it. And I'm relieved, very relieved. I thought someone was out to blackmail me. You have no idea.'

'Blackmail. Some skeletons, Mr McFarland?'

'Wouldn't you like to know?' He laughed. 'Can I get you a pastry?'

'No, thank you,' she said. 'Can you tell me a little bit about the hotel project in North Beach?' McFarland's face drained, his eyes lifeless, a rabbit in the clutches of an eagle, knowing its fate and knowing there was nothing to do about it. 'My partner has learned that that there is an effort to build a hotel in North Beach. I imagine that either makes you very happy or very sad.'

'I'm not at liberty to discuss these things. You seem to move from one embarrassing topic to another.'

'They could be linked, couldn't they? Maybe that was what Mr Warfield was writing about. Could that be? I mean, he wanted to preserve North Beach the way it was. He wanted it historic without the tee shirt shops.'

'I think our discussion is over, Miss . . .?' He stood.

'Paladino. You guys are usually pretty good with names.'

'Potential voters. You? Doesn't matter.' He smiled, but his smile was a knowing fake.

'You're walking a tightrope, Mr McFarland.'

'So are you,' he said, holding the smile before turning and leaving.

# Thirteen

'You look relaxed,' Lang told Carly.

He heard her come in and went to her office. It was time to commiserate on the list.

'So?' she said. It was sharper than intended.

'I like that in a woman.'

'What?' she asked.

'Swatting away compliments with acerbic wit.'

'Acerbic? Your new word for the day?' She smiled.

'Inspired by you.'

' "Relaxed" is a compliment?'

'I meant it that way. Lunch?' he asked.

'No,' Carly said. She began to realize she was overreacting. She was feeling guilty – or maybe just strange – about last night. Why, she didn't know. Nothing happened, other than sleeping with a client who was an outlier of sorts. Then again, in the eyes of Noah Lang, William Blake was a murder suspect. And he was, of course, if she remained objective. She took a deep breath. 'Thanks for the offer. Let's do have lunch. We need to talk, don't we?'

'We do. And we need to eat.'

At the bottom of Potrero Hill is an area called 'Dogpatch'. It's a small neighborhood characterized by quaint little houses that survived the 1906 earthquake and by its proximity to the Bay. It is part of an old dry dock area with abandoned cranes, empty warehouses, vacant administrative buildings and a huge, brick former steel foundry. The area was prime for redevelopment – but all was rusting and quiet.

Further in the residential area, not far from the San Francisco Chapter of the Hell's Angels, was Lang's destination – Piccino. Lang was not a gourmand, but he had two areas of expertise – Margherita pizza and crab cakes. And Piccino was definitely one of the top five pizza places in the city.

The two private investigators sat outside at the small corner restaurant, Lang with the pizza of his obsession and a glass of Italian red and Carly with a bowl of potato, leek and Parmesan soup and a glass of French white. The September sun was expected and performed well. And the people walking by made people-watching worthwhile. It took a few moments for the two detectives to focus on the list – the seemingly ponderous list.

Agnes DeWitt, they agreed, was off the list. Low on the list now was Samuel McFarland, who had an alibi that could be substantiated. In his case he would have had to conspire. Carly suggested that watercolorist Lili D. Young and publisher Bart Brozynski would not likely outrun Warfield, climb a fence and stab him, though it was not an impossibility. And neither of them would hire it done.

They hadn't peeled many off the list. And they had widow Elena, wandering son Mickey Warfield and realtor Ralph Chiu to go.

'Nathan Malone admitted to killing a man,' Carly said. 'Whitney Warfield knew who, when, how, where, and why.'

That seemed to perk up Lang.

'Who?'

'He wouldn't tell me.'

'Wow.' Lang thought that was some confession. 'What about Wiley?' he asked.

Carly shrugged. 'I don't see the anger or the fear. He's putting on an exhibition of his early work, though. And he was very secretive about it. And you?'

'Hawkes could have, the mistress could have. Don't know why either would. But they're both difficult to read, particularly Hawkes. He's not fond of people, it seems. And your friend, Mr Blake?'

She was ready this time.

'And what about him? Why would he pay to have someone, in addition to the police, meddling in his affairs if he had something to hide?'

'Gamesmanship. Arrogance.'

'He's not arrogant,' she said too quickly. 'I mean, he doesn't really come across that way. Yes, he has an unusual occupation.'

Lang smiled. He had nothing against professional companions. In some ways it was a more honest relationship than many of those sanctified by society. But he enjoyed seeing her ears grow red. He pulled a sheet of paper from his jacket and handed it across the table as the server picked up the empty plate and bowl.

'Thanh followed the private detective who rousted us the other day. Before going to his office, he stopped at an apartment building very briefly – to drop off something or pick up something, but more likely to report on his activities. This is the list of people who live there. Anyone ring a bell?'

She looked it over carefully. 'No. Can I have this?'

'Sure. I kept a copy. It might mean something, it might be something totally unrelated.'

'What are you up to?' she asked.

'Mr Chiu at three and then I have to track down the widow. You?'

'Just the kid.'

'Mickey Warfield is probably not a kid,' Lang said.

'No. And I have a question I want to pose to Wiley.'

'The photographer?'

'Yeah. I don't think he'd murder anyone, but he was nervous – maybe just about his show. Maybe he knows something he wasn't telling. I don't know. I'd like to pin it down.'

A lot of what Lang did was boring. Stakeouts, searching through records, or trash, tailing people as they went through their mundane errands, and questioning people. Interviewing people in this case had become particularly boring because he was asking the same questions and getting a whole lot of nothing in return. But this was part of his job description.

Chiu's real estate office was on Geary, the main east–west traffic artery, running from downtown's bustling shopping district out to the usually lonely Ocean Beach. Along the way there is a stretch devoted to small businesses – printers, mattress shops, tire retailers, laundromats, computer repair shops, small travel agencies and real estate offices – and tiny restaurants of all ethnicities.

Once mostly Russian, Chinese families had moved into the neighborhood often called the Richmond or the Avenues. On the window of Chiu's office were pictures of homes, with their prices and details printed out below in English and Chinese. Inside there were three desks. Two were occupied by women. That pretty much identified Mr Chiu as the slightly plump, slightly balding man sitting at the remaining desk. And if it didn't, then the nameplate – in English and Chinese – did.

There was nothing pretentious about the place, nothing decorative except for the calendar showing an unidentified tropical paradise. Chiu looked up, noticed Lang, then looked down at what appeared to be his appointment book. He stood, didn't smile, and motioned for Lang to come to him. He looked puzzled, but not troubled. A Caucasian as potential home purchaser? Not a problem.

Chiu, dressed in a tan cotton suit, blue shirt and red, white and blue tie, handed Lang his business card. Lang reciprocated. Chiu studied it, face frozen in seeming indifference. He sat. Lang sat.

'You have a Chinese-sounding name, Mr Lang.'

There was a hint of a smile.

'People say that,' Lang said. 'You have property in North Beach, Mr Chiu.'

He nodded slowly, weighing. 'You interested in buying or leasing?'

'Interested in your interests,' Lang said.

Chiu nodded slowly, but remained quiet. It seemed to Lang that he could remain quiet for days if need be.

'Hotel project?' Lang continued.

Chiu shrugged. He stood, reached out his hand. 'Thank you for stopping by. Please let me know,' he said with only the slightest accent, 'if I can help you with your real estate needs.'

'You know Whitney Warfield?'

Chiu pulled back his hand, sat down, stared across his desk. 'Who does not know Mr Warfield?'

'He was writing a book when he met his end. Revealing information about folks the folks don't want revealed.'

Chiu gave no verbal or visual response.

'A wise man and his words are not soon parted,' Lang said.

'Is this some sort of attempt at Confucius humor, Mr Lang?'

'Feeble.'

Chiu nodded. 'Not bad. Why don't you tell me what you want and we can both move on with our business?'

'You were on the list,' Lang said. 'A list of people Warfield wanted to embarrass. Why you?'

'That is a very good question, Mr Lang. Why me?'

'He was very liberal in his politics. You, I understand, are very conservative. You are a real estate agent, who, I'm guessing, is involved in a hotel project in North Beach, a project Warfield was vehemently against. I suspect the two of you crossed swords many times.'

'Many times,' Chiu said. 'If I may ask, why are you pursuing this information?'

'I'm trying to find a manuscript that was stolen from his home and may hold the key to the identity of his murderer.'

'All of that makes perfect sense, but I cannot help you. I don't have any manuscript and I didn't kill Mr Warfield. Please send my sympathy to his family.'

He stood again, this time his invitation to leave was serious. Lang had nothing left to entertain the man, who had no doubt negotiated with wily businessmen far savvier in the art of negotiation than he. Lang had no doubt underestimated the man. He may have been richer and more powerful than his modest office suggested. After all, it is mostly a Western notion, a Trump-like vanity, to build an edifice with one's name on it. Perhaps Chiu was putting all this ego in the bank.

There was something else. Given the history of the Chinese community in San Francisco it was maybe stereotypical but certainly conceivable that someone as prominent as Chiu could find a way to have an impediment like Warfield removed by folks without taking his business outside of Chinatown.

'I'm hoping, Mr Chiu, that I can be helpful to the investigation in order to prevent police and media inquiry.'

Chiu's eyebrows raised a centimeter.

'You've got my card,' Lang said, extending his hand, aware that if his analysis was even remotely correct, then an irritant, say a private detective, could be dealt with as well.

Chiu remained quiet.

As far as Lang knew, Chiu was a legitimate businessman who simply didn't want the news of a hotel to come out at an inauspicious time.

If he was involved in one of the underground gangs, the only thing Lang could think of was that Warfield knew something about it – threatened to reveal it. He'd do some research.

If Lang were ever inclined to write off Chiu as a criminal type, an old, white, beat-up Toyota Cressida following him back to his office would prevent it. Though the tail was back a few cars, Lang was pretty sure the driver was Asian.

'I feel like I'm just stirring up the snake pit,' Lang said into his cell. He had parked a block from the office and was heading toward it. 'I don't feel like I've made any progress. Do you feel any closer or do you sense a direction here?'

'It's early yet,' she said. 'One thing to keep in mind is that we've been hired to find out what we can. What we can,' she repeated. 'If we decide at some point that we're not making progress, then we'll file a report and bill him for any time beyond his advances.'

'Only a sane person could say that.'

'Thank you. Or was that a compliment?'

'Your guess. I gave you a compliment the other day and you spit in my face.'

'I did not,' Carly said.

'Wait, you said advances. Plural.'

'Did I?'

'Have you come in contact with our Roaming Romeo?'

'We're covered for expenses,' Carly said.

'Did he give you the money in person?'

She thought a moment. William had placed an envelope on a table. She could reply in the negative without being dishonest.

'No.'

'That was awfully tentative,' Lang said. 'You've met him again.'

'And?'

'That's my question. And?'

'There is no and.'

'Ooooh.'

'What?'

'Nothing,' Lang said. He'd reached the door and went up the steps. 'Be careful. The man's career is based on his ability to use people.'

'And you? Your career is built on . . . what?'

'Finding out things people don't want me to know. I did pretty well, didn't I?'

The office was open, but empty. He heard something stirring in the back.

'I'll talk to you later,' he said softly and closed his phone.

Lang went to his desk and retrieved a roll of quarters and moved toward the back room. There were strange flashes of light and the sound of someone moaning. Lang moved quickly around the corner.

Brinkman was sitting in his chair, smoking a cigar, sipping whiskey from a coffee cup. A small television was on his desk.

'You don't have a home?'

'My wife's sister is visiting,' Brinkman said.

'I thought your wife was dead,' Lang said, regretting he hadn't put just a little sympathy in his voice.

'You see my dilemma.'

'Are you going to live here now, smelling up the place with cigar smoke and liquor?'

'I haven't decided yet.'

'How long is she going to be living with you?'

'The world's a cruel place.'

He looked at his watch. It was getting dark earlier now. In a month or so, it would be dark at five. He still needed to talk with the widow, Elena. Maybe he'd drop by this evening. That would complete his list.

# Fourteen

When in doubt, do the obvious, Lang thought. He drove his dilapidated Mercedes up Russian Hill. The car struggled, but was otherwise equal to the task. He found Warfield's home. The sun was floating on the horizon and in deepening twilight he could see lights were on inside the home. After twenty minutes trying to find a parking place on the hill, he braved parking near a fire hydrant.

He would be only a few minutes, he told himself to relieve both the guilt and the fear of receiving an expensive fine.

He knocked on the door to a handsome two-story home. It was far enough from the edge of the hill to forego a view from inside. But a short walk would yield all of San Francisco at your feet.

He thought it might be the maid who answered. The woman was older, somewhat dowdy in an earth mother sort of way. She wore an apron.

'I'm looking for Elena Warfield,' he said.

'I'm very busy,' she said. 'Who are you?'

'My name is Noah Lang. I'm a private investigator looking into Mr Warfield's death.'

'The police aren't enough?' she asked, anger rising. 'Who hired you?'

He wasn't sure what to tell her. 'Someone who wants to be cleared of any suspicion.'

She looked at him warily. 'It's true? What you say?'

'Yes.'

'Come in.'

It was a small entryway with a small table, a chair and wastebasket holding umbrellas. Through the arch was what appeared to be a living room. Pleasant enough, but not staged, as many do, as if it were about to be photographed for *Architectural Digest*. He followed her through a formal dining room into a large, well-lit kitchen. Pots and pans – far from shiny and new – hung on hooks over a center workstation. The stove, which she was now tending to, had six burners and steam rose up a vent. It was not a pretty kitchen, but it was a serious one.

'You expecting guests?' Lang asked.

'Not today,' she said, then realizing what all of this looked like, she continued. 'Tomorrow night people will be over. Relatives, friends . . . after the service.'

'You're cooking for them?' he asked.

She smiled at him, broad and friendly, revealing an unexpected beauty. 'I'm not a martyr, Mr . . . I'm sorry, I've forgotten your name.'

'Noah.'

'This is therapy, Noah. What else would I do? My brother is making all the funeral arrangements, a sister is working with the Church and that leaves me with nothing but questions.'

'Maybe I can help you answer them.'

There was a cutting board with chopped vegetables – red, orange and yellow peppers – on one side of the board and garlic and onion on the other. There was fennel and oregano and on the counter blocks of some sort of hard cheese.

'Maybe,' she said, continuing to work. 'Have you had dinner?'

'I will,' he said.

'I'll put on a little pasta. Take me only a moment.'

'Is your son helping you?' Lang asked.

She looked back sharply. 'Mickey is Whitney's son.'

'I'm sorry.'

'You couldn't know. He's no good, like his father.' She seemed embarrassed at having said it, then changed her mind. A look of determination on her face, she added. 'Without the talent to redeem him.'

'Does he stay here?'

'He crashes here,' she said. 'That's what they say, don't they? Crashes? He says that. Almost fifty years old and he talks like he's a child. Crashes? Can you imagine that? When he is drunk or broke or has nowhere to go he stays here.'

'Is that often?'

'Too often.'

'Did Whitney get along with his son?'

She shook her head as if she'd just been told her village had been destroyed.

'The two of them are the same. Drink. Women. Arguments. Mad at the world.'

'Tell me about your husband.'

She filled a pot with water and put it on to boil. 'You like penne?'

'Penne's good.'

'His family was in New York. One brother is all that's left. And he's coming out tomorrow morning. Whitney was some sort of big shot when he was young and he decided to move out here for a while. He and some friends of his thought this was the place to be for people like him.'

'People like him?'

'Writers, artists.'

'Who came out with him?'

'A bunch of them. Some painter named Hawkes, a writer friend . . . what was his name? Malone. Nathan Malone. Another artist, a very big man of absolutely no morals. Anselmo something or something Anselmo. Some others. They palled around together for a while.'

'Was Whitney close to anyone?'

'Less and less. He'd get so angry at his friends.'

'You two stayed close.'

'We stayed together. Why?' she asked, shaking her head. 'Why I don't know. We fit in our odd way, I suppose.'

'You know who might want to kill him?'

'Me sometimes,' she said, and laughed. 'Well, that felt good. Thank you, Noah. I'm sorry, the answer is anybody and everybody, I think. I'm not aware of anyone in particular.'

'Do you know a William Blake?' he asked.

'No. Should I?'

'I don't see why.'

'What about Marlene Berensen. I'm just throwing names around.'

'No need to lie to me, even if it is for a noble reason. How is she? Have you talked to her?'

'Yes. She seems to be holding up.'

'She would seem to be holding up. That's how she is. She gives you nothing . . . I mean nothing about how she feels. I would have killed Whitney if it wasn't for her.'

'How's that?'

She lifted the lid off the small pot. She dropped in a handful of pasta, then another.

'I couldn't have handled Whitney's . . .' She either couldn't find the word or didn't want to say it. 'I couldn't have handled Whitney all by myself.'

'And Mickey?'

'No,' she said, again a little sharply. 'Not from Miss Berensen. Before. I don't know. I don't want to know.' And that subject was gone, not to be revisited. 'It will be just a few minutes.' She had moved on to her cooking. 'I have an open bottle of wine. Would you like a glass?'

Lang left an hour later. It was completely dark. There was no ticket on his windshield. He had a full stomach and a feeling of well-being. He wondered though, why this woman, just days after her husband's death, was all alone.

Whitney had come to San Francisco and fallen in love with a young Italian girl. Somewhere along the line, he had a son, apparently from a third woman. And he spent most of his later years alienating his friends – at least one of them to the point where he or she murdered him.

Lang learned a little more as he dined at the counter in her steamy kitchen. He learned that pasta puttanesca, which is what he was eating, came from Naples not all that long ago and was called that because it was the kind of sauce 'a whore would make', all tarted up with anchovies, capers and black olives. He liked it and he liked the Sangiovese she poured for him.

Lang also learned that Mickey Warfield was seeing some woman whose name was Angel LeGard. Elena Warfield remembered it because she thought it pretentious and because the woman was Asian, not French. She was a suspect in Elena's mind, but somehow fitting for Mickey. She wanted nothing to do with either of them.

'Puttanesca,' Elena said smiling, referring to Angel. The name LeGard meant something to Lang as well. He wasn't certain why.

Carly stopped by Whole Foods, created a small box of various greens with some crumbles of blue cheese from the salad bar and two Vietnamese shrimp rolls from the deli. She went back to her flat, where she dined in the living room with a glass – just one – of a light white wine. She would relax a few minutes, change into something a little warmer for the evening and trudge down to Frank Wiley's gallery. She'd just drop by. A call might act as warning, forcing him into hiding.

She found a parking space on Grant. It was good fortune born of the time of the evening. The daytime businesses had closed and the daytime people were gone. The evening revelry had yet to begin. It wasn't far to Frank Wiley's little alley. As it was on her first visit, the address was a little forbidding at night, though North Beach, the part that was away from bars and strip clubs on Broadway, was generally safe.

The bulb over the landing at the top of the outside stairway was on, setting more of a mood of desolation than light on the stairs. She climbed, taking deliberate steps. As she approached the top, she heard music – classical. She didn't recognize it. The door was ajar by maybe two feet. Inside was dark. Further in, she could see a light angling into the darkness.

'Frank!' she called out. She waited, looked down on the alley. It was empty. She called out again. Bach, she thought. She wasn't an expert, but it sounded more controlled and less sweeping than she remembered of Beethoven, not sentimental in the way Tchaikovsky is, or Mozart . . . what was she thinking? What did she know? What did it matter? She called out one last time as she opened the door and edged in, moving in the near darkness to the sharp-edged shaft of light that came through the door from the next room and on to the floor.

She moved slowly, alertly, ready to retreat quickly if need be. She pushed against the door to the lit room, but it didn't budge. She poked her head through the gap and saw Frank Wiley sprawled on the floor, his head in a pool of blood. She backed away. She would leave and call 911. She turned, went toward the door, lifting her cellphone from her jacket pocket. She may be in trouble, she thought. More light. Sudden light. She was in trouble. She turned, saw a human advancing quickly, too quickly. She saw even more light, illuminating the inside of her cranium for a split second before everything went suddenly and profoundly dark.

# Fifteen

Angel LeGard was on his mind. He went back to the office. He didn't bother turning on the lights in the reception area, moving in the familiar darkness to his own area. He clicked on his desk light and rummaged for the sheet of paper.

There it was – the apartment directory Thanh put together. And there she was – A. LeGard, apt. 307. Scotty Markham was visiting apartment 307, probably not to chat with Angel but to report to Mickey Warfield the results of the man's comic attempt at intimidation. Though, Lang thought, he probably wouldn't tell the story. 'Message delivered,' was what Markham probably said, then, 'Where's my money?'

He called Carly's cell immediately. He would gloat just a little about how he tracked down Mickey Warfield for her. It rang five times before slipping into automatic answering. 'Call me,' Lang said after the tone. 'I've got a line on Mickey.'

He leaned back, wondering why Carly hadn't picked up. It was still fairly early in the evening. He knew her well enough to know she would check to see who called and he was pretty sure that she'd pick up for him. He rarely called her. And it was never for casual conversation. He punched in the numbers again, thinking that maybe that would suggest a level of urgency if she were at dinner and wanted to be polite.

The same patient automatic response came on.

He nudged his mind back over earlier communication. She was going to talk with Frank Wiley – the photographer. Somewhere in North Beach. Maybe she was in a bar and couldn't hear the ring tone. Maybe the phone was in a jacket she checked. Maybe, maybe, maybe.

He punched in the number again. While it rang Lang asked himself if he was being unreasonable. This wasn't an emergency. The information he had for her could wait until morning. Maybe she was in the bath and would let the phone ring until she could get out and dry off. Maybe she was at the movies. Maybe she was tired and wanted the day to be over. He was being unreasonable. Still no answer. And despite what logic told him, he had a sense something was wrong.

Nothing prevented him from going down to North Beach and if all was well, he'd have a drink somewhere, enjoy the nightlife for a little while and go home. Lang checked the phone book for Frank Wiley. Nothing. He checked Google. He wasn't getting close. There was a people search program, but he didn't know how to use it. Some detective, he thought. But that was why he had Thanh hanging around. He went back into the reception area, flipped on the light and then went into Carly's office. He checked her Monthly Minder and noted that she noted she was going to see Wiley. But there was no address.

Lang called Thanh's cell number. 'Pick up, pick up,' he said as he waited.

'Helloooo,' Thanh answered.

'Sorry to bother you, but I need to find out where Frank Wiley lives or works.'

'Who's Frank Wiley?'

'One of the guys on Carly's list. She went over to see him tonight and I can't get hold of her.'

'Let me call you back.'

Lang went back to his desk. He wondered if he'd let Thanh know how important it was. Maybe three minutes passed. Thanh's call gave him an answer to that question as well as Frank Wiley's only address.

'How'd you do that?'

'You know that iPhone you bought me?'

'I bought you an iPhone?'

'You must learn to pay attention to what you sign.'

'What else have I bought you?'

'Let's just say you are a generous man. You need me to meet you there?'

'I think it's a wild goose chase, probably.'

'You are chasing geese?'

As good as Thanh was at the English language, these kinds of phrases often befuddled him. 'I can handle it, thanks.'

'You know that geese can be pretty mean,' Thanh said. 'They might just chase you.'

'A definite possibility.'

'You have experience with geese?' Thanh was playing him now.

'Wild geese. And chases. Plenty.'

Not quite nine, Columbus was lit up. The wide avenue was busy with tourists. As he drove by he could see waiters outside trying to talk the folks into coming inside for dinner, just as the barkers would try to lure them into the lurid sex shows on Broadway later. No parking spaces.

He went back around and then up Grant Street, which was still quiet. Lang wasn't sure, but he thought he saw Carly's Mini Cooper parked near Union. After another block and a couple of turns Lang found the address on an alley-like street that dead-ended. Not much light in the street. He parked his Mercedes so that half of it was on the sidewalk, allowing another car to get by if need be.

As he walked up the stairway, he reached behind him to feel his weapon, a SIG P220. If he was found with it, he could be arrested. He had no permit. He had no permit because the city didn't give out permits. At the top of the stairs he noticed the room was dark though the door was open. He nudged it further, felt the wall for a light switch. He found the switch and flipped on a dirty gold light; a light that nonetheless revealed Carly Paladino crumpled on the floor near him.

Lang knelt down, felt her neck for a pulse, relieved to find one. He moved to the other side. There was a little blood on her forehead just above the eye.

Lang reached back for his weapon and moved softly to the door where light was escaping. He pushed the door. There was an obstacle, but he had room to get by. He moved in. A man was on the floor, his head in a pool of blood. He took the man's pulse. There wasn't any. He looked around. It was a darkroom, with sinks and red lights. Beyond it was Wiley's living quarters – a small living room, a bedroom, a small kitchen and bath. Live-and-work bachelor quarters. No women lived here.

He punched in 911 as he came back to his unconscious partner. He knelt down again, touched her cheek.

'Talk to me, Carly,' he said before the operator answered. Lang informed the voice about the situation and provided the address. Need medics. He hung up and called Homicide. He was switched around twice before he talked to anyone who could help.

'I need to talk with Inspector Gratelli.'

'He's not on tonight,' this new voice said.

'He'll want to be. This is part of his murder investigation.'

He gave the new voice his name and cell number and was told to wait for a call from someone. 'Maybe Gratelli, maybe not.'

Lang hoped it would be Gratelli.

'Come on Carly, wake up. No sleeping on the job.'

Gratelli was asleep in his chair, a newspaper open on his lap, Donizetti's *Lucrezia Borgia* was coming to an end on the stereo when the discordant sound of the telephone mangled the sound of the opera. He woke, confused and angry.

'Hello,' Gratelli said, eyes beginning to focus. He checked his watch: nine twenty p.m. This was getting to be a habit. Too much sleep. He didn't sleep this much when his wife was alive.

He was told that a Noah Lang had called about a dead body and an injured woman. And that he asked specifically for Gratelli. Gratelli put the phone down to find a pen. He wrote the number on the top of the newspaper.

'Why can't people get killed during the day?' Gratelli said when Lang answered the phone.

'A photographer, Frank Wiley, is dead in his gallery and Carly Paladino was attacked.'

'Is she all right?'

'Medics are coming. She's out but alive.'

'Give me the address.'

When Lang did, Gratelli was pleased that it was at least in the neighborhood. The homicide inspector looked in the mirror in the bathroom as he put on his tie. He swept back his thinning gray hair with a palm. He didn't know Frank Wiley, didn't even know of him, even though he lived in the area. But he did know that Wiley was on the list. So, this was likely connected somehow with Whitney Warfield's death.

He was glad he didn't have to drive. He walked down his hill, to Vallejo, turned right and then right again on to Grant. He walked the narrow sidewalk on the narrow street for several blocks, then right again until he was walking up a dead-end street on the north side of the hill. It would have a been a shorter trip as the crow flies, he thought. And if he had been a crow, a straight line would be possible.

There was a fire truck in the alley, lights blinking, a black and white on the corner. He went up the steps. His muscles and bones didn't like evening work either and he felt the tightness and the pain.

Inside, Carly Paladino was awake but groggy. Noah Lang was talking with one of the uniformed police. Gratelli flashed his badge.

'Homicide.'

The other uniformed cop nodded toward the door. Gratelli went in. He reached into the dead man's rear pocket and extracted a wallet.

'Frank Wiley,' Lang said out loud.

Gratelli looked around, checked out the other rooms. There was a huge camera, the kind the press used to use in the fifties, in the corner of the room as if it had been tossed there or perhaps fallen there.

It looked as if the dead man was struck in the back of the head and then in the front, perhaps more than once.

He came back out into the room.

'What's your story?' Gratelli asked Lang.

'I got worried about Carly. She wasn't answering her phone. I knew where she went so I came over. Carly was on the floor there,' Lang pointed. 'And the body was in there. I called 911 and then you.'

'You didn't . . .'

'. . . touch anything? No. Except for Carly.'

'That's touching,' Carly said.

'You're feeling better, I see.'

'Talk to me, Ms Paladino,' Gratelli said.

'I had a few questions for Mr Wiley. I knew he didn't want to talk to me so I didn't call. I just stopped by. I found him in the other room and after I turned to leave I was hit. That's it.'

'What did you want to talk to him about?'

'About Warfield and the book. Warfield provided the narrative to one of Wiley's previous books and I thought maybe Warfield was involved in Wiley's new project.'

'And what was that?' Gratelli asked.

'Some sort of special exhibition.' She looked at the boxes against the wall. 'Maybe . . .'

'Maybe what?' Gratelli asked.

'I lost my train of thought, I'm sorry. I'm still a little fuzzy.' She looked at Lang.

'They want her to get to the hospital. Have her head examined,' Lang said.

'Nice,' Carly said.

'Go on,' Gratelli said. 'So nobody saw anything other than what I'm seeing now?'

'Right,' Lang said. Carly nodded.

'You didn't see your attacker?'

'No. I saw a figure, but he was backlit. I saw no details.'

'Him?' Gratelli asked.

'I don't know that, I guess. It was either a large person or someone wearing a big coat or cape or something. The figure seemed large.'

'You heard nothing?' Gratelli asked.

'No,' she said. 'Oh, wait – there was music on when I came in. Classical.'

'I didn't hear any music when I arrived,' Lang said, obviously picking up on the contradiction.

'Smell anything?' Gratelli asked.

'No, sorry.'

Carly took her light raincoat off and handed it to Gratelli. Maybe he shouldn't have been so casual with them. There was nothing to say that one or the other or both were guiltless here. They had a client to protect. He'd have to be careful.

The crime scene folks arrived, as did another set of uniformed cops.

'Leave your jacket,' Gratelli said to Carly. He looked at Lang. 'You too.'

'Something in there I need to get,' Lang said.

'So get it,' Gratelli said. Gratelli thought Lang didn't look too eager. 'Go ahead.'

Lang pulled out the olive green Sig from the pocket of his jacket. He gave Gratelli a sheepish smile, tucked it in the back of his jeans and pulled out the tails of his shirt to hide it.

Gratelli closed his eyes, shook his head.

'Good thing this guy wasn't shot,' he said. 'Get out of here. Both of you.' Gratelli looked around, caught one of the uniforms by the sleeve. 'Get out in the neighborhood and start asking questions.'

He wasn't at all hopeful. It was a short alley. Not many lights on. Perfect place to commit a crime, just as Warfield's death happened at a perfect time. Warfield was killed with a pen. Looked to Gratelli as if Wiley was beaten to death with a camera. Who says two isn't a pattern? Maybe someone was trying to deliver a message with a poetic twist.

Carly didn't want to go to General. In the midst of the craziness there, the doctors are the best at stitching up knife wounds and digging out bullets. She wasn't convinced. Instead they went to a hospital near Pacific Heights where the ambience was more like a nice residential hotel. Quiet, organized.

As they waited for the film to come back and the doctors to analyze it, they talked about the case. Lang said he was done with his list and thought he could find Mickey Warfield if that was OK with her. She was fine with it. A little groggy yet, she was nonetheless able to construct simple, logical sentences.

'Generally speaking, what do you think?' she asked.

'I don't know. We've been through the list, now where are we? I feel like we will end up with Colonel Mustard with a wrench in the library. Maybe we should gather all the suspects in the parlor and turn the lights out.'

'That's a good idea,' Carly said.

'You don't mean it,' Lang said. 'You mean it, don't you?'

'Not exactly like you think.'

The doctor came in. They wanted to keep her overnight. Probably nothing at all, but there was some swelling. They wanted it to go down before they released her.

'My car,' she said to Lang.

'Give me the key,' he said. 'We'll take care of it. Tonight. Call me in the morning. I'll come get you.'

'Thank you. You've been . . .' She shook her head, didn't continue.

Outside the hospital, Lang flipped open his phone, called Thanh.

'Can you do me a quick favor?'

Maybe it was all the activity, but Lang's energy hadn't flagged as it usually did in the evening. Maybe now was a good time to visit young Warfield and complete the first run-through on the list. The list? It had taken on its own life, hadn't it?

# Sixteen

Lang picked up Thanh on the corner of Polk Street and Sutter. He was a PIB tonight, PIB standing for People in Black. It was still *de rigueur* in some circles. Lang was pretty sure that Thanh belonged to or at least infiltrated many social circles and he knew the fashion codes for each.

Tonight, Thanh's assignment was easy. He needed to get Carly's car parked safely – close to her home. Thanh agreed. Next stop for Lang was Angel LeGard's apartment, but not before Thanh filled him in on Markham.

'Dishonorably discharged from the Navy where he had been . . .' Thanh shrugged '. . . something called a "seal". From then on, he was doing the PI thing.'

'Navy Seal,' Lang said out loud. It was hard to believe that this forlorn, overweight, barely successful PI was a trained killer, spy, survivalist. Certainly he was tougher than he looked. He was also an underachiever.

Lang rang the buzzer for apartment 307.

'A delivery for Angel LeGard,' Lang said into the intercom when she answered.

'What kind of delivery?' she asked – no fool she.

'Flowers,' Lang said.

'Really,' she said not quite believing. 'Come on up.' Her tone had changed to 'what the hell'.

'You have no flowers,' she said, not looking all that disappointed.

'You noticed. And you're not completely dressed.' She was covered, sexily so, in a silk slip the color of salmon. She wore nothing underneath, he was sure.

'You noticed,' she said. 'What is it you want?'

He wanted *her*, but he couldn't say that. Beyond the sensuous, twentyish Asian woman he believed to be Angel was a dimly lit living room and the voice of Phoebe Snow.

'Mickey Warfield,' Lang said.

'What a letdown,' she said. 'He's not here. He doesn't live here.'

'He's here often, though.'

'How do you know that?' she asked.

'I know a lot of things nobody else cares about.'

'He owe you money?'

'No. I want to ask him some questions about the death of his father.'

'He'll be here in the next hour or so. Maybe you can ask me some questions for a while. About anything.'

'Are you two friends?' Lang asked, trying to keep the conversation going.

'I have lots of friends,' she said, then reconsidered. 'Not that many. Come in. Anything I can do for you while we wait?' Her expression left him in little doubt as to the meaning of her question.

'Am I supposed to answer that?'

'You police?'

'Not really. Private. Licensed. What do you do?'

She smiled. She shrugged. 'I'm versatile.'

'Lady of the evening?'

She shook her head no. 'I make do though. All I have is Scotch,' she said and went to a sidebar and poured them each a drink, though he had not accepted the tacit offer.

Her English was impeccable, better than most native speakers, which meant she was second- or third-generation Chinese or that she was schooled young and was smart.

'You're Mickey's girlfriend, right?' It seemed to be obvious, but Lang figured he hadn't really nailed that down and he had more than one motive to ask.

'We have an understanding.' She handed him the drink and then took possession of the sofa and he sat across from her in an amply upholstered chair.

'And that is?'

'None of your business,' she said smiling again.

She held her sexuality back, but only slightly, perhaps just enough to keep Lang interested. He had to be careful. Angel LeGard was probably a lot smarter than he was, at least in this kind of situation. Lang had been led foolishly astray more than once by the involuntary flow of blood to a destination beyond his control.

She took a sip of her Scotch.

'I have no money, Angel. I'm one payday from being thrown on the street,' Lang said, slightly exaggerating.

'Money isn't everything.' She sat up, leaned forward, her breasts preceding her. 'Let me see your badge.'

Lang pulled out the leather folder, flipped it open. She took it, stared at it under the dim light by the sofa.

'Is that it? No badge?'

'We aren't allowed badges.'

'It's like a driver's license or something.' She pulled a business card from the other side of the leather case. She read it. 'Noah Lang.'

Lang nodded.

'Noah. Like the boat.' She put the card on the table. She handed his license back, again leaning forward, knowing that his eyes were devouring her, knowing that he knew she knew.

'Sorry to disappoint you. It'd be nice to have something shiny in silver with eagles and snakes.'

'It would.' She smiled.

Then there was silence, the atmosphere thick with it. It was uncomfortable for him, but she seemed to be bearing up well. After a short spell – and it seemed like a spell to him – she had mercy on him.

'No more questions for me?' she asked with a smile.

She was definitely in control of the territory.

'You could go slip on something less comfortable,' he said.

'You're not going to get off that easy,' she said. 'You know how I meant that, right?'

'OK. I do have a question. What does Mickey Warfield do for a living?'

'Got me,' she said.

'Where does he live? He doesn't live here.'

'No, he doesn't live here, but he is paying some of the bills.'

'I see,' he said. He tried to be uninterested in the information. A doctor, maybe, acknowledging a symptom. She saw through it.

'Doesn't mean he owns me.'

She was sultry. The room, warm and small as it was, seemed luxurious, with everything bathed in a gold light. And the music. And the slow motion. And her beauty? It was criminal. He could be in one of those sensuous, moody Wong Kar-Wai films – *In the Mood for Love* or *2046*. The fact that she was Chinese made all of this more than a fleeting celluloid sensation.

He'd have to stop watching so many movies.

'You *do* expect him this evening?' he asked, trying to break the mood.

'Are you getting nervous?' Angel asked.

'Things to do, places to go,' he lied.

She smiled knowingly. She took his glass and freshened up his Scotch.

'I don't like being alone,' she whispered in his ear as she delivered his glass.

He didn't have to see her. She enveloped his senses.

'Vanilla,' he said.

'And jasmine and oil from orange blossoms.' She was still there, her lips touching his ear ever so lightly.

The key in the lock was jarring. Lang felt himself blush, despite the fact that the temperature of his body was already up a few degrees.

Angel was heading for the door as it opened.

'Angel,' the man's voice said.

Lang turned back to see the cheerful face of a late-fortyish man turn sour. He stood, turned toward the approaching Mickey Warfield.

'And you are?'

'You know me, don't you? Noah Lang. Private investigator.'

Warfield looked at Angel who maintained an observer's expression, but Lang noticed she put her glass on top of his business card.

'I fooled her to get inside,' Lang said.

'No one fools Angel,' Warfield said, now looking a little amused. 'You don't look the worse for wear.'

'Scotty Markham did his best.'

'Maybe I should have hired you.'

Warfield was a big guy, but not fat. Six-two. A barrel chest wrapped in a tweed sport coat over an expensive black tee shirt. It was a comfortable, cool look that didn't look too orchestrated. His hair was the color of old rust. His skin also had a rust-colored cast as if his freckles were too close together.

'I don't scare me either.'

'Look, it wasn't personal,' he said, tossing two sets of keys on the table. One set belonged to a Jaguar.

'It felt personal,' Lang said. He felt more comfortable facing Warfield than he did his girlfriend. But he advised himself not to get carried away with matching macho with macho.

'I could use one of those,' Warfield said, nodding toward Lang's drink. Angel obeyed graciously, not in a subservient way, but not offended either. 'So, what do you want?'

'The first thing I want is to find out why you're so sensitive about my looking into the death of your father. The second thing is to find out why you are so difficult to find. And the third is what you have to gain from your father's death.'

'It all goes back to your first question. This is none of your business. None of it is your business. As far as I'm concerned,' he said, nodding toward Angel who was bringing him his drink, 'you know too much already.'

'Your father wrote a book revealing a lot about a lot of people who didn't want their secrets told. The question is – did his son have a motive to kill him? You have just made the case for me.'

Warfield looked puzzled for a moment, then he nodded. 'Why don't you finish your drink?'

'It's all right. You can have the rest of it,' Lang said and went toward the door, but turned back briefly. 'Nice to meet you, Angel. Thanks for the hospitality.'

'You've been warned, Mr PI.' The man said it plainly and firmly.

'That's very kind of you,' Lang said. 'Have a nice evening.'

Outside he spent a few minutes canvassing the neighborhood. He found a new black Jaguar parked down a block. He wrote down the license plate number. Not sure that was the only Jag in the neighborhood, he went a block in each direction. It wasn't the kind of area one would park a late-model luxury car. It wasn't the kind of neighborhood to go wandering around in late at night, either.

Lang went home. Buddha was by the door as usual and guided his human room-mate to the kitchen whereupon Lang fixed the feline a late dinner.

'A little candlelight?' Lang said as he put the dish on the low counter. Buddha gave him a look that Lang took as disapproval. Buddha didn't appreciate sarcasm either, apparently.

Lang plugged his cellphone into the charger, put his pistol on the table and opened an Asahi 'Super Dry' as he peered into his refrigerator for inspiration. He pulled a frozen crab cake from the freezer and defrosted it in the microwave. He boiled some water for pasta and chopped two small cloves of garlic into tiny pieces.

It all came together in twenty minutes. Olive oil, basil from his plant outside, and garlic for the pasta and a thawed crab cake in a small skillet. Once the cake was cooked, he put it on a separate dish, and put everything else in the skillet, stirring it up until some of the pasta was crisp. Finally he topped it with some grated pecorino cheese.

'Pasta Crabolini,' Lang said to Buddha, who looked as if he were impressed. Perhaps it was the lingering aroma of crab.

After Lang put Chet Baker on the stereo, he took his plate of food and second beer outside. The air was still warm and if there was a wind the force of it was blocked by the homes. The sound of Baker's trumpet drifted out to his little table in the near darkness. Lang took a deep breath and relaxed. Life was good at the moment. And Lang had learned to appreciate these fine, small moments. He'd call Carly in the morning, pick her up if he needed to. He'd also run the plates on the Jaguar, maybe get an address on Warfield the Younger.

The second murder, though he couldn't be absolutely sure, lent credence to the idea that Warfield's, and now Frank Wiley's, deaths were connected to the list.

Carly Paladino wanted her bed, her bath, her wine. As it turned out, she wanted her sleep. The nurses did not let her drift off for too long, it seemed. By morning she had been awakened and had looked into a little flashlight at least ten times.

When the doctor did his rounds at eight, he told her she could go home, but to be alert for signs that might suggest she needed further treatment. While she had been disoriented only briefly after being struck, the fact that she had been unconscious was serious.

'No aspirin,' the doctor said, pulling out a pad and prescribing some other pain medicine if she needed it. 'Someone needs to check in with you periodically. You have someone who can do that?'

She thought of Nadia. Maybe.

'Yes, I'll be fine.' Getting out of there was worth some risk, she thought.

She called Lang who, though a little groggy, said he'd be right there. He brought her coffee and she sipped it as he drove her home.

'I've met Warfield's kid,' Lang said, as they drove down California toward Fillmore. 'Why don't you give him to me?'

Lang didn't tell her that he wondered if Mickey Warfield would escalate. First, hire some muscle to scare off an investigation. Then, when that failed, murder someone who might prove problematical.

'That might be good,' Carly said. She seemed defeated. 'I'm supposed to rest for a few days.'

She didn't look too happy about it.

'Looks like the game is getting serious,' Lang said.

'Are we causing any of this? The deaths, I mean.'

'It's us or the police.' He nodded toward her. 'And now, it's personal.'

She looked at him. She liked him more that second than she had since she met him. And there were a couple of really good moments. She considered herself pretty strong and definitely independent, but it didn't hurt to have someone taking care of your back. She hadn't really had that since her father died – a long time ago.

# Seventeen

After dropping Carly at her place and seeing her to the door, Lang stopped for coffee at Quetzal on Polk Street. He called the office to see if Thanh was in. He wanted his sometimes assistant to check on the Jaguar. But it wasn't Thanh who answered the phone.

'Brinkman, Paladino and Lang.'

'That you, Brinkman?'

'Last time I looked.'

'You're answering the phone?' Lang asked. To an outsider it would seem to be a dumb question, but Brinkman never answered the phone, which was understandable because it was never for him.

'It's not exactly engineering a soft landing on Jupiter.'

'How is it that Brinkman is first?' Lang knew better than to ask, but he did anyway. 'You said "Brinkman, Paladino and Lang".'

'Alphabetical order.' His tone suggested Lang's intelligence was in question.

'But if that's the case Lang is before Paladino.'

'I never knew you were so petty.'

It was hopeless.

'Is Thanh there?'

'If he was I wouldn't be answering the phone.'

'Thank you. You've been most helpful.'

The coffee was good. The place was busy. All of the half-dozen iMacs on a counter near the door were occupied. Lang was seated by a window that overlooked busy Polk Street. Watching the people walk by, he noticed that the neighborhood, once called Polk Gulch and Polk Strasse – and now by order of the merchants, Polk Village – seemed to attract Middle-Easterners as well as Vietnamese. A copy of the *Fog City Voice* was abandoned with the dishes on the table next to his. He picked it up. The cover said it all. There was a collage – a digitized photo of Whitney Warfield, a partial map of North Beach, and an artist's rendering of a hotel. All of this was under strategic drops of blood. At the bottom of the cover, it read: 'Did Warfield's opposition to North Beach Hotel sign his death warrant?'

The story went on for six long pages. Lang was amazed at the skill of the writer. There were no accusations, only questions, subtle and sometimes far-fetched implications. Was there a hotel being built in North Beach? If so, Warfield was opposed to it. It was possible the land that the hotel was to be built on could have been owned by Mr Chiu. And if that was the case this was the district represented by Council member McFarland.

The story, quoting 'sources close to the investigation', indicated that Warfield's missing book might have implicated the players the story mentioned and that they had motive to kill Warfield to keep him quiet about the secret plan until developers were ready to reveal it. Big bucks and intricate political maneuvering were required for the project's success. Timing was essential.

It was a great non-story with the thin plotlines augmented by the often bizarre assortment of characters surrounding Warfield. The late author's flattering obituary was a sidebar to the story. Lang finished his coffee and copped the paper to show Carly.

At the office he made some calls and, before noon, Lang had his second major surprise of the day. The Jaguar young Warfield was driving last night was registered to Daddy's mistress, Marlene Berensen.

Shortly after noon, Carly called.

'I'm not going to make it,' she said wearily. 'Oh, I didn't mean it the way it sounded.' There was a faint laugh. 'Sounded pretty dramatic. What I mean is, I'm not going to be able to just hang around the flat for three days. I'm ready to scream now.'

He told her about the article in the *Fog City Voice* and then about finding out that young Warfield was driving the car belonging to old

Warfield's mistress. Carly came to life. She wanted to read the story. She wanted to talk about the case, and she was willing to offer lunch in exchange for Lang's visit.

Carly could see that Lang was impressed with her flat. He looked around, wide-eyed.

'I know,' she said. 'It's a great flat. I could never have afforded it from my work. My parents bought this place a long time ago. And I inherited it. And the furniture.'

'It's great,' Lang said. She not only lived in Pacific Heights – at the outer edge – she had a nice place and looked at home in it.

'Come on out to the deck,' she said. 'Some wine? I have an open bottle of Pinot Grigio.'

He nodded. He figured it was two-bedroom and one bath. At one time this would be considered just a nice, comfortable home. But now, with a fireplace, high ceilings, and a terrific location, Carly could sell the place and live in Mexico for the rest of her life. Never have to work again.

She was also a good cook. Lunch was an omelet made with Brie and mild sausage – a joke on him, he thought – and some sautéed potatoes and Italian parsley. A lot fancier than Eddie's Cafe on Divisadero. Below them was another flat, this one with a Japanese garden, not exactly Zen, but with the simple elegance that the Japanese seem to bring to whatever they design. Gravel, stone, grass and shredded bark changed the texture beneath manicured trees and bushes and around little islands of flowering plants.

'No wine for you?' Lang asked.

'Not for a while. The good doctor doesn't want me to have any fun.'

'Are you feeling all right?'

'I don't know how to explain it, but my head feels numb. It doesn't hurt. There's just a dullness to everything.'

'Maybe you need to nap a bit.'

'Maybe,' she said, and then, to change the subject, 'I think we're making progress. Agnes DeWitt is off the list, right? Too old.'

'And too lovely,' Lang said.

'Samuel McFarland has an alibi.'

'He could have hired someone,' Lang suggested.

'I thought of that. But there's too much poetic justice, too much symbolism in the way they died for this to be a hired gun. We can take Frank Wiley off the list.'

'Being dead isn't an alibi,' Lang said.

'But Warfield and Wiley getting killed – each with the tools of their trade?'

'I can't imagine Elena Warfield jumping a fence to stab her husband with a pen.' He shrugged. 'I don't want to be sexist or ageist, but I can't imagine a seventyish woman with a heaving bosom . . .'

'Heaving bosom?'

'They would have to heave, I promise you.'

'You just wanted to say "heaving bosom".'

'Well, true. How often do you get a chance to use that in a sentence?'

'I'm not sure Lili D. Young could do it either.'

'Speaking of heaving bosoms?'

'She's a big woman,' Carly said. I'm not sure how quickly she could get around, let alone climb over the fence.' She remembered how difficult it was for the artist to get to her feet.'

'You said you thought the attacker was a big person, remember?'

'Memories are fading in and out a bit. I'm not sure what I really saw.' Half through, and only picking at her eggs, she picked up the copy of the *Voice*.

Lang thought for a moment. 'You know, Warfield could have gotten over the fence after he was stabbed with the pen.'

'Last burst of adrenaline?'

Lang nodded. 'He didn't even have to be chased. He knew his attacker, but didn't know he was being attacked. He turned to leave. Bang.'

'It was a puncture wound. No bang.'

'Squoosh then.'

'But the attacker had Warfield's pen,' Carly reminded him.

'Good point. But how did the attacker get his pen and then kill him?'

'Maybe Warfield was physically subdued.'

'Maybe the killer asked to borrow the pen,' Lang said.

'Then Warfield turned his back?'

'Another good point. We don't know what we thought we knew, which proves we don't know what we don't know. That Rumsfeld, he knew what he was talking about with known knowns and known unknowns.'

'Got the war wrong,' Carly said.

'Now, you're nitpicking.'

As Carly read the article, Lang constructed the revised list in his head.

Marshall Hawkes
Marlene Berensen
Richard Sumaoang

Ralph Chiu
Mickey Warfield
Bart Brozynski
Nathan Malone

Lang considered William Blake a suspect as well, but would keep that to himself.

'Wow.' Carly looked up from the article. ' "Sources close to the investigation" – I guess that would be me.' She shook her head. 'I fed him the story.'

'Seems like you asked the cat to babysit the canary,' Lang said. 'If it makes you feel better, I was used a couple of times as well. With Richard Sumaoang, he asked questions, I answered. I asked questions, he didn't. Maybe we need to take a couple of refresher courses in the art of the gumshoe.'

'What's the plan?' she asked. She seemed tired.

'The plan is for you to go to bed and rest and I'll see what I can do to eliminate the people on the list . . .'

'Not eliminate them exactly, I hope.'

Lang laughed. 'Eliminate them as suspects,' he said patiently, 'until we find someone we can't eliminate . . . as a suspect.'

She nodded.

'You know,' Lang said, 'that story might move things along. Anybody asks, tell them you planted it.'

'Thanks. You going to the service this evening?' she asked.

'Should I?'

'If you would,' she said. 'See who shows up?'

Noah Lang was good to have around in a crisis, Carly thought. She smiled as she climbed into her bed. He was also quite good at creating one.

It was still warm. The sun would keep the air warm for a couple more hours. Lang decided he could avoid the office and still get some work done on the case. Round two was about to begin. He decided to drop in on Richard Sumaoang. Maybe he could get the artist to be a little more forthcoming.

Richard's place was in the Haight, off Cole Street. It was a short, single-family Victorian in need of – ironically – paint.

A woman of forty or so answered the door. Even without make-up, and probably not expecting company, she was attractive. She eyed Lang as if he was going to try to sell her some aluminum siding.

'I need to talk to Richard,' Lang said.

'What about?'

'That's between Richard and me.'

'OK, so we both have a secret. I'm not telling you where he is unless you talk to me about why.'

'OK. I want to talk to him about murder. How does that make you feel?'

'Whose?' she asked, unaffected by Lang's attempted shock, delivered in his best threatening voice.

'His maybe. But if you'd rather play games, I'll drop by some other time.'

'C'mon,' she said, motioning with her dirty-blonde head.

He followed her through the house. It was an artist's home. Plants in old coffee cans, rugs Sumaoang may have made himself, a sofa that was once a Chinese bed. The place spoke of comfort, color, and non-traditional but very individual taste. The kitchen smelled of ginger and there was fruit and bread scattered about. Cheerful Latin music also permeated the rooms. There was a sense of life, of living. It was a happy place, Lang thought, until he arrived.

Sumaoang was outside. A huge sheet, maybe fifteen feet by twenty, was on the ground, rocks scattered at the edges to keep the large drawing from taking flight and taking the artist with it. He was using a chunk of charcoal to sketch out his vision.

'We've got company,' the woman shouted, as Lang descended the couple of steps into the back yard.

'Go away, Mr Lang,' the artist said, standing and turning toward the interloper. 'We've had our meeting and that was it.' Sumaoang was shirtless and if there had ever been any question about his fitness, it was instantly dispelled; he had the physique of a man many years younger than he was.

'Between you and your girl, you could hurt a guy's feelings.'

'Apparently Lana and I haven't tried hard enough.'

Sumaoang seemed to want to divert Lang's eyes from his work. He moved to the other side of the detective, so that wandering eyes would see only the back of the house.

'Frank Wiley's dead,' Lang said.

'I read the papers,' Sumaoang said. He came to the edge of the wooden steps, where Lang stood, to retrieve his iPhone. Lang took note of the seeming dependency. Perhaps it was new.

'Yeah, good. An informed citizenry is a good citizenry.' Lang didn't know where he came up with that. 'But I wanted to get as much infor-mation from you while you were still alive.'

Sumaoang smiled. 'Are you for real?'

'Unless you're the killer,' Lang said, meaning what he was saying and looking directly into Sumaoang's eyes, 'you are in danger. You know something, I bet, whether you know you know it or not.'

Back to Rumsfeld, Lang thought. Unknown knowns.

'I can't help you,' Sumaoang said, after giving it some thought. His tone wasn't belligerent anymore.

'What was Frank Wiley working on? We know he was putting together an exhibition.'

'We hadn't talked in a long time. I don't know. And I don't know what Warfield would have to say about me that would warrant my wanting to kill him. I was a wild kid. I did what rebels did then. Got lost in drugs and sex. Marched against the government. Vietnam. Threw rocks. Probably hung out with criminals of various sorts, certainly political enemies of the state. But I'm not ashamed of any of it. I was on the right side. If I knew how to put words together, I'd include all of it in my memoirs.'

'Who were Wiley's closest friends?'

Sumaoang thought a moment. 'He worked with Malone on his first book. Maybe Wiley had a book deal going with his exhibition. He would have gone to Warfield or Malone for an introduction or narrative.'

'Anybody else?'

'No.'

'Anybody he didn't like?' Lang recited the list that Blake had provided.

'Hawkes, probably. Wiley didn't like Hawkes and the feeling was mutual.'

'Why?'

'I don't know. Hawkes could be a little prissy. He never fit in with the gang. Hawkes and Warfield were close. I don't know if they liked each other, but there was some sort of understanding. That it? I've got work to do.'

'Thanks.'

'You can go out the side.'

# Eighteen

Lang stopped for another cup of coffee and called Carly. He wanted to let her know he was anxious to talk with Malone about Frank Wiley's death. He also wanted an excuse to check in on her.

'Sure,' she said, 'but this is boring. I'm up. I'm walking around. Why can't I be working?'

Lang didn't have an answer, but apparently Carly did.

'I think I've just answered my own question. Let me go along with you to see Malone. But am I missing something? Why Malone?'

'Malone, Warfield and Hawkes all knew each other from New York. And he worked closely with Wiley on the first book. Maybe he knows something about what Wiley was up to before his death.'

'Good, yes,' Carly said, but she sounded a little unfocused.

'Tomorrow,' Lang said.

'What?'

'Tomorrow,' Lang repeated. 'Tomorrow morning we'll visit with Malone. Could you set that up? I'll revisit Hawkes this afternoon. I'll give you a call later to find out what's going on with Malone.'

'You're checking up on me. You're trying to make sure I'm all right.'

'Business is business, Carly.'

'What does that mean?'

'I don't know. If you wanted a partner who made sense . . . well . . .'

'OK, OK.'

Lang constantly surprised her. He seemed so irresponsible. It was part of his demeanor. Yet he wasn't. It was just that he went at reliability from an odd angle. It was somehow connected to his failure to apologize for being himself. Ever, she thought. But she rethought, as she – still in her oversized cotton pajamas – lazily climbed out from beneath the thick comforter, and out of bed. 'Ever' was too long a time. She had only known him for a few months. She wanted to say he wasn't normal, but that wasn't right either. He wasn't average. He wasn't predictable.

Why was she going on so much about him? She went to the kitchen to see if the coffee she made earlier was still drinkable. Inside the thermal pot, the coffee was not hot, but warm. She would make a sandwich. She would try to get her thoughts together. After all, she had a client and she owed it to Mr Blake to devote significant time to his case.

A peanut butter and jelly sandwich and bean soup. She smiled. She was nine again.

Maybe she was the one who wasn't being responsible. Was she pulling her own weight? Lang had taken on more of the case. He was taking the lead, it seemed. She sat in the living room, on the sofa, sipping her coffee and relishing her sandwich in between waves of insecurity. If she were to diagnose herself, she would conclude that she was getting a little too emotional. Maybe from the concussion. She'd have to admit she was feeling a little sorry for herself at the moment. Frightened, possibly.

She took a deep breath. 'Buck up, you old broad,' she said out loud. She could shake it off. She'd have to shake it off.

Her cellphone called out. It was Gratelli. He asked the question she knew he would ask.

'I'm guilty,' Carly told him. 'I didn't mean to be a source close to the investigation. I guess I'm a little naïve when it comes to journalists.'

'Maybe we can fix that. What was your take on Bart Brozynski?'

'Seems too shameless to worry about any exposure. I think he'd relish being in someone's tell-all book.'

'OK,' Gratelli said. 'I'll handle the pugnacious publisher. Anything else.'

'McFarland was out of the country. Lang doesn't believe the wife could have killed her husband, based on her physicality. It's the heaving bosom defense.' She waited for Gratelli to laugh. He didn't. She wanted to move on quickly. She thought about telling him that both Warfields, father and son, had links to the mistress, but decided to hold that back for now. 'I don't think Lilli D. Young could have done it,' she said, trying to give him something. 'She doesn't move that quickly. If both murders were committed by the same person – and that's an "if", I know – I don't think she could have done them.'

'We've tracked down Mickey Warfield. He has an alibi for the night his father died. A girlfriend. Girlfriends are girlfriends, but it is an alibi.'

'I'll pass that along to Noah. What about a will? Insurance?'

There was a pause. 'You won't be calling up the *Fog City Voice* when I tell you what I know?' Gratelli asked. If there was humor intended here, Carly didn't hear it.

'No.'

'You promise?'

'I promise.'

'We're still wrangling with the lawyer on the will, but there were two insurance policies. Both substantial. Elena Warfield was the beneficiary on one. Marlene Berensen was the beneficiary on the other.'

'The son, Mickey?'

'Not so good for Mickey.'

'Thanks.'

'Don't forget me,' Gratelli said and hung up.

Carly felt better. She felt involved. Didn't take much, did it? She answered the phone and a little progress fell in her lap.

Hawkes was not happy. But Lang thought that was probably the artist's natural state.

'Do you just drop in on the CEO of GE?'

'I don't have reason to,' Lang said, seeing Hawkes's narrow face through the twelve-inch gap between door and door jamb. 'I thought you might have some insight into the death of Frank Wiley.'

'I don't,' Hawkes said.

'He was going to have an exhibition of his photography. Do you have any idea what it was going to be?'

'Why would I?'

'He was a kind of historian, as I understand it. He chronicled the characters who hung out in North Beach . . . their lives. And you were part of that.'

'Not really. It was a scruffy bunch and in the scheme of things I was never really part of the hangers-on.'

'He didn't photograph you?' Lang asked, not sure why, except that would be a connection.

'No, not me.' Was his answer even more abrupt than usual? Hawkes recanted a little. 'Maybe, but it would have to be when I was young and foolish.'

'You knew all the players, right?' Lang asked. 'Your past, Mr Hawkes . . . we can't seem to find out much before you moved out here.'

'I didn't ask you to look.'

'Of course. Just curious. I'm told you're from New York.'

'Mr Detective, I'm sorry someone found it necessary to kill two people of my acquaintance and your concern. But it is not my problem. I have no reason to talk to you at all, much less open up my life so you can peck at it.'

'Just trying to find the truth,' Lang said. It was a weak, silly-sounding statement and he wished he could pull the words back before they reached Hawkes's ear.

'We're through here,' Hawkes said. No anger, just a sneering statement of the obvious.

The door shut.

Lang stopped by his place, supplemented Buddha's bowl of dry food, engaged in a monologue with the patiently attentive feline and would have liked to go for a swim. Too long between any kind of workout.

Instead, he stopped by Namu, several blocks west on Balboa, where he talked them into fixing him the fish sandwich with kimchee tartar sauce. He had a beer and watched the young men doing happy hour with sake at the bar.

After the service he'd come back and watch an Asian movie. Korean, perhaps. And he'd have a few bottles of Asahi Dry. Extra dry. That should finish his attempt to get the bad taste out of his mouth and banish the prissy Hawkes and what was likely to be a stuffy church service from his thoughts.

Lang was a little buzzed. He couldn't remember another day when he went on a coffee-drinking binge as he had all this morning and afternoon, stopping several times to refill his sad little paper cup. Usually he was a take-it-easy kind of guy. Not today. He was getting through a marathon day. Thing was, he was rarely this motivated.

Lang wasn't sure what he'd gain by going to the service for Whitney Warfield. It was an inappropriate time to talk with people about the murder.

Saints Peter and Paul was a San Francisco landmark. Grand and historic, it presided over North Beach as if it were castle to the kingdom. Nearby St Francis of Assisi didn't hold a candle, Lang thought sadly. Joe DiMaggio and Marilyn Monroe had posed on the church's front steps and the baseball great's final services were held inside. They would do no less for Whitney Warfield, who would have loved the drama though he railed against all organized religions – and everything organized, for that matter.

Inside Lang looked around. The interior was tastefully ornate for the most part. The only high drama was Christ on the Cross. But even that, sanguine as it was, was less lurid than he remembered from his own brief and now seemingly ancient experiences with religion.

The interior was at least three stories high. Grand chapels and other sacred nooks and crannies were off to the side. The choir loft was high and perched over the entrance. He went up the steps to the loft and using a little spyglass he gazed down on the hundreds of folks below. People were talking but in low tones and there was a low-grade buzz emanating up. Then it was as if someone had turned the volume down slowly. The chatter diminished. There was the sound of wood creaking as people settled into the pews.

Someone in robes stepped up and began to speak. Because of the cavernous space, each electronically enhanced word echoed slightly, giving it special authority. However profound, spiritual or mundane, the reverberation also made the words impossible to understand. Lang didn't try.

He remembered his own early Latin, which he spoke in sing-song fashion:

*Myfathercanplaydominoesbetterthanyourfathercan.*

Lang spotted Marlene, who had regained her attitude. She was three rows behind Elena who was in the front pew. Hawkes stood on the side in the back near the confessionals. Sumaoang, his mourning attire put together as best he could, was there with his girlfriend. Chiu was there with two other men, younger, who were obviously no slaves to fashion. He didn't know some of the players by sight – McFarland, Malone, Lilli D. Young. Agnes DeWitt even showed up, looking frail and elegant.

Of those on the list he could recognize, all were in attendance – except the newspaper publisher and Warfield the Younger.

# Nineteen

At home, he called Carly one last time in the evening. His excuse was to check on the proposed meeting with the writer, Malone. Carly had set it for ten. He'd pick her up at nine forty-five.

'You seem in control of your faculties,' he said in a way that Hawkes might have put it.

Damn, he thought, the man continued to haunt him.

'That's the nicest thing anyone has ever said to me,' she said, a Southern Belle drawl creeping into her voice.

Gratelli, at his desk nursing a cold cup of coffee, called the *Fog City Voice* publisher to request he come to the Hall of Justice for a little chat. Bart Brozynski asked politely if Gratelli could come to him.

'I smashed three vertebrae in a fall,' Brozynski said. 'It's painful for me to move and a car is hell. You mind?'

'When did that happen?' Gratelli asked.

'Three weeks ago.'

'Tell you what,' Gratelli said, 'you give me the name of your doctor, maybe we won't have to talk after all.'

'That's disappointing,' Brozynski said. 'I'd like to know a little more about the deaths of Warfield and Wiley.'

'So would I.'

'Does that mean the police have no suspects . . . a dead end, maybe?'

'You're putting words in my mouth,' Gratelli said. 'I know how that works. Right now we're talking about you.'

'I didn't kill them. I try not to create news. There's so much existing news that isn't reported. You like the story?'

'The difference between what you do and what I do is that I have to back up what I say with facts. Innuendo rarely works in the courtroom.'

'I beg to differ with you, Inspector. If the glove doesn't fit . . .'

'I think that proves my point,' Gratelli said.

'Then we're both happy,' Brozynski said.

'Let's not tempt fate,' Gratelli said, 'and call it a day.'

Gratelli would check with the physician and the hospital. He could get conditions and dates and that would either put Brozynski in the skillet or out of it. He'd bet that the cantankerous old publisher, for whom he held a begrudging respect, wasn't lying.

'Up late last night?' Carly asked Lang as she scooted into the passenger side of Lang's car.

He nodded. But her face still had the look of inquiry. He smiled.

'A Korean film about some young man who occupied people's homes when they weren't there and had a fetish for golf,' Lang said.

'An art film?'

'Yes. Korean art film. I was in the mood for Korean movies.'

'You were in the mood for it?' she asked.

'I had kimchee tartar sauce on my fish sandwich.'

'You are impressionable, then?'

'I must be. And I like themes. I watch *The Godfather*, I want a pizza or linguine, that sort of thing.'

'Did I tell you that Nathan Malone admitted to killing a man?'

'Yes.'

'You're not shocked?'

'No, I suppose not,' Lang said. 'Why did he kill?'

'Passion, maybe.'

'Well, let's hope he's not in a passionate mood this morning.'

'What are we going to ask the dangerous and deadly Mr Malone?' Carly asked.

'About Frank Wiley. About the exhibition. Maybe there was a book in the works. Maybe Warfield's book was illustrated. Maybe with Wiley's photographs.'

She nodded. 'I thought that too. Not just Malone. Somebody else would have to know what Wiley was up to.'

'A publisher, maybe. If there was a book. A printer and a framer if there was an exhibition,' Lang said. 'Malone was OK with me coming along?'

'I think he's interested in the story – or at least what we know of it. He's a writer, his curiosity is involved; he's part of it, his ego is involved.'

'And if he didn't do it, he has to begin to worry if there's a pattern and if he fits it.'

Malone answered the door himself. He looked relaxed in slacks and a sweatshirt over a blue, button-down shirt. While his face revealed his true age, his movement was that of a younger man.

He looked at Lang and then at Carly.

Smiling, he said, 'After the last time you felt you needed a body-guard?'

'This is Noah Lang, my partner,' Carly said.

Lang and Malone shook hands.

'My wife has gone to the market,' he said, 'so we have the house to ourselves.' He led them back to his office. 'I bared my soul to Ms Paladino when last she was here.' He stopped, turned, looked at Carly. 'I'm not sure there's anything left.'

'Since we talked,' Carly said as they continued their walk to his office at the back of the house, 'Frank Wiley has been murdered.'

'Yes, I heard. But I know nothing of it.'

They arrived. Malone sat in his desk chair, allowing Lang and Carly to take the two upholstered 'guest' chairs.

'Maybe you know more than you think you do,' Lang said.

'That's very kind of you, but as a writer I'm more inclined to know less than I think I do.'

'You worked with both of them – Warfield and Wiley – on a book,' Carly said.

'I did. The third of a trio,' Malone said. 'I'll let you in on a little secret. We didn't sit on the floor in the living room, eat popcorn, and put a book together with scissors and glue. Warfield went off to write his part. I did mine. And Wiley did what he had to do with the photographs. The publisher has people who put these things together. Once we understood what our role was, we hardly spoke.'

'You didn't pal around with them?'

'At one time, as I told your partner, Warfield and I closed a few bars. But Wiley was all light and dark and Warfield and I were boisterous boasters who used, or tried to use, words as swords, and argued about subjects Wiley had absolutely no interest in. Then I grew up, got married, and became mature and stuffy. Warfield was left to cause chaos in the china shop all on his own.'

'You had no dealings with Wiley after the book?' Carly asked.

'I'd see him around. He'd begun to photograph buildings, so it wasn't unusual to see him. Before that he was obsessed with portraits.'

'He take a photo of you?' Lang asked.

'Yes. Many.' Malone smiled, stifled a laugh.

'Some humorous ones, I take it.' Lang said.

'Probably most of them. But somewhere floating in the universe may be a naked photograph of me, thankfully of my much younger self. Even so, it's as if the world hasn't suffered enough. It was during all that summer of love stuff. We were supposed to be comfortable with our bodies. You're too young to remember.'

'You know anything about Wiley's latest project?' Carly asked. 'What it was about? Maybe he came to you for a little collaboration?'

'No. He wouldn't have. And if he did, I wouldn't have. In the end my life was only tenuously attached to the North Beach he loved. The neighborhood began to loom less large in my life. It was just a few years. Some nice years. But it would be misleading to put me with the writers and artists who were an integral part of North Beach history.'

'All right,' Carly said. 'Thank you for seeing us.'

'You find out anything?' he asked.

'No. We're stymied,' she said.

'And the police? What are they thinking?'

'They're trudging through the evidence. We're not in the know.' It was a small lie, she thought. But after the article in the *Fog City Voice*, she was more cautious.

He nodded, stood. It was the signal to leave.

'Thank you again,' Carly said, standing up.

Malone followed them to the door.

'Good luck,' he called after them.

'The wife was there,' Carly said once they were outside. 'She was in a robe carrying a glass of something and having a hard time moving down the hall. She looked sloshed.'

'Not at the market?' Lang said, smiling.

# Twenty

'Lunch?' Noah said as they went to the car.

'One track mind,' she said.

'No, not really. I have other tracks. Food, movies and . . . OK, let's just say two tracks.'

L'Osteria El Forno was a tiny storefront restaurant tucked away amid the tourist spots on Columbus in North Beach.

It was her choice, but Lang had eaten there before and thought it was a perfect place to lunch – if they could get in. What was it, he thought, that Yogi Berra said about such places: 'Nobody goes there anymore. It's too crowded.'

Maybe because it was still early, there was a surprisingly short wait to sit at one of the nine or so tables inside. None of them, it seemed, were more than a few feet from the kitchen. The place had high ceilings and the patina that comes from age was real not cosmetic. The walls were an appropriately faded Tuscan sun color and the waiter was young and handsome and smiling and Italian.

'So this means you'll have to watch *The Godfather* or *Goodfellas* tonight?' Carly asked. 'Maybe a Fellini film?'

'Depends on what I have for dinner. If I go to a German restaurant, I might watch *Das Boot*.'

'Are there German restaurants still around?'

'Yes. Shroeder's downtown. Schnitzel House, South of Market. Suppenküche in Hayes Valley. There's an East German place . . . Walzwerk . . . on South Van Ness.'

'You are a walking city guide.'

'I'm a male living alone . . . nearly alone . . . Buddha doesn't cook.'

She ordered some sort of fresh, cold salmon dish and he ordered the pumpkin ravioli and a glass of Sangiovese. They shared a small cheese, tomato and basil pizza.

'Do you ever eat anything green?' she asked.

'Basil is green,' Lang said.

'C'mon,' she said.

'On St Patrick's day.'

'What do you think of Malone?'

'Seems too sane, too self-satisfied. That's just a gut feeling. That doesn't take him off the list. But he said something interesting that may seem obvious now. The publisher puts a book together. If – and it's a big "if" – Wiley had a publisher to follow up on his planned exhibition, they might have something interesting.'

She nodded. 'And if we could get into Wiley's, we could look at the photographs that are part of the exhibition and get a sense of . . . something.'

'Can we get in?' Lang asked.

'One way or another,' she said.

'I like your attitude.'

'That's because it's your attitude.'

'I won't hold that against you.'


There were no police visible on the short, usually empty street where Frank Wiley lived and died. The afternoon sun provided no cover for their climb. At the top they were greeted with what they expected. Criss-crossed yellow crime tape provided a spiderweb of forbiddance.

'Do we?' Carly asked.

'No.'

'What do we do?'

'We get a stapler, a couple of flashlights and come back tonight.'

'This was a trial run?'

'We needed to find out what we needed. Let's get some gelato.'

'We need gelato?'

'Need?'

'You have no idea what you're doing to me. I'll get big as a house. What did you get from Hawkes?'

'Attitude. He doesn't know anything and he doesn't really care to know anything if you can believe him.'

'Do you believe him?' Carly asked as they turned on to Columbus.

'I don't know what I believe.'

'Some good news,' Carly said as they dodged the mix of neighborhood inhabitants and tourists in shorts and baseball caps. 'Brozynski, according to Inspector Gratelli, isn't very mobile. I noticed that when I visited with him. I just thought he was too lazy. Apparently, he took a tumble and smashed some vertebrae. The timing was such that it's doubtful the guy has the agility to be the murderer. Not for sure, but reasonable doubt. And I had that anyway.'

'The murders sell newspapers, Carly. Sort of like a mortician killing off a few folks because business is slow. Lime,' Lang said when they entered the shop and noticed the vast array of flavors.' He looked at Carly. 'Green. Are you happy?'

'Thrilled. My life could end now.'

'I take it Gratelli called you. What else did he say?'

'Nothing.'

Carly had the pistachio gelato with dark chocolate as the second dip. She spooned a bite.

'A nosy question,' she said.

'That's what we're paid for.'

'But this is personal. You don't have to answer.'

'I'm so grateful.'

'You ever thought of being a dad?'

'Too late.'

She thought about saying 'Not really', but decided that might imply something she wasn't ready to imply.

'You ever regret not having kids?' she asked.

'I try to minimize regrets. The great philosopher Sinatra.'

'You mean "shoobee doobee do"?'

'I was thinking of something else, but yeah, that will do.'

'You'd have made a great dad,' Carly said. She watched his face to see if she was going too far. But he continued to be a bit of a mystery.

'Why's that?'

'You are so even-keeled.'

'You said I was "lackadaisical" earlier.'

'Sensitive too.'

'You want to be a mother?'

'A great defense is a good offense. No, I'm too selfish. And I don't have a green thumb or whatever color of thumb I'm supposed to have to raise children.'

'Let's meet back here tonight, at eight,' Lang said. 'We'll go in under the cover of darkness. Wear dark clothing.'

'And a mask?' she asked, smiling.

Carly was feeling better. The kind of damp cloud that seemed to have occupied her brain was gone. Having Lang fully on board and whittling down the names on the suspect list gave her a sense of optimism.

Mickey Warfield
Marshall Hawkes

Marlene Berensen
Richard Sumaoang
Ralph Chiu
Nathan Malone

That was the list now. And it was progress she could relate to William Blake. Sweet William, she thought as she climbed the steps to the office. She admonished herself for her momentary lapse into sentimentality. In her many years at Vogel Security, she would have never imagined her life to have taken such an odd turn. Living was no longer abstract. It was real. And she believed she was beginning to like the idea. But it was not without risk. That was obvious now.

Inside the office, Thanh looked like a punk mechanic. He was wearing black coveralls. His hair was slicked back in early rock style.

He smiled. 'You lose Noah?'

'He's parking the car,' Carly said. 'You look like you're ready for anything.'

Lang was in the doorway.

'Perfect,' Lang said to Thanh.

'Of course it's perfect,' Thanh said. 'But what did *you* mean by it?'

'You're dressed for the break-in tonight.'

'Finally, some fun.'

Carly looked at them, shook her head, but she wasn't really perturbed or confused or disgusted or anything of the sort. She just had an image to keep up.

Lang was feeling antsy. He decided to revisit Marlene Berensen. This time he would drop by her place unannounced. The car registration listed an address on Mallorca in the Marina. Though it would be diffi-cult to find a parking space – that was true all over town, except for the tops of some steep hills – it was even more difficult to get to the ritzy neighborhood from South of Market by bus.

The Marina was named for the obvious reason that it was home to a couple of marinas where small yachts and sailboats were tied up. It also had a couple of yacht clubs. In Lang's mind the neighborhood was defined by Chestnut on the south and the Bay in the north. The eastern border was Fort Mason and the western line of demarcation was the Presidio. The homes were, for the lack of anything more descriptive, Mediterranean; two- and three-story houses of stucco, painted in brave pastels or restrained sun colors. Most of the homes edged up to the sidewalks. Whatever outdoor living was to be done was in the back or, in some cases, in a courtyard.

The people who lived there were likely over sixty-five or under forty. The younger ones had a golden retriever, a kid or two, and possibly a nanny. The older ones were sitting on real estate that had appreciated at least a thousand per cent since they bought it and they just might sell it to move to San Diego or Fort Lauderdale.

Marlene Berensen was an exception. She was between forty and sixty-five, had no kids and no dogs. She did have Mickey Warfield and that was what Lang wanted to talk to her about. She was also unhappy to see Lang.

'Hi there,' Lang said.

'Go away,' she said. Her hair was up. She was without make-up. She wore sweats. Even at less than her best, there was something about her. Something smart and sexy.

'Nice to see you again,' he said. 'I wanted to talk to you about some developments in the case.'

'I'm not interested. Go away.'

'You know Frank Wiley was killed,' Lang said, looking over her shoulder into her home.

'I don't know Frank Wiley. I'm sure he will be missed. But not by me.'

Her sexy, gravelly voice probably came from years of smoking and drinking and whatever it took to be a fun mistress, he thought.

'A photographer in North Beach. Worked with Whitney Warfield.'

'Goodbye.'

'One more thing. Mickey Warfield. You know him, right?'

She shrugged. 'Whitney's kid. So?'

'So, you two are close?'

'What makes you think that?'

He looked beyond her. From what he could see of the room behind her, there was a sort of frayed elegance to the decor. Kind of like her, he thought.

'You let him drive your Jag,' Lang said.

A slight tremor appeared on her face. She tried to overcome it with more attitude, a narrowing of the eyes and a sneer.

'I lent him my car. So? Don't you have something to do besides wandering around asking petty, annoying questions?'

'It's what I do best,' Lang said.

'There are adult learning classes available throughout the city.'

'Are you and Mickey having an affair?'

'If you bother me again, I'll call the police, get a restraining order and sue you for everything you have.'

Marlene Berensen shut the door.

\*     \*     \*

Carly spent the afternoon working with Thanh. Together they used various Internet sites to determine the finances of those folks remaining on the list.

Ralph Chiu had holdings that were in the several millions. As one might guess, they were primarily real estate. Chinatown, the Richmond, and North Beach. He was also involved in various new condo developments South of Market and in rapidly developing Mission Bay. He was a partner in five hotels. He could be connected to a Chinatown Tong; but then what successful Chinese businessman couldn't? Many were as legitimate as any chamber of commerce.

Marshall Hawkes was worth nearly $2 million. He owned his own condo and was doing well in the art market. Top credit rating.

Marlene Berensen was on poverty's doorstep. She had a poor credit rating and heavy payments on her home in the Marina. She had no clear source of income.

Richard Sumaoang was dodging creditors as well. He rented his home in Cole Valley near the Haight.

Whitney and Elena Warfield were pretty much breaking even. They owned the home outright and even though the royalties were diminishing each year, they were solvent. A couple of certificates of deposit. And Whitney owned a half interest in a bookstore, which was also barely holding its own.

Nathan Malone was comfortable. His royalties were more than ample to keep him in the style to which he had become accustomed.

Mickey Warfield had no visible means of support and was, for the most part, off the radar in financial terms.

Carly wasn't sure what any of it meant, but the increased focus on the remaining suspects might be coupled with other information which, if they were lucky, could help them narrow the list even further. Copies of this new information were put in the folder Thanh had created for each one on the list.

# Twenty-One

Thanh went first. Carly and Lang followed a couple of minutes later. Lang had a large gym bag. Inside were flashlights, a stapler, some spare crime tape, a small crowbar and small digital camera that worked well in low light.

When the two of them turned the corner into the small dead-end street they saw Thanh scaling the second floor, feet on the sill of one of the windows. The glass opened out and it took Thanh only a few seconds to slide something in and slip the lock. In a couple more seconds he was inside and had shut the window.

By the time Carly and Lang reached the top, Thanh had the door open. Lang undid just enough of the crime tape to allow Carly and himself to crawl in. Lang handed the others a flashlight each and kept one for himself.

'What are we looking for?' Thanh asked.

'We don't know,' Lang said. 'Maybe we'll know when we find it.'

'Or maybe we won't,' Carly said. 'OK, I found something.'

'God, you're good,' Thanh said.

'Shut up,' Carly said. 'The day I visited Wiley, there were four stacks of four.' Her flashlight shined on some wrapped packages that appeared to be large pieces of art. 'One of the stacks only has three.'

'You counted them?' Lang asked in disbelief. 'Why would you do that?'

'I don't know. I was taken by the symmetry . . . the neatness. I don't know why. I just do those things sometimes.'

'And you notice that one is gone?' Lang asked, still not quite believing.

'Yes. It's obvious. One stack is different from the rest.'

'Very observant, grasshopper,' Thanh said, then to Lang, 'I think she's smarter than you are.'

'Who isn't?'

The three of them wandered through the front room, into the second room, which was a small office – desk, files, storage closet and a small darkroom. Beyond that was a hall. A bathroom was on the right, a kitchen on the left. The hall eventually led to a larger space, where a bed, stereo system, a comfortable chair and a table for two completed the inventory of his estate.

'It's all quite modest,' Carly said.

'A man of small appetites, apparently,' Lang called out from the kitchen. 'There's no alcohol anywhere. Canned food, chili, soup. Pizza in the freezer.'

It seemed odd to Lang that in one of the greatest food towns of the world and in the center of the Italian quarter, there was a freezer with several Tombstone pizzas.

Thanh sat himself at Wiley's desk and went through it and the filing cabinet that butted up against it.

There wasn't much to look at. The three of them ended up in the office, going through his records, searching for something significant. Thanh came across a folder that contained correspondence with Blue Monkey Press.

Wiley had written them inquiring about the possibility of publishing a book of photographs of Beat poets and artists – naked.

A return letter was a politely phrased rejection.

Wiley sent a second letter with a further enticement. There would be a narrative by author Whitney Warfield. Again, a polite rejection.

Frank Wiley wasn't easily deterred. This time, he said that best-selling author Nathan Malone would do a major introduction and that Warfield would do the narrative. Did Malone lie or had he never been contacted? The subjects included some legends of the movement, including Allen Ginsberg and Malone himself.

This seemed to have done the trick. Blue Monkey Press offered an advance – a small one, but an advance just the same. The book was to be published after the exhibition, pending final approval of the contents.

Thanh took notes: the time frame for the book, the amount of the advance, and the name and address of the publisher. As he was doing this, Lang investigated the darkroom and Carly thumbed through the proof sheets – many of them marked up with symbols she didn't understand.

For the most part she ignored all the photographs of structures and focused on any photographs of people. There were thousands, most of them clothed. She recognized a few of the subjects. Some were nationally known. Some were local legends. And some were just street folks and some of them probably friends. William Blake was among those photographed. Clothed and unclothed. He was handsome.

'We have to look at the photographs in the other room.'

They carefully undid the brown paper wrapping and the tape. Thanh used his cellphone to snap a photograph of each photograph. There were fifteen of them, not quite life-size. All in black and white. All with dark backgrounds, light only on the flesh of the subject. Even in the light from a flashlight, it was clear this was taken with a large-format camera. The detail was rich and perhaps a little gruesome. Modesty might not be the only objection.

'Not exactly glamour shots,' Thanh said.

'Looks like those photographs of fleas blown up a thousand times,' Carly said.

There was something powerful about them, Lang thought. Whether Wiley had revealed his subjects' true characters or just a frightening vision of an aspect of their characters, he didn't know. But, as Thanh said, these weren't glamour shots. Some of the subjects might object.

'Did you come across a folder of release forms?' Carly asked Thanh.

'I don't think so.'

'Could you look? They would need permission from the subjects to exhibit or publish the photographs. Without it, Wiley couldn't legally have a show, let alone publish a book.'

Thanh went back to the office area to check the files.

'Maybe we can match permission forms with the photographs here to find out which photograph is missing,' she said.

'You think that's the link? The photograph?'

'Maybe,' Carly said. 'One is missing. Maybe Wiley sent it back to be reframed or something.'

'Or someone really doesn't want to be seen naked and is willing to kill over it,' Lang said. 'Quite an ego.' His cellphone squirmed in his jeans.

'Lang.'

'I need to see you,' said the feminine voice.

'Who is this?'

'Angel.'

'Angel?'

Carly looked up. It was too dark to see if she was smiling.

'I'm busy at the moment,' Lang continued.

'I need to see you. Tonight. Come when you can. But come, please.'

'Got a date with an angel?' Carly asked.

The two of them finished rewrapping and restacking the photographs as Thanh made a list of names on the permission slips he had found and the dates they were signed. There were more than a hundred of them.

It had taken them several hours to do what they had to do and it was nearly one a.m. when the crime tape on the front door was reaffixed as carefully as possible.

The three of them walked back to Lang's Mercedes together.

'Who's Angel?' Carly asked.

'Yes,' Thanh said, 'who's Angel and why am I asking?'

'Angel is Mickey Warfield's girlfriend and alibi for his father's murder.'

'She wants to see you?' Carly asked. 'Why?'

'She likes me.'

'Really?'

'It happens. By the way, how's your friend William?'

Carly was thankful that it was too dark for him to see her blush.

'Don't be mad,' William said, flicking on the light by the sofa. 'I didn't look in your closet or open any drawers.'

'William . . .' she said.

'I'm a firm believer in mixing business with pleasure.' He stood to help her with her coat. He wore jeans and a white shirt, top two buttons open at the neck, sleeves rolled up. A black cashmere blazer was draped over the sofa. 'And you're late.'

'I must have forgotten to put our meeting down in my appointment book,' she said.

He smiled again. 'I wanted to check in. With Wiley dead, maybe there is some news?'

'No,' she said soberly. 'No news. We've interviewed everyone on your list, some of them twice. We've eliminated a few.'

'Who?'

'So far we are still looking at Mickey Warfield, Marlene Berensen, Ralph Chiu, Richard Sumaoang, Nathan Malone and Marshall Hawkes.' She'd been over the list so many times, she had the remaining suspects down cold.

'Down to six.'

'If the murderer is on the list.' She headed toward the kitchen. 'Would you like some wine?'

'I put a bottle of Primus on the counter, if you're interested.'

'Oh, yes, I see. By the way, how well did you know Frank Wiley?'

'I didn't.'

'Not at all?'

'No.'

'Strange,' she said, plucking the cork from the bottle, 'there was a proof sheet of photographs of you in his studio.'

'There was?'

'Nudes.'

'Oh . . . yes . . . My God, I had to be seventeen,' he said, coming into the kitchen.

'That would have been illegal,' Carly said.

'No, not really. And besides I've always been slightly illegal.'

'You knew him though,' she said.

'You are having a crisis in confidence, here?'

'No. Just want to make sure all the cards are on the table.'

'It was a long time ago. It was Anselmo's idea. I used to model for Anselmo. Wiley came over during one of our sessions, where I was, as always, without some or all of my clothing. Wiley, straight as an arrow, I'm sure, was just beginning to photograph human beings. Like most artists, he found something especially challenging about nudes. That's it. Didn't see him much. Different crowds. I've passed him on the streets. But that's it. We didn't have a lot in common.' He smiled. 'Frank was poor and straight.'

She poured the wine and handed him a glass.

'Did you know any of the others?'

'Never met Mr Chiu or Mr Sumaoang. I've met Nathan Malone at cocktail parties, but we weren't each other's type in any sense of the word. I was aware of Mr Hawkes, mostly through Anselmo. The two disliked each other intensely.'

'Why?'

'Anselmo said that he had been Hawkes's mentor and that once Hawkes got going he not only never acknowledged the help, but acted as if Anselmo was beneath him. Never met Mickey Warfield. Marlene . . . Marlene has appetites. It's been a few years though. As you know, I'm a professional companion. She used to have a large disposable income. There came a time when Marlene didn't.'

'Didn't have any money.'

William nodded. 'And you saw me naked?' He smiled and turned to walk back into the living room. 'May I put on some music?'

'You were seventeen and, yes, I saw you naked.'

'Did you approve?'

'Of what? Your body or your posing naked?'

'Doesn't matter which,' he said. 'He looked through the stack of CDs and put on some slow, quiet jazz.'

'You know, about the music . . . I'm thinking maybe it's late.'

'It is late. I put on music appropriate to the hour.' He smiled. 'Don't try to get rid of me.'

Angel looked as if she had been in bed.

'You gave up on me,' Lang said.

She nodded, giving him a faint, innocent smile. She looked softer tonight. Maybe it was the light, or near lack of it.

'You were asleep?' There was only the one lamp lit in the room. The light was behind her and her nakedness beneath a sheer nightgown was apparent.

'In bed, but couldn't sleep,' she said. 'Come in.'

She stepped aside and once he was in, she shut the door behind him. He thought about turning on more lights to change the ambience, but indecision brought about by the conflict between lust and logic came to a passive end.

There were fresh flowers – white, long-stemmed tulips – in a vase beside the lamp. On the table near it was a small folded card, the kind that comes with delivered flowers. The smell of tobacco and whiskey hung in the thick, quiet air.

'Beautiful flowers,' he said to move things along.

'A drink?' she asked.

'Yes.'

'Scotch all right?'

'All right.'

'I have pretty much anything you want tonight,' she said.

He resisted saying, 'I bet you do.' He could have said it. She loaded the sentence with innuendo.

'Scotch is fine.'

When she disappeared, he looked at the card.

'A small gesture for your generous help.' It was signed with what appeared to be an 'M'.

He took the glass from her.

'You wanted to see me?' he asked, sitting in the chair he sat in last time, giving her the sofa, the only spot in the room where light fell.

'To tell you something,' she said. 'I don't know what to do. I am frightened to do something, I'm frightened not to.'

'And you think I can help you decide?'

'I'm not sure I can think clearly,' she said, finally sitting on the sofa.

Looking at her, he wasn't sure he could think clearly either. It had been a while since he had been with anyone. This was purely physical, but it was strong. He knew the night wouldn't be just a bit of business about making a decision. She was seducing him with every move. The obviousness of it would have been humorous, if his mind was engaged in any kind of analytical thought. He'd find all this funny – tomorrow.

'I lied about Mickey being with me the night his father was killed. I lied about that. He wasn't with me that day or that night.'

'You could have told me that over the phone.'

'I want to do more than just say that.'

'You are trying to decide whether to tell the police or not.'

'Yes.'

'You told me, Angel. This is my case and I'm obligated to do something about it. Just like the police.'

'I know.'

'So you've decided.'

'I have more to tell you.'

She sipped her drink, leaving him leaning forward, waiting for something perhaps more shocking than eliminating Mickey's alibi. There was a little more to it. To ask someone to provide a false alibi was even more incriminating.

She told Lang about her life, coming from Hong Kong as a child. Once rich, she was now reduced to getting by as best she could.

'I had servants,' she said, as she fixed him another drink. 'Our family did, I mean – a cook, a gardener, a driver. It's quite a comedown. Baths were drawn for me. I didn't learn how to bathe myself until I was separated from them.'

She had a long, sad story. It might have been true.

'There's something else you wanted to tell me,' Lang said, after she seemed to have exhausted her autobiography.

'Yes,' she said. She was being coy.

'So?' Lang asked.

'But I'm not going to tell you until morning,' she said, glancing at her watch. 'Finish your drink.' She stood, slipped off her nightgown and walked toward the bedroom.

# Twenty-Two

Carly woke enveloped in the warmth of his body, his flesh against hers. The memory was vivid and difficult to shake – not that she really wanted to. She had to, though. Nothing would come of it.

She scooted away from him and, as she pulled on her robe, he stirred.

'Morning,' he said.

'Morning.'

'You slept well,' he said.

'I did. Coffee?'

'Please,' he said as he tossed aside the bedclothes. His body was firm, smooth, and appeared younger than it probably was. 'You mind if I hop in the shower?'

'Please don't hop,' she said. 'It will spoil everything.'

She went to the kitchen, put the wine bottle in the recycling bin, placed the glasses in the sink and set about making coffee.

She didn't know what to think. Although far from being a prude about such matters, Carly had never really had what could be called casual sex. She could still count her sexual partners on the fingers of . . . both hands. She also felt, though she didn't know why, that she was cheating. On whom?

By the time the coffee maker gurgled it's last gurgle and let out a telltale, steamy sigh, William Blake was in the kitchen.

'So who hit you?'

'You just now noticed?'

'No, I just now mentioned it. The light of day turns me from romantic to pragmatist.'

'Don't know. It happened when I went to visit Wiley. Somebody clunked me pretty good.'

'Would you know him if you saw him?' He poured his own coffee.

'Not sure it's a him, but no, I wouldn't. I didn't see anything. But I have a question.'

He looked at her, waiting.

'Am I aiding and abetting a fugitive?'

'It's not official yet,' William Blake said. 'You are aiding and abetting a person of interest, so say the newspapers.'

'Lang thinks you might be the murderer.'

'It's not a novel thought. But I don't hurt people. Not intentionally. I make them feel good.' It was obvious he was reconsidering his words. 'I try to make them feel good. Do you feel good?'

'I'm not the client. You are.'

'You're right. And I put an envelope on the bedside table for you.'

'The bedside table?'

'If you want you can think of it as for last night . . .' He looked at her repressed grin. 'It isn't. But if it excites you . . . And, Carly, you would never be my client. You are not nearly rich enough. Last night was because I wanted to. Very much.'

He kissed her cheek and quickly downed his coffee.

'I'll check in from time to time. I hope no one else dies.'

'I . . . uh . . . agree,' she said, not sure how to take the parting wish.

Go away, Lang thought. The pounding and shouting bounced against his monumental headache. Sleep. He just wanted sleep. He wanted everything to go away. Maybe he could just die. That would be OK. The pain would go away, then, wouldn't it?

Slowly the shouts became clearer.

'Come to the door, Ms Chang. Come to the door now, please.' The 'please' was urgent, somehow both begging and demanding.

There was a thud, then a crash. Footsteps on the floor, voices calling out for Ms Chang. He didn't want to open his eyes. That would make it real. He opened in time to see distorted, out-of-focus faces looking down at him, arms coming toward him, hands grasping him, pulling him up. Then turning him around, forcing him back on the bed. His arms were pulled behind him.

'Dead,' he heard.

What? He was dead?

'Noah Lang. Jesus Christ,' Lang heard, but couldn't see. His face was pressed into the bedding. Where was he?

'Turn him over,' the voice said.

Though he still could not see clearly, he could make out the face of Inspector Stern and in moments, beside that face, the face of Inspector Rose.

'What's going on?' Lang managed to say, but the headache was the worst he'd ever had and it was painful to speak, to move. To add to the punishment someone had pulled open the blinds, sending piercing shafts of light into his tormented brain.

Rose wrapped a blanket around Lang's nakedness.

'We had a saying in the Navy, Lang,' Stern said. He was in his usual slightly too small suit and a tie that seemed on the verge of cutting off the cop's oxygen supply at the neck.

'I don't want to hear it,' Lang said. He was beginning to get his bearings.

'Find 'em, feel 'em, fuck 'em and forget 'em. Yours apparently added kill 'em.'

'What?' He turned. Angel was still in bed, naked and quiet. 'What?'

'She's dead, Lang,' Stern said. He seemed to take pleasure in delivering the news.

There were several people in the room, a number of them in blue uniforms. Some were wearing white.

'I got it,' a uniform said, his latex-gloved hand holding what appeared to be an ice pick.

'That matches the body,' a man in glasses said.

'Well, that didn't take long,' Stern said.

'What happened?' Rose asked.

'I don't know.'

'You usually go to bed with dead women?' Stern asked. 'Oh, that's right, you've been with dead women before.' He referenced cases, one fifteen years earlier and one more recent, each of them involving a dead woman.

'You don't know?' Rose asked.

'I don't remember anything. I came over last night because Angel asked me to.'

'Miss Chang asked you to come over.'

'Miss LeGard,' Lang corrected.

'Chang,' Rose said. 'Doesn't matter what name she gave you.'

'Why did she ask you to come over?'

'She wanted to tell me something.'

'Tell you something,' Stern mimicked with disgust. 'Jesus!'

'What did she tell you?' Rose continued in calm tones.

'She told me that she lied when she alibi'd Mickey Warfield the night of his father's death.'

'She did, did she? Then you killed her.' Stern's face was contorted in anger.

'Right. Then I crawled in beside her because I was too lazy to go home.'

'She want to sleep with you?' Rose asked.

'Yeah. She also had something to tell me, but I had to wait until morning. All I remember is following her to the bedroom, maybe getting into bed. It's vague. That's it. Now I have the worst headache I've had in my life.'

'How much did you have to drink?'

'A glass and a half of Scotch. You have the picture?'

'She slipped you a Mickey?' Stern said, obviously finding the idea preposterous.

'Mickey is right,' Lang said. 'I think "Mickey" is just right.'

Rose looked at Stern. Stern shook his head, anger subsiding or turning into a general distaste for the universe.

'Scene of the crime, Rose,' Stern said. 'We got him. Right there. Got drunk as a skunk, had a blackout, killed her.' He laughed. 'Poor, dumb son of a bitch. If we find your prints on the weapon, Lang, you are toast.'

'Let's get him tested,' Rose said.

'For what?'

'Drugs and alcohol. Let's get some facts.'

'We got the facts,' Stern said.

'Now,' Rose said. 'I'm not blowing a case because you have a Johnson for Lang.'

Stern stifled himself. And the process, Lang thought, looked painful.

Lang had never seen Rose take over like that, but he was glad he did. Stern was ready to administer capital punishment on the spot and this wasn't good cop and bad cop. Over the years Stern had developed an intense dislike for Lang. Rose didn't care enough to have feelings one way or another. He was, though, the saner of the two.

Lang was allowed out of handcuffs so he could dress. He looked back as they took him from the bedroom. They were putting Angel in a body bag.

In the car, heading toward the Hall of Justice, Lang tried to remember the night before. He remembered climbing into bed with her, remembered a deep kiss, remembered his hands on her warm body, exploring. They were making love when his memory ran out.

'We'll run a few tests to see if you have something in your system that would put you out,' Rose said.

'But listen here,' Stern said, looking back over his shoulder from the driver's seat, 'you could have drugged yourself.'

'So, you're saying there's no way out here?'

'I'm just saying what I'm saying,' Stern said.

'Why would I kill her?'

'God knows,' Stern said. 'People don't need reasons.'

'Why would I set myself up? You don't make sense.'

'For a guy found in bed with a dead woman, I wouldn't go around talking about somebody else not making sense,' Stern said.

'What else did Angel tell you?' Rose asked.

'Nothing. She was going to pull the alibi from her boyfriend Mickey. Mickey, you guys ought to know, is somehow connected to Marlene Berensen, Warfield's mistress.'

'In what way, connected?' Rose asked.

'I don't know. But this is connected to Warfield's death and Wiley's.'

'I know,' Rose said.

'No, you don't fuckin' know,' Stern said to his partner.

'Whether Lang is a slime ball or not is an open question. I got your back there,' Rose said to Stern. 'But he's not going to randomly kill some woman he's balling and if he did, why an ice pick?'

'Who uses an ice pick these days? Why?' Lang asked.

'She might be cold,' Stern said, 'but she wasn't frigid, was she, Lang?' Lang didn't answer. But he did have a question.

'Who called you?' Lang asked.

Neither cop responded.

'C'mon, guys,' Lang continued, 'you didn't just drop by to say hello. You were told where to go.'

'We ask the questions,' Stern said. 'Don't we, Rose?'

'How far is up? Why are we here? What happens after we die?' Rose asked.

'What was a lowlife like Noah Lang doing in bed with a suspect's girlfriend?' Stern asked.

'That's a question,' Rose said. 'Takes Stern only a moment to catch on.'

They were on their routine. Lang wouldn't get anything. Maybe Gratelli could help.

Lang was allowed to sit in homicide, at Rose's desk. Stern wanted to book him. Rose wanted to let him go. A compromise was reached. They would push for the fingerprint match. If Lang's prints were on the ice pick, it was over for the private detective, no matter what happened with the tox screen. Lang wasn't relieved. If someone went to the trouble of killing Angel while Lang was unconscious beside her, there was little reason to believe the killer wouldn't have wrapped Lang's fingers around the handle. But he wasn't in a position to negotiate.

'I'm going to make a call,' Lang said, 'are you cool with that?'

'Call to your heart's content,' Stern said. 'You might try for a presidential pardon. My money says you're gonna need it.'

His first call went to Chastain West, the defense attorney who provided Lang with most of his work. This time, instead of West hiring Lang, it would be the reverse.

'Tough times,' Lang said.

'What's up?'

'I may be up for a murder charge. I'm here at homicide. Can you break away anytime soon?'

'Yeah. Give me an hour.'

West was one of a handful of people Lang could count on. He believed in the idea of justice and would often take cases when there was absolutely nothing in it for him but seeing that the weak or the poor weren't trampled upon.

Lang called Thanh and explained the situation. Thanh was surprisingly emotional and, for a moment, he seemed panicked.

'Let me think,' Thanh said. 'We'll do something. You tell Carly?'

'Next on my list. Is she there?'

'No.'

'I'll catch her on the cell. We need to get a line on Mickey Warfield. Every move he makes. You might pick up the trail at Marlene Berensen. She lives in the Marina. He uses her car sometimes and who knows what else?'

'All right.'

'We need to go deeper on Mickey's life. We don't know what he does for a living. We don't even know where he lives, unless he lives with Marlene. If that's the case then that's very, very interesting. Can you find out?'

'I'm on it. Anything else?'

'Yeah. If you have the time. Find out about gang activity in Chinatown in the last few years. Has there been any? Who was involved? Find out if Ralph Chiu has any suspicious associations. Keep Carly in the loop.'

Carly Paladino was still adjusting to being her own boss. After years of regular office hours at Vogel Security, nine to six or seven, weekends off, she found it odd that work could be done when it needed to be done. That working until midnight some nights meant that she might hang out at home until noon. Saturdays and Sundays were whatever she wanted them to be.

She spent this Friday morning at the Ferry Building, wandering through the farmer's markets. Because it was late September, she was aware the amount and variety of fresh produce would soon be in decline. But there were fall vegetables and fruits. Her head felt normal and she reluctantly admitted that while last night caused her to engage in a little critical self-reflection, she felt good. Relaxed. Renewed. She also felt somewhat relieved that this was not an affair. Not an affair, she repeated in her mind as she looked at what might be the last of the really good local tomatoes.

Her cell had beeped several times. Finally, she worried that it was truly urgent.

'Lang here,' the voice said.

'Hi, Noah.'

'I'm in a bit of trouble.'

'What kind of trouble?'

'Murder trouble. I'm being arrested for the murder of Angel LeGard aka Chang.'

'What?' Carly heard him. She just needed a moment to process it.

'My fingerprints were found on the handle of the weapon that killed her.'

'I don't understand. This Angel Chang . . .'

'Mickey Warfield's girlfriend.'

'How did they connect her death to you?'

Lang cleared his throat. 'I've only got a minute. They just told me about the prints. As they say in the movies, "I wuz framed."'

'Noah, tell me how they came to you.'

'When I woke up she was beside me. Dead. The police were coming through the front door.'

'Someone dumped her at your place? It doesn't sound . . .'

'No, I was at her place. Things . . . developed,' Lang said. 'I think that in the process, she put something in my Scotch.'

'Noah . . .'

'I gotta go. Not my idea . . .'

Click.

Carly didn't know what to think. She wasn't even sure what she felt. There was anger. Was it because Lang had acted unprofessionally? Or was it that she didn't like the idea that Lang was sleeping around?

'Well, you're a prize hypocrite,' Carly said out loud and to herself. Life should be clearer, she thought.


# Twenty-Three


And there it was. After all these years, after all these close calls, Lang found himself in jail. He was surprised that he had not been before. And, for an experience that was now only an hour old, he was also surprised at how frightening it was. He wasn't fearful of his life or limb. He wasn't fearful of inmates or guards. He was fearful of the confinement, the sense that he was no longer in control of anything. It was a mix of claustrophobia, which he knew he had, and the strange reality that he could be lost in time and space. After only an hour.

'Big baby,' he said to himself.

He was relieved to see Chastain West. The man was dressed as usual in low-key style – browns today of various textures, perfectly, self-consciously chosen, as were his movements and words. He was a handsome black man, a little silver around the temples suggesting that even his wisdom was cool.

'Who shall I hire to investigate?' Chaz said, smiling, seemingly not concerned. 'You're busy, it seems.'

'Not busy,' Lang said. 'Need to be busy. Can you get me out?'

'Not before morning. And then, I don't know. I don't know what they're charging you with yet. Murder, do you think?'

'Maybe. She's dead. I was there. My fingerprints were on the weapon.'

'The big cop said ice pick. Ice pick?'

'Yes.'

'How strange. Who uses ice picks these days?'

'You can work with Carly Paladino. She's a partner now. And this is connected in some way with the investigation we were both hired to do.'

'By whom?'

'Some mysterious gigolo named William Blake.'

Lang filled him in. The rules had been relaxed and the two of them spoke for at least two hours. 'I need to get a message to Thanh to stop by and feed Buddha.'

'Feed Buddha?'

'My cat,' Lang said, checking his attorney friend's face for a sign of disapproval.

'Good for you,' Chaz said. 'I have three. Perfect companions for people who don't need constant approval.'

The world was full of surprises. He never pictured Chaz having cats. Probably he had never really pictured Chaz beyond the time they spent together, not all of it business. Sometimes they had a couple of drinks somewhere jazz was played. Lang was partial to the Blues and West tended toward the pure and progressive. But they could meet in the middle on music and most things.

'You have any ideas about who killed the girl?'

'The obvious is Mickey Warfield. He had a key.'

'But she was his alibi for another death, right?'

'Yes, that's a problem. If she was telling the truth, she was going to the police to retract her alibi statement.'

'Did he know that?' West asked.

'I don't know. Maybe he knew her well enough to know she wouldn't be reliable. The thing is, she claimed to have something else to tell me. To get me to stay she said she'd tell me in the morning.'

'That's why you stayed, to hear what she had to say in the morning?' West asked, voice dripping with sarcasm.

'All right. All right. It wasn't the smartest move I ever made.'

'The bad news is that they have a weapon. That means they have means and opportunity. But they're extremely shy of a motive . . . unless there's something else you haven't told me.'

'I don't know what they could come up with as far as motive. I gain nothing from her death. And it would be extremely stupid for me to hang out after I killed her. I think Inspector Rose understands that. Not sure what Stern thinks. Or if he thinks.'

'Murder usually puts bail out of bounds, but I can use the shaky case as leverage. I'll know better when I understand which judge is handling the arraignment. Maybe I can get the police to back off altogether. Who is in charge of the Warfield investigation?'

'Inspector Gratelli.'

'Good. He's a pragmatist.'

Gratelli ran into Stern and Rose on the third floor of the Hall of Justice building. The third floor was lined with San Francisco City and County Superior Courts, the courts that handled felonies. They stood next to an old telephone booth. With the phone long ago removed by Ma Bell, the booth was merely a glass enclosure. People still slipped inside the booth to make calls on their cells away from the din of those gathered in the marble-walled echo chamber they called a hallway.

'I understand they found Rohypnol in Lang's system,' Gratelli said to Rose.

'What does that change?' Stern asked defensively. 'He could have drugged himself to avoid suspicion.'

'Why wouldn't he just have left?'

'Maybe she drugged him and he realized it. Before he passed out he killed her.'

'Possible,' Gratelli said. 'I just don't buy it.'

'It's not up to you to buy it or not,' Stern said. 'It's between us and the prosecutor.'

'Sorry, Stern. I'm taking it.'

'You can't.'

'Actually, I have. It's part of the Warfield–Wiley deaths. The girl was Mickey Warfield's woman. She was the son's alibi on the night his father was killed. I don't see motive for Lang. It doesn't make sense.'

'Christ,' Stern said bitterly.

'C'mon, Stern,' Rose said, touching Stern's elbow.

Stern jerked it away.

'It's just not right. Lang gets away with murder.'

'I didn't say he was getting away with anything. We're holding him for a while,' Gratelli said. 'We'll see what comes up.'

'Fingerprints, Gratelli,' Stern said. 'Fingerprints.'

Gratelli nodded. 'I know. But is he that stupid?'

'He's a lucky son of a bitch,' Stern said. 'This isn't the first dead woman he's been connected to.'

'I know. He's in that kind of business.'

Stern wasn't convinced.

'I need to work with you guys,' Gratelli said. 'Everybody's got their eyes on this one. We can all come out on top or we can blow it.'

He looked at Stern. Stern gave no sign he was going to pick up on team spirit.

Gratelli noticed Chastain West standing a few feet away. He was pretty sure the defense attorney was waiting for one of them.

'I need your help. I hope I can count on it,' Gratelli said.

Stern and Rose went off with Stern still mumbling. Rose turned back, winked. West approached.

Gratelli nodded a hello.

'You here about Lang?' Gratelli said, aware that Lang was West's prime investigator.

'I am. He didn't do it.'

'That's all I needed to hear. Let me get my key to his cell and I'll go let him out right away. Anybody else you want me to let out?'

Chastain smiled.

'I think this is one of those two birds with one stone kinds of thing,' West said. 'Somebody wanted to silence the girl and wanted someone else to go down for it, maybe put him out of business.'

Gratelli nodded. 'That's how I have it figured.'

'I'm a little wary of your sarcasm.'

'No, I do have it figured that way. Lang's a little slippery. He bends the rules. I don't think he'd kill some girl. And he's too smart to leave his prints on the weapon and hide it in such an amateurish spot. Let's go talk to him. You have the time?'

Lang was surprised to see West and Gratelli together. Gratelli sat on what approximated to a bed. West stood, leaning against the bars.

'You guys look like the Governor said no,' Lang said.

Gratelli might have grinned or he might have had a cramp, Lang thought.

'What do you think happened?' Gratelli asked.

'I was invited over to Angel's place. She told me that she was with-drawing her alibi on Mickey . . . that is, being with him the night his father was killed.'

'Why you?'

'I don't know. I had been trying to find Mickey and couldn't. In the process I discovered that he was a regular with Angel. I stopped by to see her. Maybe she thought we hit it off. Maybe she knew from the start that I was due for a set-up and didn't know everything about what was planned for her.'

Gratelli nodded, but didn't speak. West was quiet as well.

'She's a sexy woman,' Lang said. 'Was.'

'What's the last thing you remember?' Gratelli asked.

'Climbing into bed.'

'You were doped,' Gratelli said.

'A headache like that and no memory of what ought to be very memorable says you're making a lot of sense. I had one drink and part of another. I don't black out that easy.'

'Who?' Gratelli asked.

'The likely candidate is Mickey. He has a key.'

'If Warfield and Wiley were killed by the same guy, then it wasn't Mickey. Young Warfield was in a San Mateo jail. DUI – driving under the influence.'

Lang didn't hide his surprise. 'Well, all I know is he tried to frighten me off the case once before by hiring some dumb muscle to scare me.'

'And you didn't scare?'

'No. Maybe it was just that he didn't like me messing around in his business. Then again, I've been teasing the snakes.'

'These snakes have names?'

'All speculation.'

'Speculate,' Gratelli said.

'I picked up a tail after talking with Ralph Chiu. Seems as if there's some top-secret hotel being planned for North Beach.'

'The *Fog City Voice* opened that up already,' Gratelli said.

'But maybe not all the players. Maybe not the whole plan. I mean, I don't really know.'

'Then there's the list,' Gratelli said.

'Yeah. Sumaoang, Hawkes, Malone, Marlene Berensen. Something fishy with Berensen and young Warfield.'

'You heard of a William Blake?' Gratelli asked.

'The name's floated by now and then,' Lang said, hoping that he could dodge any extended conversation about Carly's client. 'I never met him.'

'We're going to let you out, Lang,' Gratelli said. 'You think you can keep away from crime scenes and public spectacles?'

'I'll try. What's with Stern?'

'If you give him a reason, he'll shoot you. What did you do to that man, anyway?'

'I seem like a lucky guy to him. He doesn't like lucky guys.'

Again the expression. Maybe that was Gratelli's smile.

'Let's go talk to the DA,' Gratelli said to West. 'Get Mr Lucky out on the streets again where he'll no doubt get into trouble.'

'One more question,' Lang said.

'You're not in a hurry to get out of here?' Gratelli asked.

'What's the real reason you're letting me go?'

Gratelli didn't answer right away. Maybe he wanted to get the words right, Lang thought. Maybe he had to come up with something believable.

'I believe you. You wouldn't be that stupid. And, keeping you here is counter-productive. I want the killer to know that we're not buying it – that he . . . or she . . . is in trouble. Not only are we still looking, but so are you.'

'You're poking at the snakes too.'

'Lang, listen.' He leaned forward. His face was hard as stone. 'We were working together, you and I?'

Lang nodded.

'Now you're working for me. You're not a free agent. Legally, because this is a murder case and you are a PI, you shouldn't have been involved anyway. There's more. You are still a suspect. Even if you weren't a suspect, you're a material witness. So we proceed carefully, under my direction. You have less than nothing. I want to see your partner right away.'

'Same little heart-to-heart.'

'Yeah. You don't have a problem with that, do you?'

'No,' Lang said.

'If you screw with me, you're back in here in a heartbeat.' It was a matter-of-fact statement. No huffing and puffing. No macho attitude. That's when Lang understood. Gratelli was a helluva lot tougher than Rose or Stern. And the old inspector was right . . . for the most part.

West hung back.

'You didn't say much,' Lang said.

'It's my famous silent strategy.'

'You'll have to fill me in on how that works.'

West laughed.

'We liked what he was saying, didn't we?' West said. 'Why interrupt him?'

'We're not home free,' Lang said.

'But you're going home.'


Thanh agreed to meet her, but asked if they could get together at Quetzal, a coffee house on lower Polk. He was working on his bike – a vintage motorcycle of undetermined brand identity – and pieces of the machine were scattered about.

He had to live somewhere in that area, Carly surmised. It didn't matter. Quetzal was fine with her.

As usual, she didn't know who or what to expect. What she got was a handsome fellow in battered jeans and a grease-stained sweatshirt. It amazed her that this sometimes delicate flower could take engines apart and do whatever needed to be done. Thanh, she concluded, would be much handier on a deserted island than anyone at her former employer's firm and better equipped to deal with reality than either William Blake or Noah Lang.

Thanh smiled when he saw her, his hair disarranged and a cheek smudged with black. He explained that Lang had asked him to do a couple of things. But not much had been done yet.

'I couldn't get a line on Mickey Warfield,' Thanh said, sitting down. 'I called around. Called Marlene, pretended to be a friend. Called again, pretended to be a bartender with a message. Nothing. No bite. As far as I know, he could be in Sweden.'

'Why Sweden?'

'First country to come to mind. I like Swedes. Not when they talk, but when they look at me.'

She smiled.

'I wanted to go out there, but my bike wouldn't start. I'm fixing it now, which is why I look so butch. Anyway, Ralph Chiu is a member of a business association, a Tong. That's not uncommon and it doesn't mean anything really. Not all of them are criminal. No one's real sure how much of that kind of crime still exists in Chinatown. And as a Vietnamese, I have no special access. We're not generally loved by the Chinese.'

Carly's cell played out its tune. She checked it. It was Lang. She pushed the screen and said hello. He said hello.

'You're out?'

'Yep. Free as a bird,' Lang said.

'That was quick. Is it over?'

'Dunno. But you are supposed to go see Gratelli.'

'Why?'

'He wants to read you the riot act.'

'Why?'

'Just to scare you. Mostly because you're hanging out with me, so he wants to make sure you're not contaminated with the wild ass virus.'

'The wild ass virus?'

'I have a mind of my own and he thinks that might have rubbed off on you.'

'I'm insulted. I have my own wild ass virus.'

'Go see him. We have to keep him happy or my wild ass will land back in jail.'

'When?'

'Now.'

# Twenty-Four

Gratelli didn't scare her. He could have been one of her father's skinny brothers. But she knew the man had spent decades in homicide. He wasn't a sweet, harmless old man. A smart person wouldn't try to play him.

'You have to clip his wings,' Gratelli said. 'At least for a while. I appreciate your help. But since last we talked seriously there are two more bodies. You are connected with one and he is unfortunately very intimately connected with the other. We're no longer operating subtly below the radar – anybody's radar.

'We understand.'

He gave her a long look, measuring, it seemed, her sincerity.

'We understand. We do,' she said, trying to stop short of overdoing it.

'Paladino,' he said. 'Your family from here?'

'Yes. Restaurant in North Beach.'

Gratelli nodded. 'Paladino's?'

'That's the one.'

'I'm quick. Used to eat there, when my wife was alive and when my kids were young and at home.'

'I probably brought you glasses of water.'

'Family style. That whole thing is pretty much gone now.' He shook his head. 'Times change. I don't know why it continues to surprise me. What do you have on this thing?'

'We're down to Mickey Warfield, Sumaoang, Marlene Berensen, Malone and Hawkes. Oh and Ralph Chiu.'

'We're trying to find Mickey to talk to him about his girlfriend's death. He's not an easy man to find.'

'We know,' Carly said. That would be Lang's top priority, Carly thought.

'Don't let Lang rough him up too much. OK?'

He was reading her mind.

'He's top of the list, don't you think?'

'He is a person of interest. What's the angle on Chiu? Anything?'

'Don't know,' Carly said. 'A little research. He is influential in a Tong. Maybe Whitney Warfield was going to reveal a little secret, maybe who killed Allen Leung.'

'Don't get ahead of yourself,' Gratelli said. 'First, many of the Tongs are legitimate business associations. Second, aside from Leung's murder in '06, there's not a lot of violence there anymore. Crime has moved from women, drugs and guns. It's white-collar now. Identity theft, credit card fraud . . . things like that. And with the change, a lot less blood-letting.'

'Leung's murder is still unsolved, I'm told,' Carly said, pressing it.

'I don't think either one of us knows enough about that,' Gratelli said. 'Correct me if I'm wrong, there are those who believe he was killed in order for someone else to move up the ladder or maybe revenge for some real or imagined slight. A number of people, important people, believe that Leung was killed at the request of the Chinese Communist Party. Leung was a staunch believer in democracy. He put his money and his energy where his mouth was, as I understand it. He didn't want the Chinese mainland to have any influence here and was a mighty thorn in the CCP's side. That's a story anyway. One of the many. But who knows? We don't.'

Gratelli looked at her and continued. 'All I'm saying is don't get caught up in the stereotypes.'

'At the moment all we can do is list the names and speculate on possible connections so we can run them down. Just like you do. We don't know that much about Chiu except that he's also involved in the hotel project in North Beach and that Lang picked up a tail after his meeting with Chiu. Asian guys in the front seat. Angel was Chinese.'

'So's a third of the city's population,' Gratelli said.

'Again, we're just seeing what matches and what doesn't. Seems suspicious.'

'It does.'

'A white Toyota Cressida. Old.'

Gratelli stood. 'Can you guys be a little less visible in your work?'

'We will.'

'You hear anything about a William Blake?'

Carly couldn't tell if there was something other than kindness in Gratelli's eyes. Did he know something?

'A poet,' Carly said.

'Not that William Blake,' Gratelli said.

'I'm sure I heard the name somewhere. Wasn't he with Warfield the night he died?' She answered a question with a question.

Gratelli didn't answer. His face was stone.

Lang understood Gratelli's concerns. If the circumstances were better for the police department, the pragmatic investigator would force Paladino and Lang to back off completely. But the timing couldn't be worse. Murder rates continued to bounce at all-time highs and the future was unclear, not to mention the additional bodies popping up. Gratelli, pragmatic and professional but short on staff and under pressure from superiors, needed the help.

Lang's money was still on Mickey Warfield's involvement though the guy's alibi for the night of Wiley's death was ironclad. Mickey hung around questionable women and down-and-out private eyes – Lang mentally acknowledged he was the pot picking on the kettle. Mickey was likely to be having an affair with his father's mistress. Some sort of strange Oedipal notion that Lang didn't want to understand, except that he bore no similarity to Mickey on that one.

Lang stopped off at his place, showered off the jailhouse stink and climbed up to his loft bed for a nap, or at least a restful way to contemplate next steps. Though Paladino was still the lead in this case and he would respect it, he now felt like he owned some of it. Being framed for murder tended to do that. The blow to Paladino's head had already made it personal for him. Sleeping with a corpse made it even more personal.

And back to Mickey, it was obvious. Mickey knew the girl, contributed to the rent, had a key to her place, and might very well have had motive to get her out of the picture. Maybe it was macho revenge for Lang sleeping with her. Maybe he had an inkling she was going to turn on him in the witness box. That was a twofer.

Buddha appeared at the edge of the loft. Lang had put down food, changed the water and freshened the litter box before climbing up. In the small space, Lang talked with him for a few minutes. The dark brown cat blinked his golden eyes and went to sleep, face looking out over the room. It wouldn't take much to awaken the sleeping sentry.

Things were in motion, Lang thought. He had instructed Thanh to find and stay close to Mickey. Paladino said she had some follow-up to do, but was vague about it. What was Lang's next step? Sleep, apparently. When he awoke, it was dark.

It was Thanh's call that woke him. Bike repaired, Thanh had looked around. No sign of Mickey. Marlene's garage housed an old, Navy blue Volvo. No Jaguar. Nor was the sleek sports car parked anywhere near Elena Warfield's place. Thanh also cruised North Beach. Nothing.

Getting around on a motorcycle was easier than scouting from behind the wheel of a car. Lang suggested Thanh scan the neighborhoods surrounding the strip clubs beyond North Beach. There were a few on Market and over on Jones. Look in the areas where there are massage parlors. Long shots, all of them, but it wouldn't surprise Lang if these kinds of places were the man's regular stomping grounds. And if nothing else, he lost Angel. Obviously, he needed something more than the attractive, but mature Marlene Berensen to keep him happy.

As long as he was conjecturing, he could build a case that Mickey Warfield, whose vocation was unknown at the moment, worked with the Chinese underground. That would explain his connection to Angel and her ambiguous feelings for him.

Lang shook his head. Get something solid, he told himself.

And that went for food. Lang was hungry. He climbed down from the loft, slipped on a robe and after a visit to the bathroom, headed toward the kitchen. Not a lot there. He'd have to improvise.

He had a can of crabmeat, a couple of slices of stale bread and some old pretzels. OK, he thought, checking the refrigerator. A couple of eggs. Some mustard. Half an onion. A bit of ginger. He had what he needed. Crab cakes and a little pasta. Something green? He had some basil outside. That would have to do.

He looked at his watch. A few minutes before midnight.

                              *     *     *

Carly had gone home early. By six, she had talked to the *Fog City Voice* publisher about gangs in Chinatown. He gave pretty much the same response as Gratelli. She asked about Chiu. He knew nothing, but was interested in knowing something. She begged him to wait. She was sure of nothing at the moment. Too many pieces of the puzzle and very few of them in place.

She threw some cocktail shrimp into a bowl with some fresh spinach, created a quick dressing with olive oil, vinegar and garlic and sat in front of the Lehrer News Hour on PBS. A glass of water to drink. No wine tonight. She was still worried about her concussion and wasn't sure what alcohol would do to her brain. She was proud of her restraint, but disappointed in the progress she made on the case. She also felt a slight and foreign hollowness being alone. She blamed William. She recanted. Blamed herself. Reconsidered. Forget the guilt. It didn't matter who was to blame, she had to be more cautious with William Blake – for many reasons, the least of which was that he was not a keeper. He would admit to that without apology. And so?

Carly was not at all tired. In fact she had an abundance of energy and nothing to do with it. It wasn't until just past midnight that she climbed in bed after hours of reading. Her body, she thought, had not re-keyed itself to the unregimented routine of her new career. What sleep finally came did so after two in the morning, and even then it was spasmodic. Surrealistic dreams were scattered here and there between bouts of unwelcomed consciousness.

During her waking hours, Mickey Warfield occupied her thoughts for the most part. He was still in hiding. And that fact, in itself, was an indictment – unless of course he fell victim as well. No one else on the list carried as much freight. She wanted to talk to Lang, but she'd wait until morning. They needed to move on Mickey Warfield. They needed to push the police and conduct their own search for the bad father's bad son.

Thanh met Lang at the coffee shop at Central and Hayes. They sat outside in the cool, clean morning air.

'You owe me tip money,' Thanh said. He smiled slyly.

'Because?' Lang played along. He sipped his coffee, nibbled at a blueberry muffin. He hadn't slept after waking up at midnight. Looked as if Thanh was a little sleep-deprived as well.

'Girls, girls, girls,' he said, smiling. 'At the clubs. Tried to get information on Mickey Warfield. I couldn't find his Jag anywhere near the massage parlors or strip clubs. I stopped in at a couple of the independent clubs. One of the girls said she recognized his photo but not sure if he had been a customer or had stopped in to talk with management. I'm not charging you for the massage. It was nice.'

'You learn anything?'

'I know most of that already.'

'No, about Mickey Warfield.'

'Oh. No. But that doesn't mean anything. There are a hundred parlors here, it seems. Who knows how many parlors there are in the Bay Area.'

Lang nodded. Thanh was right. While San Francisco was a big little town, the Bay Area was huge – more than four million people. Counting all of the El and La and San Somethings, there was room for a lot of individually owned as well as organized massage parlor enterprises. Some of these towns, contrary to tourist brochures, are not cute little wholesome wine and cheese communities. Some of them, like Vallejo, Oakland and Richmond, while having their good side, are tough enough.

'You need to get some sleep?' Lang asked.

'I'm fine. Anything else you want me to do?'

'Check Marlene Berensen's place from time to time. Let me know if the car shows up. The man has to sleep some place.'

As he spoke, it occurred to him that Mickey probably had another girl. A guy like Mickey, a guy who strings along an older woman and then stashes a sexier version in an apartment he pays for might have another stashed somewhere else. But finding the girlfriend of a guy he can't find doesn't make things any easier.

He looked at Thanh, shrugged. A guy walked by with two dogs, one half limping, half hopping on three legs. Lang must have had a sad look on his face because Thanh sought to cheer him up.

'Look at it this way,' Thanh said, 'he's got one more than you do.'

The dog seemed happy enough.

As Gratelli set his coffee cup down on his desk in his office, he noticed a file had been placed against the phone so he couldn't miss it. On the file was a Post-it. 'You can thank me later,' it said. It was signed 'Ted'. Ted was a cop who worked out of the Taraval Station, which handled the far west of the city – out to the Pacific Ocean.

Inside the folder were several copies of photographs of a late-model Jaguar. The license plate indicated it was registered to Marlene Berensen. Police noticed it parked all night by itself in one of the lots at Ocean

Beach. Though technically the Beach was the responsibility of the National Park Service, the car nonetheless aroused suspicion. Gratelli had put out an alert on two people – William Blake and Mickey Warfield – both MIA. Lang had provided Gratelli with the fact that Mickey was driving Marlene's Jag and had also given him the license number. Gratelli had put that info out there as well. And now it came back.

Here was the car. Where was the driver?

Gratelli called Marlene Berensen and judging by her incoherence figured he had awakened her not just from a late night but also from an alcohol-soaked late night.

Did she know where her Jaguar was? No, she didn't. Why didn't she? It was stolen. Did she report it? She did. He'd check that. We have reason to believe that Mickey Warfield used the car regularly. She mumbled something Gratelli didn't understand, but after more prodding said that yes, he did, but he had returned it. And it was stolen. Where was Mickey now? She had no idea. He wasn't with her. She was by herself, she said, launching into a long complaint about men and the horrors of a woman growing old alone.

A sad drunk, he thought. His conversations with her earlier had suggested a different sort of person – someone who respected herself perhaps a little too much. She had a cold-hearted and unapologetic diva personality. If he could choose for her, he'd much prefer the self-confident narcissist to the whiny one.

Gratelli verified her statement that she called to report her car was stolen. It was true. The inspector leaned back in his chair, closed his eyes. It had been a difficult night. He had come to terms with his wife's death years ago. But there were times – and he wasn't always sure what triggered it – he'd suddenly miss her, deeply miss her. Sometimes he was able to distract himself. Last night nothing worked. This morning there seemed to be a residue of the mood, lighter in intensity, but a sad feeling of futility nonetheless.

Talking to a drunk this early in the morning did little to lift his spirits. Three murders, he thought, shaking his head. He called Lang and caught the PI as he walked back to where he lived.

'We found the Jaguar but not Mickey,' Gratelli said.

'Where?'

'Ocean Beach. I've got guys out there now looking around, looking for a body. The wind has swept any footprints away. The Feds let us take the car and we'll put a microscope on it.'

'What do you think?' Lang asked.

'Could be Mickey realized the car was identified and therefore too hot to be driving around in. Met someone, dumped the Jaguar at the Beach. Easy to go north or south from there. Since he has a DUI in San Mateo, maybe there's a connection down there. I'll make some calls, but I don't expect anything.'

'I appreciate your letting me know,' Lang said.

'I want to work together. We just need to keep it as invisible as possible.'

'You talk with Marlene?'

'Drunk as a skunk. Didn't know where Mickey was. Reported the car stolen. Who knows?'

'A perfect time to pay her a visit,' Lang said. 'I'm not sure whether to bring her coffee or a gin and tonic.'

# Twenty-Five

At Carly's invitation, her friend Nadia dropped by. Carly wanted to show her arts-oriented friend the photographs Thanh sent to her computer. They sat with coffee and toast on the sofa, the laptop on the cocktail table and Nadia clicking through the images.

'Goodness,' Nadia said. 'I think we should have looked at these after breakfast.' She was kidding. She found them fascinating. 'Wiley did these?'

'They were in his studio. He was preparing an exhibition, had them framed. He had proof sheets of these people and releases.'

'So what's your problem?'

'I think one is missing.'

'And you think . . . ?'

'I do. The intruder wanted something from Wiley's place and didn't want anyone to see who he was. I think the subject of the missing photograph is the person who whacked me. I think he . . . or she . . . was smart enough to not only take the photograph but all the negatives, proof sheets, and personal releases.'

'Someone who knows the business then,' Nadia said.

'Another artist or writer . . .'

'Or agent, publicist, gallery owner, publisher.'

'The list goes on,' Carly said.

Nadia nodded her agreement. 'So how does the list of the subjects match up with the list of murder suspects?' A bite of toast, a sip of coffee, she scooted forward to watch the slideshow.

'Let's see,' Carly said, clicking again through the photographs as they appeared on the screen. Of the fifteen, there were the truly famous naked and now dead subjects who wouldn't likely object. There were a couple of nudes Carly didn't recognize, but Nadia did. They were poets of the Beat and Hippie era and of North Beach. Of those on the suspect list were Nathan Malone at maybe thirty, collegiate, handsome and athletic; Agnes DeWitt looking very much like an educated lady though like the others very much naked; Richard Sumaoang, fierce and sexy: Bart Brozynski, bearish and not the least intimidated; Lili D. Young, sensuous, though slightly frightened and half her current weight; and Whitney Warfield himself, not especially photogenic, but seemingly proud of what he was able to show the world.

With the exception of Marshall Hawkes, those on the list who were missing were not surprising. Wife and son were not among the nudes, but weren't even minor celebrities. Ralph Chiu and Samuel McFarland were not artists or poets. To Wiley they would have been uninteresting subjects. Hawkes's omission presented a small concern. But did it really surprise Carly? From what she'd heard about him from Lang and Nadia, the painter was uptight, controlling. He was someone who would never have let his guard down, would never have consented to something so intimate and so revealing as a nude photograph.

'Well, what have we done?' Nadia asked, falling back on the sofa, taking a deep breath. Do we have more now than we did ten minutes ago?'

Carly admitted they didn't.

'I'd like to do the exhibition,' Nadia said.

'What?' Carly said. The word was accompanied by a look of near incomprehension.

'What an incredible draw,' Nadia said. 'Murderer's Row.'

'Isn't that a little lurid?'

'Oh, yes,' Nadia said, sitting forward again, excited. 'Exactly. Those photographs would go for ten times, maybe more, what they would have fetched. Poor Mr Wiley. We need to find out about your Mr Wiley's estate.'

It was a flicker, a quick hop and a skip across Carly's mind. But did someone want to improve the value of Wiley's work? It seemed the longest of long shots. There were others involved. And whoever carried all this out was taking a gigantic risk. To somehow collect at the end would put that person right at the top of the suspect list.

'I'm serious,' Nadia said.

'I don't doubt it.'

'The greatest San Francisco photography exhibition ever. I mean it's lurid, yes. And naked . . . that adds a lot. Involved in murders. Maybe the murderer is right here,' she said, tapping the computer screen. That's what you think, right? We could tour the show.'

'Calm down, calm down,' Carly said. 'And slow down.'

Carly saw the greed, understood that's how it always worked. Nadia was quick to pick up on the opportunity. Had Wiley made the same decision? Was Wiley documenting history or was he making a buck on the foolish decisions of these folks in their trusting youth? Carly thought how we all feed on others – herself included, she supposed – and how people are still feeding and feeding on the legend that was North Beach.

Lang found a very different Marlene Berensen than he had seen before. Gone was the haughty, threatening and elegant creature. Instead, the woman at the door was frazzled, dowdy and disoriented. Hair mussed, she wore a misshapen, gauzy gown much too apparent beneath a wrinkled robe.

She saw him, recognized him through a blinking, unfocused stare and moved out of the way in a clumsy attempt at a sweeping welcome. He entered, passing by her brewery breath.

'Would you like a drink?' she asked, shutting the door behind her. There were cigarettes and cigarette butts on the coffee table. 'Or . . .' she continued, 'more appropriately, a cup of coffee?'

'I'm fine, thanks.'

She smiled an odd smile. 'He's gone,' she said.

'Who is gone, Marlene?'

'Oh, "Marlene", is it?' She sat down with less grace than she expected and seemed to surprise herself.

'Who's gone?'

'Everybody,' she said, shaking her head.

'Mickey,' Lang said a little louder than usual and looking directly into Marlene's unfocused eyes. 'You know Mickey, right?'

'Right.' She looked confused. 'He's gone.'

'Where did he go?' Lang asked.

'Whitney's gone,' she said. 'Everybody's gone.'

He and Marlene might be sharing the same room, Lang thought, but they were in slightly different realities. Hers was, no doubt, slower, thicker.

There were those who thought that the words of a drunk were

unreliable. Others thought the uninhibited mind spoke the truth. Lang fell in the middle. The only real truth, he thought, was that they were likely to say things they wouldn't say if they were sober – true or not.

'May I use your bathroom?' Lang said, standing up.

'Be my guest,' she said, getting up and staggering toward a bottle of gin on the table by the door, probably where she set it when she went to answer his knock.

'Nice place,' Lang said, yelling back over his shoulder.

'Used to be,' she said.

For Lang the place exuded a faded elegance that made its formal beauty less cold, more hospitable. He glanced in the bedrooms. One room was spotless. The other was tossed by careless living. The bedclothes were barely on the bed. Clothing was scattered. The ashtray by the bed was full of ashes and butts. There was an empty cigarette package crumpled on the floor.

It was a red package. He examined it. Non-menthol. If he was correct Marlene smoked menthol. Even if someone wasn't particular about what brand they smoked, only few jumped from menthol to non-menthol or the other way around. Someone else had stayed there. How recently, he didn't know. There were no men's clothes in the closet, however, and no other clues that he could see in his quick inventory.

He could hear her coming and stepped quickly into the hall and pretended to admire a print hanging there.

'Sorry, got sidetracked,' he said when she came upon him.

He went into the bathroom and shut the door. He checked the shelves behind the mirror. There was a Darvon generic, a tube of K-Y and . . . a bottle of Viagra prescribed to Mickey Warfield. Lang couldn't repress a smile. Not because he looked down on those using a little helper, and not just because it belonged to the macho Mickey, but because it proved Mickey was here and what he was probably doing here from time to time. Other tubes and bottles might be embarrassing but shed little light on Marlene, other than that she was human with nagging little physical annoyances.

Lang looked around the bathroom, saw nothing else that was of interest. He flushed the toilet, washed his hands and emerged into the hallway and then into what dim light the closed blinds allowed into the living room. He found her on the sofa. She was out cold. He hoped she was just unconscious. He checked her pulse. These days, it seemed, it was important to check. She was alive, though her behavior suggested she might not want to be.

No more questions for now, he thought, but he checked what appeared to be a combination den, office, library, media room. It was comfortable, but had none of the design coherence of the rest of the house. This is where she could kick back. Then again, it looked a little masculine in its disdain for style.

The kitchen yielded nothing. The garage wasn't very telling either. Her blue Volvo was parked there. He looked inside. Nothing. He checked the exterior. He was no CSI, but he was pretty sure there was sand in the grooves of the tires. Not all that conclusive because much of the city was built on dunes and it was a very sandy place.

Her timely unconsciousness allowed him to check all the drawers and closets. No sign of Mickey or any other male. He left, locking the door from the inside. He felt sad about Marlene not being the tough, smart person he thought her to be. She had to put on a costume and manufacture an attitude. Nothing was what it appeared to be. This was not a sudden loss of innocence on his part. Early on in his professional life he had received a forced indoctrination about books and covers and how that applied to the human species. And certainly Thanh, the shape-shifting creature that he was, proved it nearly every day.

All in all, stopping by was a good investment of his time. In addition to the fact that Mickey Warfield was driving a car registered to her, the bottle of sexual performance pills in Marlene's medicine cabinet with Mickey's name on them pretty much sealed the case, perhaps not for a court of law, but for him. He wondered if that made Marlene Mickey's stepmistress. As far as Lang was concerned, Warfield the Younger was the prime suspect. It was often difficult, Lang thought, for the sons of celebrities to find their own light.

But what was the specific catalyst to the killing? Why now? Did he just find out he wasn't in Daddy's will? Was there a fight over Marlene? Hard to believe, now that Lang saw the sadly vulnerable personality and what she looked like before she went on the public stage.

He knew that Carly was keen on the murderer being connected to a missing photograph. There was a certain logic to her thinking. But there were other explanations. Time had passed between the evening she saw the photographs and the night of Wiley's murder. Maybe one photograph hadn't been framed properly or Wiley changed his mind about including it, and it was possible Carly didn't get the count right the first time.

'Lunch?' Lang asked when Carly came into the office.

'Is that all you ever think about?'

'More and more,' Lang said. 'It seems safer than some other human indulgences.'

She smiled. After a night sleeping with the client, she couldn't really fault him for sleeping with a witness. She'd like to. And he wasn't aware of her indiscretion, if one could call it that. But she liked to play fair.

'We need to talk,' Lang continued.

'And what is this thing that we're doing now?'

'C'mon, Carly.'

'Can we go back to Osteria?'

'The place with the handsome Italian waiter?'

'That would be the one,' she said. 'And the delicious food.'

'And, incidentally, the delicious food.' Lang smiled.

'What are we going to talk about?'

'Love.'

'I'm not going,' she said.

'Death,' he said.

'That's better.'

The restaurant Lang used as a bribe had a line of folks waiting for a table.

'That's the problem with good food and handsome waiters,' Lang said to Carly as they stood on the sidewalk outside. He scanned the street. There was no shortage of good restaurants in North Beach.

'How about a slice of pizza and a glass of wine?' Carly asked.

'That's always good.'

Golden Boy Pizza was a small place on Green between Columbus and Grant. Inside the customers either sat at the counter facing the kitchen or they sat at a counter facing a wall. Two of the walls and the ceiling were corrugated steel, providing a kind of Quonset hut environment. The pie was thick and good, the wine good and inexpensive.

'When I was young, I used to come here at night after drinking maybe a little more than I should,' Carly said, getting comfortable on her stool.

Service was quick. Pizza came from a large tray in the front and wine was poured.

'So what are we talking about?' Carly asked.

'All right,' Lang said, gathering his thoughts. 'As I understand it, you're thinking that the murderer is someone who was determined to remove a photograph. If we find the photograph, we find the killer.' She nodded. 'I'm pretty convinced that Mickey Warfield did it, but we know the night Wiley was killed, Mickey was incarcerated in San Mateo.'

'You're not making a great case for yourself, Noah.'

'I'm not, I know.' He took a sip of wine. 'This morning I stopped in for a surprise visit at the lovely Marina home of Marlene Berensen. This was after I learned that her Jaguar, the one Mickey was driving, was found driverless in the parking lot at Ocean Beach. Marlene was drunk on her feet and crying that Mickey was gone.'

'And your point is?'

Lang waited until he finished his bite of pizza and took a sip of wine.

'Mickey has to be involved. And this leads me to the possibility that maybe, just maybe, it isn't one person trying to hide one secret. Maybe the secret is bigger or there is more than one.'

Carly nodded. 'It's possible, I'm sure. It does seem like Mickey Warfield is involved but someone killed Frank Wiley and I am sure there is a photograph missing.'

It was Lang's turn to agree.

'So where are we?' Lang asked.

'In the dark, I think.'

'It's always darkest before the dawn.'

'You're just full of quotes.'

'And trite expressions,' Lang said.

'You spend the weekend reading Bartlett's?'

'How's William?' Lang smiled, knowing he had just stopped the attack. Damn, she thought, as she felt herself blush.

'What makes you think I know how he is?'

'I wasn't sure, but now I know. You have what gamblers call a "tell".'

'What kind of tell?'

'I can't tell you. If I told you what your tell was it would no longer be a tell.'

'So?'

'I like you having one.'

'Well, maybe you have it wrong.' She gave him a Cheshire Cat smile. Behind the smile she was cursing herself. She didn't want him going anywhere near the truth. If he did, then she lost whatever leverage she had knowing he had slept with the recently dead Angel.

'We are getting paid for this, aren't we?' Lang asked as they walked to the car.

'We are,' she said.

'In money?'

She gave him the look. It was more threatening than Inspector Stern's threatening look. Perhaps, just perhaps, he told himself, he'd gone too far.

# Twenty-Six

Lang climbed out of Carly's Mini Cooper on lower Polk Street. She wished him well as she pulled away. Lang went up the narrow stairway and toward Scotty Markham's office.

Markham sat at his desk amidst the clutter of Chinese takeout cartons and newspapers. It was as if Lang never left. Markham looked up, said nothing.

'I seem to have lost Mickey Warfield,' Lang said.

'You lost him, you find him.' Markham didn't bother putting down the newspaper.

'You know about Angel?' Lang asked.

'The Chinese chick, right?'

'Yeah.'

'Yeah.'

'You know, your hands aren't real clean where Angel was concerned. We know you went there after visiting our little office.'

'Hey,' he said dryly, 'I wasn't with her when she croaked.'

'Mickey tell you that?'

'Mickey schmickey. What do you want from me?'

'Some help maybe. You know where or how I might find him?'

'Why should I help you?'

'Professional courtesy,' Lang said, knowing how Markham would take it. 'Listen, Scotty, wasn't I a nice guy when you and your pal showed up threatening me and my friends? Did I punch you out? Did I call the police?'

'I'm not going to play with you, Lang. I don't like you. I don't care what happens to you. I have no investment in you whatsoever. So, go away.'

'How's your license?'

'What do you mean?'

'I'm working with Inspector Gratelli on this. They want Mickey too. You know, I tell him about your working relationship with him and how you stopped by to see Angel and, well, you find yourself . . . Oh, well. I hadn't really thought about it. But you're hired muscle. Maybe you killed Angel.'

'Nah, Lang. If I did I'd have done you for free while I was at it.'

'You might wish you did,' Lang said, smiling.

'Lang!' Markham called as Lang exited into the hallway.

'What is it?' Lang asked, peeking back in.

'Mickey hangs out with an old broad, Marlene Berensen.'

'I know.'

'So I gave you something.'

'The way this game is played is that you give me something I don't already have. So don't tell me he drives her Jag and stays at her place sometimes. Don't tell me that the car was abandoned at Ocean Beach and Mickey left Marlene in a drunken funk. Don't tell me he's involved in massage parlors. Don't tell me he's not in his dad's will. These are things I have. So what do you have?'

Lang didn't mind revealing what he knew.

'He's not in his dad's will?' Markham asked.

'No.' Lang smiled. 'He stiffed you. Wow.'

Markham looked away, maybe so Lang wouldn't see the anger he couldn't conceal.

'How much?'

'None of your business,' Markham said, trying to put a look of terminal disinterest on his face.

'Who else does he owe?' Lang asked.

'I'm not his accountant.'

'You have any clients in common?'

Markham didn't answer. Lang wasn't going to get anything more.

'Such a sensitive guy. Anyway, thanks for the present, Scotty. You came through.'

Markham did come through, unwillingly and unwittingly. Maybe Lang could have put the pieces together himself – staying on with an older woman in order to have a place to stay and a car to drive – young Warfield was having serious money trouble.

Outside, Lang called Thanh's cellphone. No answer. He called the office. Carly was back already. Lang asked for Thanh.

'Not here,' Carly said.

'What about Brinkman?'

'Brinkman's here.'

'Let me talk with him.'

Brinkman pulled up in his '86 Buick, a cigar between his lips, a sarcastic smile on his face. He double-parked on Polk, just outside the entrance to Markham's building.

Lang got into the car and asked Brinkman to pull up a little.

'I need you to tail a guy.'

'So far so good,' Brinkman said.

'Name is Scotty Markham . . .'

'The guy who came in to roust you?'

'The same. The one you scared to death.'

'Be right back,' Brinkman said.

Brinkman clicked on the car's caution blinkers, got out, went to his trunk and came back with a baseball cap to cover his flat-topped head and a pair of non-prescription, horn-rimmed eyeglasses.

'Great disguise,' Lang said. 'You're like a completely different guy with that hat.'

'Don't get smart,' Brinkman said. 'No one pays attention to old codgers like me. Believe me, a hat and a pair of nerdy glasses are enough. Where do you think he's gonna go?'

'I have no idea.'

'Maybe he'll just go home,' Brinkman said.

'Maybe he will.'

'What if he drives to Chicago?' Brinkman asked.

'You have something better to do?'

'You have a point,' Brinkman said, glancing up in his rear-view mirror. 'He's coming out. Coming this way.'

'Crap,' Lang said. He slipped down on the floor, cursing fate for sending Markham this way and thanking fate for Brinkman having a big, old, roomy Buick. 'Tell me when he's gone by.'

After a few moments of silence and Lang sucking in the cigar smoke air Brinkman gave him the all-clear.

'Call me if he comes back to his office in the next thirty minutes. Right now, he's going to the parking garage at the end of the block. Only one exit. Bye,' Lang said, getting out of the car. He patted the Buick on the trunk as it accelerated up Polk Street.

Lang went back, up the stairs and into the hall toward Markham's office. Markham had locked the door, but it wouldn't take much for Lang to get in. Somehow, it didn't seem like a bad thing to break into Scotty Markham's place. More like poetic justice. He looked around. He saw no one. Heard nothing. It was quiet on the second floor.

It took five minutes to get in. Longer than he thought, but not bad really. If Lang had to explain what he had learned that was of the most value in his profession, he would have to say patience.

Markham didn't take his laptop and it was left on. All the files were closed, but it wouldn't take much for Lang to look around and leave the screen as he found it. For a guy specializing in security, Markham paid little attention to it for himself. A little browsing, opening files, checking the Excel spreadsheet showed Lang the guy was barely making it. He checked the history. There were indications that Markham visited porn sites regularly. He had played more than 25,000 games of Solitaire online.

There were a few people searches, but no one he recognized. He clicked on to the Google Search and went through the alphabet one letter at a time, letting the little opening reveal where Markham had gone. Again, nothing that seemed to connect to Warfield or to anyone Lang recognized.

Boring work. He pressed the voicemail. Markham hadn't cleaned that up either, so there were thirty-three messages, the voice said. Lang played them back. There were many hang-ups. There was a guy wanting his money. There was Mickey Warfield's voice asking Markham to call him back. That was the day before Markham and his skinny friend visited Lang. A couple of calls telling him this was Markham's last chance to sign up for a warranty on his car. Lots of crap.

There was only one call that meant anything and if Lang was the kind of guy to feel cold chills he would have felt them as he heard Angel's voice. 'I'm afraid, Scotty. You have to help me.'

'Jesus.'

Lang opened the voicemail case, noticed the tiny cassette. Thank the Great Whatever for Markham's dinosaur ways when it came to technology. Lang put the cassette in his pocket. He searched Markham's desk, found another, replaced the tape he'd taken.

Lang looked around, gave the filing cabinet a cursory search, found nothing. He checked the computer screen. OK. He wiped his prints off everything he touched and left, remembering that Markham may have had more brain cells and more skills than Lang originally thought. He'd have to be careful. The man was dangerous.

# Twenty-Seven

Brinkman was on the other end of the line, on the cellphone Lang had given him.

'Markham stopped at some real estate office on Geary,' Brinkman said.

'Where is he now?'

'Inside.'

'Where are you?'

'On the sidewalk, half a block away near some old folks' home or something. Some big old nurse tried to herd me on a bus to goddamn somewhere.'

'Might have been a fun trip,' Lang said.

'I don't like old people,' Brinkman replied bitterly.

'But you are an old people, Brinkman.'

'The irony is your problem. What do you want me to do when he comes out?'

'Continue to follow him until he goes home or back to his office.'

'Got it,' Brinkman said and disconnected.

Lang wouldn't have made that connection – Markham and Chiu. If Chiu was part of a criminal Tong, it was unlikely he would hire non-Asian muscle. But it was clear there were ties between Warfield and Chiu and Markham and Marlene Berensen and the dead woman. This new observation, coupled with the otherwise irrelevant fact that Chiu and the dead woman were both Chinese and connected somehow to Markham, expanded the speculation. But how would a missing photograph, if one were missing, play into this set of circumstances? He was pretty sure Carly was on the wrong track.

He shook his head. At some point investigations were supposed to narrow. The point was to eliminate suspects on the list – not add them. In the beginning, Lang would have to admit, the case was a kind of amusing adventure. It became more intense because of the attack on Carly and the cloud that hung over his own suspected self. Then, there was the mounting body count. Would there be another?

'You were right,' Gratelli told her on the phone. 'There was a missing photograph, but it's been returned. Probably sent out to be reframed. Sorry I doubted you.'

Carly hadn't realized just how much investment she'd made in the idea the murder could be solved by locating the photograph. Gratelli's comments, while confirming her original observation skills, didn't do much for her theory. It felt like a punch to the solar plexus.

'We found it at Wiley's studio, at the top of the steps, leaning against the door.'

'Who sent it?' she asked.

'No return address.'

'Who delivered it? What delivery service?'

'Apparently none. Probably just the framer. Brown paper wrapper, that was it?'

'And the photograph?' she asked. 'Who was the subject?'

'A naked figure. Nobody I know. We'll try to find out if you think it's important. Is it?'

'I don't know,' she said, sorry that she allowed her disappointment to slip into her voice. 'You mind if I come down and take a look?'

There was a long pause.

'No. Come on down. I'll be here for another hour.'

She had already called Blue Monkey Press, the company that had the contract to print the book, and planned to go to San Mateo to talk with them and look at what they had. The problem was they didn't have final images . . . just the text, but that was sent out for typesetting in New York. They expected the proofs back soon. They'd call.

Gratelli seemed a little embarrassed as he brought the photograph, recovered in the brown paper, into one of the interview rooms. He set it on the table, nodded, and stepped out. Carly thought it amusing that a man who had no doubt frequently seen far worse found this moment distasteful.

Carly unwrapped the frame. The photograph was a black-and-white of Marshall Hawkes, a young Marshall Hawkes, naked. He was photographed from behind, looking back over his shoulder. His face was clearly visible and it was clearly Hawkes. The lighting, background and texture of the photograph were in keeping with the others. But there was something – and she wasn't sure what that was – troubling about the image. She took out her cellphone and photographed it.

Gratelli glanced in through the glass partition and when he saw her rewrap the photograph, he came back inside.

'Marshall Hawkes,' Carly told him.

'You look disappointed,' Gratelli said.

'I am.'

'So what do all these photographs tell you?'

'They were all young and may have regrets now.'

'Motive?' Gratelli asked.

'One of his subjects might not want his or her photograph on exhibit or in a book. That's still a possible motive. But my theory that finding the missing photograph would identify the killer just lost credibility.'

Carly said it because it seemed obvious and to think otherwise would be foolish. She knew she was foolish. She didn't fully believe what she said.

Carly called Nadia to say that her theory of the missing photograph was kaput. But Nadia wasn't to be deterred. She wanted to do the show. She would talk to Wiley's kin or whomever. She would put on the show – 'Murderer's Row'.

'You said Wiley was unimportant, an archivist. So did the people at Reed Fine Arts. So what's the big deal?'

'The hook. The media won't be able to resist. You know,' she said, catching the greed that crept into her voice, 'this will give Wiley the stature he no doubt wanted and help the people he left behind.'

'You're a saint, Nadia. Anybody tell you that?'

'Only people who think sarcasm is cute . . . or want something.'

'How about coming with me tomorrow? You can break away for a short trip to San Mateo, can't you?'

'You bet. I need to talk with the publishers . . . set this whole thing in motion.'

When Lang learned from Carly that she planned a morning trip to San Mateo he asked her to stop by the local police station. He wanted to verify that Mickey Warfield spent the whole night in their custody the night of Wiley's death. Just as the appearance of the photograph was the kink in the chain of Carly's theory, so too was Warfield's DUI the obstacle in Lang's argument.

On the other hand, there was this seeming coincidence that the publisher of the 'lost' manuscript was located in San Mateo and that Warfield the Younger had made a recent trip there. There are lots of reasons to go to San Mateo, but there were a lot of other places to go to. Mickey's San Mateo trip was worth looking into.

'There's a great Chinese restaurant in San Mateo – Little Sichuan. Check it out for lunch. And there is the king of all gourmet super-markets across the street. Draeger's. Nothing like it in San Francisco.'

'Food, food, food. I gain five pounds just talking to you.'

'It's all I think about that I can speak of in polite company,' Lang said.

'I'm polite?' Carly seemed genuinely surprised at the adjective.

'If we stretch the definition a little.'

'Are you in the office?' she asked.

'I am.'

'Could you spray my orchid?'

'I'd be honored,' Lang said.

'What does that mean?'

'I have no idea. It was what popped into my head. I've never been asked to spray someone's orchid. I wasn't sure what you meant.'

'What do you mean, you didn't know what I meant?'

'Came out of left field. Suddenly. I thought maybe it was a euphemism.'

'For what?'

'I couldn't begin to guess.' He meant 'wouldn't', but it was better to say 'couldn't'.

'Goodbye,' she said.

Brinkman came in, muttering something before he hit Lang's office. All Lang heard was a sudden outburst.

'Oh, God, I hope that's jelly,' he said. He had taken off his jacket and was examining his forearm, touched it, and brought it to his lips. 'Thank God.' He noticed Lang looking at him. 'You get old, you don't know what in the hell is growing on you.'

'I understand,' Lang said.

'Splotches and moles and liver spots . . .'

'Yes. About Markham . . .'

'. . . rashes, strange hairs, little bits of . . .'

'Again, thanks for the preview,' Lang said loudly, interrupting. 'You have me looking forward to my golden years.'

'Markham left the real estate office and went to a bar on Geary,' Brinkman said. 'McKinney's. He was in there a couple of hours.'

'You go in?'

'Yeah, had a beer, watched him talk to the bartender. Markham wasn't just another customer. He had four glasses of Guinness and walked out like all he had was a bowl of noodle soup. Obviously old friends. Then he stopped at Burger King and went to Daly City. His house, I'm guessing, 'cause he had a key to the front door. You want any of this in writing?'

'Nope, thanks. Have you seen Thanh?'

'The little sprite blew through here shortly before you called. He was in a hurry.'

'I think I was followed,' Lang said, moving to the window and looking out. 'I decided to walk from Polk Street. I needed to think. And there was one Asian guy on foot and another in a car – a silver Honda – seemed to be circling the blocks.'

'How could you tell? Every other car on the road is a silver Honda.' Brinkman said.

True enough, Lang thought. Hell, he might have been tailed every moment of the day and night and only spotted them twice. If these were the same guys who were in the Toyota Cressida, they changed cars. Smart. Having tailed so many in the past, he was more sensitive than most to being tailed himself. He was impressed. The question was: did he pick up the tail after talking with Chiu or was that merely the first time he saw them?

On telepathic cue, it seemed, Thanh arrived. Lang went out to the reception area to greet him. He was very ordinarily dressed – gray cotton slacks, a pressed striped shirt and a tan corduroy jacket. Other than noticing his natural good looks, no one would give him a second glance. It was perfect. It seemed the shape shifter anticipated what was expected of him.

'You have time to tail the tail?' Lang asked.

'Sounds sexy.'

'Maybe not so sexy. Maybe interesting, requiring guile, craftiness and skill.'

'I guess that leaves only me,' Thanh said, smiling.

'You have your bike?'

'I do, all tuned up and humming.'

Lang called Brinkman in and explained.

Lang went out first, walked a few blocks and picked up a cup of coffee and came back to his beat-up Mercedes.

'You comfortable back there?' Lang asked.

'Is the bear Catholic?' Brinkman replied from his post scrunched down in the back seat.

'Glad you're happy.'

It was starting to get dark when Lang drove to Howard Street where, after paying the fee, he pulled in line for a car wash. As he moved up in line he noticed Thanh arriving and parking just across the street. When his Mercedes was just inside the drive-thru and out of view of those following him, Lang got out, took off his stocking cap and gave it to Brinkman who climbed behind the wheel. It was Brinkman who drove the car through and out on to the street when he was finished. If the plan worked, Brinkman would drive a few miles and get out, letting the tail see that it wasn't Lang. When the guys gave up, Thanh would tail them to see where they would go. It was a gamble, but not a bad one.

The result didn't give Lang exactly what he wanted, but was still more than helpful. As Lang sat on the sofa in his converted laundry space with Buddha in his lap, he got the call from Thanh.

'You were thinking these guys were Chinese, right?' Thanh said.

'I was.'

'Chances are they're not Chinese. I followed them to the suburbs in Daly City. The mailbox says 'Bantay'.

'And?'

'That's a Filipino name.'

Lang realized he'd fallen victim to his own narrow view. Not only was it likely he had a tail long before he realized, it was possible the tail began after he questioned Sumaoang the first time, which meant he'd been watched for a while. No way to be sure. Now, he had to be careful again not to stereotype. If they were Filipino, it didn't necessarily lead back to the tough-minded artist just because he was Filipino too. Nothing else led there particularly. And who was to say that Chiu, who might just be a legitimate but savvy businessman, or anyone else, couldn't have hired a couple of out-of-work Filipinos to do some work? Still, in his heart or mind – whatever it was that generated hunches – it seriously brought Sumaoang back into the picture.

'That's interesting,' Lang said after a pause.

'It is,' Thanh said. 'You were hoping this would lead right back to the suspect. It might have, but there are phones, you know?'

'I know.'

'What do you want me to do?'

'Go have fun somewhere. I'll have to figure this out.'

He didn't want to bang on Sumaoang's door again, but he'd take a chance that Alighieri's might be a regular evening destination for the passionate artist.

Later, he apologized to Buddha, encouraging the little brown cat off his lap, and prepared to go out.

# Twenty-Eight

Carly wanted the evening to be over. She was eager to visit Blue Monkey Press and see what they had, but that had to wait until business hours. Though her theory about the missing photograph wasn't even much of a theory anymore, she couldn't let it go. Maybe what the printer had would shed some light.

A glass of Pinot Grigio, a chicken breast sliced in two thin pieces, lightly coated in seasoned breadcrumbs and sautéed, a tomato, and a dozen slender spears of asparagus roasted for 12 minutes in the oven with a sprinkling of salt, pepper and flakes of pecorino, constituted dinner.

She was too antsy to read so she broke a personal rule. She sat in front of the TV to watch *Gosford Park* for the third time. As wonderful and as rich as the movie was, her mind went adrift several times. She slipped back to the night of her attack at Wiley's studio. The vision of it – the details – were getting clearer, but no more revealing. The person who attacked her moved quickly. The form, against the back light, was not as large as she first thought, but slender, and the cape she thought she saw might very well have been one of the wrapped photographs. Might well have been, she thought. Might well not.

The seemingly symbolic weapon in the case of Wiley's death was a camera – fitting enough for a photographer – just as the pen was fitting for Warfield. Just as, she thought, an ice pick, for the woman in bed? Some sort of sexist male statement, perhaps. This suggests a single killer. Someone who is in decent physical shape, savvy, and deadly playful.

She shut off the television mid movie, did her dishes, had a second glass of wine on the back deck, and then climbed in bed. Before switching off the light, she called Nadia to say she'd pick her up at eight. Despite Nadia's objections, they would get an early start on her short trip to San Mateo.

'I can go without you,' Carly told her, when Nadia's whining continued.

'OK, OK, OK.'

Carly put her head on the pillow. In the still darkness, she could hear her own breathing. She could hear the building settle. She could hear the light wind against the trees outside. And she picked up a familiar though no less exotic scent on the pillowslip. William Blake lingered. She slept.

Sumaoang was not happy to see Lang, but he did not seem surprised. The artist, in a booth with non-bourgeois-type guys flanking him, looked up as Lang entered Alighieri's back room unchallenged – the guardian of the inner sanctum being in the john or smoking out back. But Sumaoang challenged him, putting his palms up to indicate halt. He crossed and uncrossed them quickly – a sign that Lang was to proceed no further, that he was to go away. Sumaoang closed his eyes as if it was the only way to contain the anger bubbling up inside him. Perhaps he thought Lang would be gone when he opened them. Sumaoang was wrong.

'You knew I was coming,' Lang said, nodding toward the cellphone by Sumaoang's water bottle. Lang pulled a chair up to the table. 'Why the drama?'

Sumaoang, who had put his hands in his lap, or at least under the table, tried to stare Lang down. Lang didn't know why people, the male of the species in particular, thought that a mean stare would melt an opponent. On the other hand, if there was a gun under the table, that would be truly intimidating.

'I used to be a cop,' Lang said. 'The "look" doesn't work. If you didn't want to see me, you shouldn't have put a tail on me.'

Poker face. Expressionless. It finally broke into a smile and Sumaoang shrugged. He looked at each pal and they excused themselves. The look apparently worked on them, Lang thought.

'They were supposed to be pretty good,' the artist said.

'Who said?'

Sumaoang just smiled.

'You don't want me to find out who is killing all these people? Unless you're the killer, you ought to be worried.'

'I know. I also want the book. You blame me?'

'I don't know. How dark is your secret?'

Sumaoang didn't answer.

'The thing is, I know you are not rolling in money. Hiring twenty-four-hour security – two of them – can't be cheap,' Lang continued.

Nothing.

'Are you desperate?'

Sumaoang smiled.

'Or are you not paying for it?'

The artist looked down at the table for a moment, lightly twirled his iPhone, before looking up and pasting on a smile.

'Gotcha,' Lang said. He stood. 'Thanks.' Looking down the way Sumaoang did was a tell. His physical responses to questions, or lack of them, had been consistent until then. Sumaoang, if he was a player at all, wasn't acting alone.

'You're really attached to that phone. I didn't peg you as a high-tech guy.'

'You obviously have a special talent for being wrong.'

'We all have our gifts. By the way,' Lang said, looking around, 'what's so special about the back room?'

Sumaoang smiled. Didn't answer.

'What's so special about these folks?'

'It's not who we let in,' Sumaoang said, 'it's who we don't. Tourists. Bankers. Insurance salesmen. And sleazy private eyes.'

'Murderers?'

'Oh, very different,' the artist said. 'Depends on who they murder.'

Lang found the situation humorous. Warfield might never have his last hurrah, but he had certainly stirred up his old friends and enemies, leaving them in the terrible wake of his death. He wasn't going to be forgotten; he wasn't, as Dylan Thomas – one of the few poets Lang could recall – had advised, going 'gentle into that good night'.

For Noah Lang, going into that good night for a few hours of sleep seemed appropriate. Sleep was overtaking him even as Chet Baker's voice inhabited his mind. He was distantly aware that Buddha was at the edge of the loft as usual, looking down, making sure there was no movement below.

San Mateo is half an hour or forty-five minutes south of San Francisco depending on traffic and one's opinion on speed limits. It is a thriving area that benefits from its location on an interstate between San Francisco and Silicon Valley and minutes from the area's busy international airport.

Nadia was uncharacteristically quiet as Carly's Mini Cooper purred like a car twice its size on 101. Carly had already talked to Lang, who filled her in on Richard Sumaoang and his Filipino posse. She agreed that it clouded both their theories. On the other hand, one didn't have to be a murderer to pursue what appeared to be a most embarrassing exposé.

The trip was a waste. Except for the food paradise that was Draeger's. Rarely did she have the chance to ooh and aah at the luxury super-market – vast selections of high-quality chocolates and wines, a deli that went on for ever, baked goods that doubled as art masterpieces. She and Nadia took the escalator to an upstairs that featured fine kitchen and dining paraphernalia, including such things as Versace teacups. But really all she had to show for the trip was an apology from the manager of Blue Monkey Press.

The mock-up and supporting materials to Warfield's tell-all could not be found. The wispy-haired owner explained that they had thought at first they couldn't find it because it had been sent out, but then they realized they'd been burgled. The place had been broken into recently, but they had found nothing missing – until now. It hadn't occurred to him that this kind of thing would be stolen and he had therefore not checked, even after Carly's call.

Carly remembered to check with the San Mateo police about Mickey
Warfield's DUI. The story was verified. He had been in jail the night
that Frank Wiley was killed. He was stopped at three a.m. The police
allowed her to see the arrest report and the mug shots. She thought,
no matter all the great advances in technology, it was still impossible
for a man to be in two places at once.

This was not going to be good news for Lang. But it was another
lead followed to the end. Mickey Warfield did not kill Frank Wiley –
personally. On the other hand, the San Mateo police should have charged
Mickey Warfield with theft in addition to driving under the influence.

Vincente Gratelli was in no hurry to get to work. The Chief was
complaining about overtime because the Mayor was complaining about
the budget – the city was deep in debt and the Mayor was running for
Governor – and because the daily newspaper was hammering them on
unsolved murders from one side and overtime on the other.

This morning, Gratelli was feeling 'puny' as he would put it. He
wasn't exactly sick, but his sinuses were full and deadening the brain
and his stomach was just this side of turning. He poached an egg, which
he put on a toasted English muffin. To soften the acid in his coffee he
uncharacteristically made it half milk.

He may not have gone into the office, but that didn't keep his mind
from going to work, propelled it seemed by the news that the body of
a slightly heavy-set, red-headed, middle-aged white male had been found
in an old steel mill in a dry dock at the foot of Potrero Hill. The call
had come in last night as he prepared for bed. A routine patrol in the
abandoned dry dock area indicated the old brick steel foundry's front
gate had been breached. When the officer investigated further he found
the body – fully dressed – on the floor. The wallet was missing. The cop
on duty at homicide thought it might be the missing Mickey Warfield.
Gratelli thanked the cop and said he would call later to see if the victim
could be identified.

Gratelli could feel it in his sour belly. Mickey Warfield. If it were
Warfield, he would put Rose and Stern on it. Have them revisit Marlene
Berensen. He didn't want to get ahead of himself on this, but it seemed
like the people on Carly Paladino's list were getting eliminated one by
one.

Still in his robe and wrinkled pajamas, he finished his egg and coffee
at the Formica table in the kitchen as he turned the pages of the *Chronicle*,
more out of habit than interest. He set the dishes in the sink and went

to the phone. He wished he could not think about work. Maybe read a book. But he couldn't. Paid or not, he needed to follow up.

It was Mickey Warfield, the medical examiner said an hour later. Maybe it was good Gratelli wasn't at the office. The murders were piling up and no one in the chain of command beginning with the Mayor – not to mention the constant nattering of some members of the board of supervisors – would be happy about it. Cut the overtime. Solve the murders.

'Ooooh,' Gratelli moaned with disappointment bordering on despair. 'Cause of death?'

'Neck snapped,' she said matter-of-factly.

'Put up a fight?'

'No bruises on his hands. But he might have been punched a couple of times before the *coup de grâce*. Contusions under his right eye.'

# Twenty-Nine

Noah Lang didn't like the news of Mickey the Younger's demise. His feeling had nothing to do with the senseless loss of life, but that the dead cannot be cross-examined. Gratelli had called Carly, who called Lang. This, coupled with Carly's verification of Mickey's whereabouts on the night of Wiley's death, did little to promote his theory of the murders.

Lang climbed down the ladder from his loft carrying his frustration on his shoulders. He put the coffee on, shook some dry food into Buddha's bowl, and plunked down on the sofa. He allowed himself a few seconds to feel sorry for himself. Back to square one. Or maybe just back to square three. He felt a jolt of energy. He hadn't figured it out, exactly, but maybe they had been looking too narrowly. Given what all the people on the list had in common . . . it was an idea, a thought with a little electricity to it.

He went to the kitchen, picked up his cell, flipped it open and pushed the button for Carly.

'Did you have lunch in San Mateo?'

'Too early.'

'Good, let's have lunch.'

'Noah, Noah, Noah,' she said.

'A business lunch. You tell me what you found out . . .'

'I can do that in a minute and a half,' she said.

'And I have an idea, but I need your input.'

'Input?'

'A bull session, we used to call them. Carly, I need your very valuable, no-nonsense, linear thinking.'

'Thank you.' Her tone wasn't heartfelt.

'Lunch?'

'All right.'

'Could you sound more excited?'

'No.'

'Meet you in North Beach at one.'

'Where?'

'City Lights. If one of us is late, we can browse the books.'

Carly didn't see Lang coming. She was in a relatively dark corner of the basement where the mystery section resided. City Lights was a great bookstore. She remembered sneaking away from her parents' restaurant when business was slow and heading over to City Lights. There was something almost sacred about the place. History was made there. Literary giants hung out there. Third floor, poetry. Main floor, literature – real literature, including a section of small, handmade books – and uncommon magazines. Downstairs was another main floor – travel, women's studies, philosophy, and mystery.

'You're hard to find,' Lang said.

'And you chose to become a private investigator?'

'You presuppose talent is a factor in my decisions.'

'Let's see if we can get into this little place I know,' Carly said.

'Break in?'

'It's crowded.'

Lang, in his many trips to North Beach, never noticed The House, a narrow-fronted restaurant on the first block of Grant from Columbus. Perhaps it was because there was nothing Italian about the restaurant. It was small, the decor modern, and the food, though nothing on the outside would provide a clue, had a strong Asian influence.

The two of them were seated at the only table by the window, which meant they could watch the goings-on inside and out.

Lang waited for things to settle, for their order to be taken, for the drinks to be delivered, before he launched into his scattered thoughts about the list and the deaths.

'I'm kind of at a loss for words,' Lang said once the cheerful server had brought him a glass of rice beer and Carly her usual Pinot Grigio.

'That's a rare condition,' Carly found herself saying. For some reason she wanted to needle him.

'It is. What I'm about to suggest is: I don't think we have a killer.'

'We have more than one,' she said, nibbling on the sesame-soaked cucumber skins from the little bowl in front of them.

'How long have you been harboring that idea?'

'It's what's going through my mind. Especially now that Mickey is dead.'

Lang nodded. 'Well,' he said, deflated a bit. His approach wasn't so novel after all.

'You thought that was a pretty clever deduction, I bet.'

'I did.'

'We were locked into a specific solution the moment we began. The list. Someone on the list did it. Could be some ones.'

'There are pieces to this,' Lang said. 'The murders, stealing the manuscript, deflecting the investigation . . .'

'The missing photograph,' Carly added.

'I thought it came back,' Lang said.

'Yes, a photograph came back.'

'. . . the killing of Angel. Mickey's relationship with his father's mistress and his sloppy old private eye's contact with Ralph Chiu.' He stopped. 'Shit.'

'What?'

'I assumed that because Mickey was having an affair with Angel, or something, that Scotty Markham worked for him. Maybe Markham was working for Chiu.'

'A real estate deal maybe,' she said. 'And lots and lots of deep, dark secrets, including a man who admitted to murder. We got to where we are now by poking and speculating. The question is, what do we do now?'

'Eat,' Lang said, leaning back so the lovely lady serving could put the appetizer in place – white shrimp and chives Chinese dumplings.

'What do we do now?' she repeated.

'Just last night I discovered Sumaoang was the one who had these guys following me, not Chiu.' Lang shrugged. 'Gain one, lose one. But I don't think Sumaoang was paying the boys who were tailing me. We're being pulled in multiple directions.'

She sipped her wine.

'I like my life,' she said. 'I was worried that I made a mistake leaving the comfort and financial stability of Vogel Security. But how could that compare to the fly-by-the-seat-of-your-pants operation I'm involved in now?'

'Precisely,' he said, smiling. 'Who could possibly be comfortable knowing what's coming next?'

'The sesame glazed salmon, I hope.'

And it came. As did the grilled chicken breast with black bean mushroom sauce – and he was not disappointed.

Mickey Warfield had been dead at least seventy-two hours when he was found eight hours ago. This, Inspector Vincente Gratelli learned from the Medical Examiner herself, who understood the urgency of the case. She was working directly with both CSI and the Crime Lab as well.

Gratelli sipped the coffee he had brought with him from Caffe Trieste, his first and best cup of the day. He sat behind his desk, noticed Rose and Stern taking a young Asian into an interview room. After scanning the serious parts of the newspaper he thought about Mickey's death and the timeline of the deaths. Mickey couldn't have killed Frank Wiley because he was in a jail cell in San Mateo. And he couldn't have killed Angel LeGard because he was already dead.

He shook his head. None of the pieces seemed to fit. He made a mental note to let Carly Paladino know. He preferred talking to her rather than Lang. Was he feeling fatherly? Was that the reason? He hoped so.

Gratelli pulled Rose out of the interview room.

'What have you got?'

'Not sure we have anything,' Rose said. 'We were tailing Lang and his gal Thursday and this guy was tailing them too.'

'Why?'

'Don't know. Filipino. Babbles away as if he doesn't understand English.'

'Get that Filipino cop up here. You know, what's his name. He speaks Tagalog.'

'There's some stuff all mixed up here, Vincente.'

'I know. None of it makes sense. Murders, why? Looking for the book as if it's a treasure.'

'A treasure in reverse,' Rose said.

'How's your partner doing?' Gratelli asked.

Rose shrugged, smiled. 'Stern is Stern is Stern.'

'My old partner was a lot like him. He's confused by the fact that he cares so much, covers it up by being a stubborn, sometimes stupid, rock.'

Gratelli regretted his comments immediately. It wasn't like him to psychoanalyze, or say anything about other cops, good or bad. That's how he had stayed out of trouble all these years. But he often thought of his partner. Everyone thought he was tough, but, in fact, he was ill-equipped to deal with evil every day.

'Forget I said anything,' Gratelli said just before Rose went back to the interrogation.

'Forgotten.'

It was probably the death of the Chinese woman that got to Stern most. Women and children. Same as his partner.

Time to wrap all this up.

# Thirty

Lang and Carly entered the lobby of their small office building. They were both prepared to walk the two floors to avoid the glacier pace of the elevator, but there was a yellow cone on the second step and yellow tape across the entry. At first Lang thought it was a crime scene, but there was a little sign that said 'Pardon our dust'.

Lang went closer, looked up. There was a portion of a ladder visible.

It didn't feel right, but there were many times when he had let suspicion get the better of him and the situation had turned out to be harmless. He looked at Carly.

'That happen often?' she asked.

'No.' He pressed the button.

'Something wrong?'

'Maybe.'

The elevator was on the first floor, but it took thirty seconds for the lumbering doors to open. They stepped in. Lang pressed the button to close the doors as if the elevator would pay attention – and then the floor number. The doors closed, banged open, then closed again.

The gears locked in place, the windowless room groaned.

'This is going down,' Carly said.

'It is.' Just as he attempted to stop the elevator, the dim light expired and the elevator clunked to a stop. Then it moved again.

'It's still going down,' she said.

Lang flipped open his cellphone and punched in the code for the office. Nothing happened. Inside the thick, steel-lined elevator and in a basement, no signal went out.

The elevator came to a rough stop. There was a long moment of silence and the doors opened. The only way they knew that was the sound and slightly, ever so slightly less darkness.

Lang pushed Carly to one side of the elevator and he stood on the other, away from the opening.

The guns fired, explosive sounds and the pings of bullets against the elevator walls. Lang hoped luck would keep both of them out of the way of ricochets.

Lang flipped open his phone and punched in the code again, this time with a prayer. He slid the phone out on the floor into the darkness.

'Can't see anything,' Lang yelled out as if he were communicating with the assassins. What he wanted, hoped, no begged for, was that Thanh or Brinkman was picking up on the message. 'Who are you and what the fuck you doing in our basement?'

'Time's up,' the voice said.

'You made a mistake,' Carly yelled out. 'This makes it a standoff.'

'We'll just come get you. If you had a gun, you'd have fired it.'

It was Scotty Markham's voice in the darkness. Lang didn't figure the guy would go this far.

'Come on over, Scotty, see for yourself,' Lang said. He hoped someone upstairs was listening to all this and figuring it out.

'He said "we", didn't he? Two here, at least,' Carly said in a whisper. 'Another outside to let them know when to take control of the elevator.'

New sounds in the darkness: *thooot*, *phut*!

'What was that?' a voice asked. It wasn't Markham's.

'You weenies, you're a disgrace to tough guys everywhere,' Lang said. 'Somebody put some trash in the chute. Scared of a little trash? How are you doing with the rats? They like the dark. Crawl up your leg.'

'Shut the fuck up,' Markham said.

'I have to admit, I didn't think you were too bright,' Lang said, 'but I never figured you for this. This is low.'

'High and mighty, that it? You're about a year and a half off being me.'

'No, Scotty. I'm not adept at snapping a man's neck.'

'A little practice.'

'I'd have a hard time, stabbing a woman with an ice pick. Truly cold-blooded.'

'You sound like a high school kid majoring in dance,' Markham said.

On one hand, Lang wanted this to be over, but the fact that the other guys had guns meant he couldn't push it. He and Carly were living on a bluff.

'What's that?' said the other voice.

'What?' Markham said.

'I heard something.'

'Rats, I tell you, and not the Disney kind,' Lang said. 'You don't believe me.'

'I believe you're dead,' Markham said.

Lang sensed someone, something, coming closer.

There was a thud, something soft but heavy hit the floor.

'Eddie,' Markham said. 'Eddie!'

'Things not going according to plan?' Carly asked.

'I told you those rats are big,' Lang said. He whispered for her to see if the doors would close. If not she was to get down to the floor.

Lang saw Markham's face light up briefly as he tried to use his cell-phone.

'I see you,' Lang said, slipping out the elevator and to one side, and heading toward where the light was.

Markham fired in Lang's direction.

Something hard hit something soft and there was another thud.

'Just two of them?' It was Thanh's voice.

'Inside anyway,' Carly said.

'Brinkman went after the post outside,' Thanh said.

The lights came on. There was a thick lump of apparel on the floor not too far from the trash dumpster beneath the chute. Carly was sure there was a human being inside. Between the boiler and the elevator was the crumpled body of Scotty Markham. Over Markham stood Thanh, in a gray pantsuit, a baseball bat in his hand.

'You will reimburse for the dry cleaning,' Thanh said, brushing off the grime and nodding toward the dumpster and trash chute. 'It was a dirtier, but faster ride than I thought.'

Carly called Gratelli.

Lang felt for Markham's pulse. Dead. Then the other guy. A little luckier.

When Brinkman opened the cellar door, the feral guy from the previous visit preceded the old PI into the room. Behind them came the whooping of the police sirens. Lang nodded for Thanh to leave.

Uniforms arrived first and everyone had to play nice until things were sorted out. In less than twenty minutes a perturbed Stern and an amused Rose arrived. Carly intercepted Stern who, face full of reddening anger, headed toward Lang.

'These guys were waiting for us,' Carly told Stern. The cop nodded but his eyes were still on Lang and his body language was that of an angry dog pulling against the leash. 'They were going to assassinate us. Had the elevator shut down . . .'

'Yeah, yeah.' Stern was gathering calm, however slowly. His cell rang and he answered. It seemed to keep him busy for a little while.

'I don't know if either of Markham's cohorts know anything,' Lang said to Gratelli as the older inspector came in. Gratelli looked the place over, medics now working on the second guy, CSI working with Markham's corpse, while the third member of the gang, the feral guy, was handcuffed and cowering in a dark corner. Rose was talking to him, but that seemed to be the way it was. Rose was talking. The feral guy wasn't.

'And we can track Markham back to Chiu?' Gratelli asked.

'Yep. Nothing more than they talked after Markham learned Mickey Warfield wasn't going to get an inheritance. And on top of that he was missing.'

'Worried him a lot,' Gratelli said.

Carly thought the inspector may have smiled.

'Warfield's body is found and Markham goes homicidal on you guys.' Gratelli raised his eyebrows. 'Why?'

'We're getting close,' Lang said.

'Why did the girl have to die? The alibi? Why would Markham care?'

'Maybe Markham didn't care about the alibi. She wanted to tell me something else, remember? Maybe about Chiu.'

Gratelli nodded. 'You know, all we have to do is sit back. Just let them kill each other and the killer will be the last one standing.'

'Can I ask you a favor?' Carly asked.

Gratelli nodded.

'You know the list? Get the last two months' financials. Checking, savings.'

'What do you have?'

'Nothing yet. Not sure what I'm looking for.'

'Yeah, you do.' This time Gratelli's smile was unmistakable. 'I've got some of them. You need all of them?'

'Please,' Carly asked.

'You'll let me in on it, won't you?' Gratelli asked.

'I will. Thanks. If there's anything there, I'll definitely get you involved. It wouldn't work otherwise.'

Carly, Lang and Brinkman spent thirty minutes answering more questions, most of them the same questions phrased differently. The police found the identities of both surviving attackers and both had records – one for armed robbery and the other several arrests for beating up people, including his wife.

While Stern may have liked to lay something on Lang, the crime scene was pretty clear. It was consistent with the consistent stories told by the two intended victims. The only people using bullets were the attackers. Who actually bought the bullets seemed to trouble Lang more than it did the police. And the two attackers said that Markham had invited them along for backup. Their weapons told a different story.

As Stern passed by Lang, he shook his head.

'Do you believe the fucking luck?' he said to the air.

On the stairway going up to their offices – Brinkman stubbornly waiting for the elevator to be put back in service – Carly asked Lang, 'Why did you have Thanh sneak out?'

'We want to keep his superhero status secret.'

'Can you ever be serious?'

'If we acknowledge his special powers, we'll have to pay him more.'

'Cut it out, will you.'

'Seriously, think about it, he's kind of a secret weapon. And any undue attention by the authorities, especially our favorite detective Stern, might complicate his life – and ours.' They were quiet for a while, but as they entered the office, Lang pulled Carly aside.

'We've got to put an end to all of this, don't we? You have any idea how we can do that?'

'I do,' she said. 'Let's have lunch.'

'We just had lunch.'

'Let's have a coffee break.'

'North Beach?'

'Yep.'

'Let me have a few minutes with Thanh first.'

Carly headed down the hall to the restroom.

Lang found Thanh at the reception desk, head in hands. He looked up, eyes searching Lang for news.

'How bad were they hurt?' Thanh asked.

Lang would have lied, but the truth would be in tomorrow's newspaper.

'Markham didn't make it,' Lang said.

Thanh nodded. If killing Markham bothered him, he didn't show it.

'You want me to stick around?' Lang asked.

'You can if you want, but I'm going home to shower and change.'

Thanh smiled. It was faint, barely noticeable. But it was a smile.


# Thirty-One


Coffee in North Beach, Lang knew, was likely to be good, wherever they went. There was Graffeo, maybe the best in the city, but they didn't serve it in cups, just beans in a bag. There was the famous – and not just for the coffee – Caffe Trieste. It was often wonderfully loud and one might hear an aria or two. But for a quiet spot with in-house roasting Carly and Lang settled on Caffe Roma.

Not all kickback and homey, the interior was sparkling clean with an Italian feel that was more stylishly modern than one would expect in an old Italian neighborhood. Great wines lined one wall. Art hung on other walls. Carly ordered a latte, Lang a cup of the pick of the day. As they sat, Lang noticed that while the patrons of Caffe Trieste seemed to lean toward the artistic, the clientele of Caffe Roma tended to attract the establishment types. Suits and laptops. Everyone was entitled to a taste of Bohemia, he thought.

Carly arrived at the table with her latte and a small plate of cookies, which she intended to share.

'Kind of like recess,' she said, smiling.

'Where I went to school, we weren't that civilized.'

'Your school was a reform school?'

'Yes.'

'Oh.' She laughed. 'It was a wild guess. Just being silly.'

'Silly is good. You should be silly more often.'

'Seems to be the direction I'm going, thanks to you and your friends.'

'It's the process of decorporatization. We remove dress codes, rigid hourly expectations, competition for the boss's favor, and doing things we don't believe are right,' Lang said.

She smiled. Despite this slightly arrogant litany, Noah was right.

'But we still have a case. Murders to solve. We should get back to business.'

Lang nodded.

Her expression was serious now. 'What do you think? Where are we?'

'I don't know,' Lang said. 'Let me reiterate.' He stopped for a moment. 'When do we iterate? Anyway, we've been operating on the assumption that this was the work of one of the people on the list.'

She nodded toward him. 'I see. Not one, but more than one. There were a number of people who didn't want to see this book come to light.'

'Including your client,' Lang said.

'Our client, Noah. Why would he hire us and then try to kill us?'

'Point taken. So we have this: Whitney Warfield was murdered. Angel LeGard was murdered. Frank Wiley was murdered. And now Mickey Warfield is murdered. And these people, generally speaking, weren't the real players.'

'Whitney was killed to keep the book from surfacing. Angel was killed because, we think, she was pulling the alibi for Whitney's son on the night of his father's death. And possibly because she knew something else damning that had to do with the case or not. But why on earth was Wiley killed?'

'There we are,' Lang said, taking a sip of coffee and watching a line gather in the front for coffee and cannoli.

'More than one,' Carly repeated.

'Which ones? I still have trouble seeing Agnes DeWitt involved in all this.'

'Don't let your attraction to her cloud your judgment,' she said, smiling.

'She is a charmer.'

'I have an idea.' Carly leaned over the table. 'Trust me?'

'Hey, it's your case.'

'I'll get back with you.'

Considering the events of the day, Lang was surprisingly relaxed. He would have to go through some additional police interviews at some point. Fortunately, neither he nor Carly had used a firearm, which would have raised all sorts of issues. Lang took the credit or the blame for using the baseball bat on the two victims and Brinkman had taken his shotgun out to his Buick once Lang tied his prey to some pipes.

This meant that at the moment the case, the only case they were working on at the time, was now completely in Carly's hands. It was too late in the day to go prospecting for new work. Thanh had completed all of the accounting for the month. Brinkman was at home, probably nursing a bottle of Scotch.

The evening was before him.

He gave it some thought. He could call Maura, a masseuse whom he engaged from time to time. Their occasional meetings had been going on for three years. He justified it because she worked for herself, was not part of any sex trafficking ring, and had chosen this line of work because she preferred it to others. Unfortunately, waking up beside a dead woman had destroyed what was left of his libido – at least for a little while. He had no desire to go to a bar, or even a restaurant that required him to be his formal self.

Buddha waited by the door.

'Yes, well, here we are. No offense to you,' Lang said to the cat who had already walked toward the kitchen, expecting Lang to follow, 'but this scares me. I'm relatively young, Buddha. I come home to a cat like, well, pardon my stereotypes, like a maiden aunt or an old guy who lost his mate.'

Buddha stopped, turned back.

'I know, that was unkind. I know that. Thing is, I don't knit doilies and I don't go to see the revival of *Cats*, but I *live* with a cat and seem to have no other life.'

Buddha, Lang thought, may have regretted stopping to listen to such garbage. The brown creature walked gracefully toward the kitchen, where his water was changed and his dry food bowl replenished.

Lang checked the cabinets and refrigerator. Aside from a few condiments, he might as well be on a deserted island. Not even a coconut. He didn't feel like going out, but he pretty much had to if he wanted to eat and . . . drink.

'You want something? A little crab, maybe?'

Lang walked down to the Panhandle, the narrow sliver of Golden Gate Park a few blocks from his converted laundry space. A few blocks to the East was Falletti's. He'd find something there. Maybe a bottle of decent, cheap wine or a beer he had yet to try. Some sausage to throw in a bit of pasta or a piece of fish.

He began to feel better as he walked the few blocks on the path under the trees before the park ended at the Department of Motor Vehicles. The smell of eucalyptus was in the air. Dogs chased things – sticks, Frisbees or bright green tennis balls. Bicyclists and runners traversed the paths. Elderly folks were getting a bit of fresh air and exercise.

Lang took a moment to sit on a bench. Yes, he told himself, stop rushing. It only hurried the end, didn't it? Not the end of the case or the day, but the end of it all. He took a few deep breaths and allowed himself to re-enter the present, a slower present, a more pleasant present.

He wandered inside the grocery unhurriedly, the evening now out before him in the most pleasant way. Even so, at the perimeter of his consciousness, he thought about how this case might all come down. And it was coming down. He could feel it.

Perhaps William Blake was telepathic or just extremely intuitive. She wanted to talk to him. And now, there he was, sitting on the sofa. He was sipping what appeared to be a Martini. He wore a camel-colored cashmere V-neck sweater with a white tee shirt beneath and tobacco-colored pants with a deep crease. His feet were sockless inside some brown Gucci loafers. He looked comfortable but not all that happy.

Carly felt as ambivalent as he looked. She was glad to see him, but had never quite gotten over his lack of respect for her privacy. She was entertained by his unpredictability as much as she believed it to be self-indulgent and immature.

'Doors have locks for a reason,' she said, more harshly than she intended.

'If I were a little freer,' he said, raising his eyebrows, 'if I didn't have to hide or look over my shoulder . . .'

'All right,' she said. It was a fair point. 'Are you blaming me?'

'No.' He stood, put his hand on her shoulder. 'I'm getting antsy. Another death. Mickey Warfield. This is what I wanted to avoid. Are we getting close, Carly?'

She nodded. 'I have some questions for you.'

'How about I fix you a drink? Martini?'

'Sure. Not too strong.' She followed him to the kitchen. 'How did you end up with Whitney that night?'

'He called me,' William said. He put some ice in both glasses as he cut a sliver of lime. He waited. 'Wanted to meet me there.'

'Whitney knew your number.'

William nodded. 'Friends and friends of friends. I don't want my name on a billboard, but can't be too hard to find or I'm in trouble.'

'Why Alighieri's?'

William paused for a moment. A moment too long in Carly's mind. 'It's where he holds court.'

'When?'

'Every night after eleven.'

'Every night?'

'Every night. Everyone there knows his schedule. He has late-morning coffee at Caffe Trieste, writes in the early afternoon, has dinner, writes in the evening, and at ten thirty or eleven shows up at Alighieri's where he drinks and pontificates the night away. He works really hard to get a buzz before closing.'

'You say "everyone knows".'

William smiled. 'I'm sure the president is unaware of Whitney's habits, but the natives know.'

He drained the water off the ice in the glasses and put it in the shaker along with additional ice. He poured an infinitesimal amount of vermouth and a more substantial amount of gin into the ice. He didn't shake the container but swirled it for a few seconds and then poured the contents into the glasses. He snapped the lime peeling and rubbed the rims of the glasses. He handed one to Carly.

'You said we were close to the end on this,' William said.

She wasn't sure how much she wanted to say. Not all the pieces were in place and they wouldn't be until she could get the people on the list together – including him – in one room.

'You read or watch any of those old British mysteries?'

William nodded and smiled.

'I need a place,' Carly said. 'A place where I have enough room to put up sixteen large photographs and have maybe fifteen or twenty people in a somewhat relaxed atmosphere.'

William took a deep breath, suspicion and amusement on his face. 'I know of a place.'

'Really?'

'Alighieri's. The back room. When do you want it?'

'Just like that?' Carly asked.

'Just like that.'

'How can you do that?'

'I own the place,' William said.

'You own it?'

'You look surprised. I'm not going to be beautiful for ever,' he said, grinning. 'I have a few investments. What I do is similar to playing sports . . . there comes a time, you know.'

There was obviously more to learn, Carly thought.

'Alighieri's is the place where all this began,' Carly said.

'It was.' He walked back into the living area. She followed. 'I promise you,' he said as he settled into the sofa, 'I didn't kill anyone. Ever. And I have never hired anyone to do anything nearly that evil. Faced with fight or flight, I always choose flight.'

'I noticed. Anyway, I didn't accuse you.'

'Directly.'

The Martini was good. It was also strong.

'I'll cook,' he said. 'Am I getting too comfy?'

'When this is all over, will I ever see you again?' Carly asked.

'No. Probably not.'

'Then you're not getting too comfy,' Carly said. 'Dinner sounds lovely.'

'And?'

'And that might be lovely too.'

It was settled. Alighieri's back room at ten. Ten was determined because, as Carly soon discovered, there was to be a prelude to the Alighieri get-together – services for Frank Wiley at St Francis of Assisi that would begin at eight. A phone call to Nadia was helpful. She would set up sixteen large easels to display the photographs as well as arrange the tables for the evening's event. Nadia saw it as a launch to her very own show of Wiley's 'art', as she now described it.

Over dinner Blake asked Carly to tell him about all her loves.

She laughed. 'A boy when I was very, very young. He went away.'

'That's the sum of it all?' Blake asked, comfortably embedded in the large sofa next to Carly, sipping wine from a large glass.

'Love? Maybe that's the sum of it all. I let my life drift,' she said. She looked at her wine, swirled it a bit, not out of any attempt to enhance the flavor, but to allow the debate in her mind about what to tell and what not to tell. What would reveal too much about herself. And what would no doubt bore him to death.

'Go on,' he said. 'We have the night ahead of us.'

'There was Peter. We were together for a long time. I would describe it as an interim relationship, a long, long interim relationship.' She looked up from her wine and saw him staring. 'Don't look at me like that.

I didn't lead him on. He was to me as I was to him. We had a lot in common, including a lack of passion for the other. And . . . he left me. A job in Seattle. Didn't even invite me to go along. And it was absolutely fine.' She thought William looked doubtful. 'True. It was the beginning of . . .' she gestured broadly enough to almost spill her wine '. . . this!'

He nodded.

'In whatever time I have left on this earth, I want to live a little, not sleepwalk through it.' Was she being a little loud? Maybe she needed to put a cap on it. 'And I'm getting a little silly.'

'A little silly is fine,' William Blake said. She remembered Lang's comment about letting go a bit. She didn't say anything. 'What about dreams? Are they important?' he asked.

'Short dreams sometimes,' she said, 'like this one. They're nice, aren't they?'

He nodded.

# Thirty-Two

Carly woke up to the sounds of the shower running and the smell of coffee brewing. The light that squeezed between the broad-bladed Venetian blinds was intense. She had slept well, surprisingly well considering how difficult it was to sleep beside another living creature. Unless William had slipped out to sleep on the sofa during the night, this was a first. How could she be so trusting?

She just was, she thought. She reached for her cell and punched in Lang's number. Without going into detail, she explained the event that would take place that evening. Would he make sure those on his list, those remaining, were in attendance?

'How am I to coax the unwilling?'

'You're just the first step. I'm going to ask Gratelli to make the invitation more formal. But you might mention that we have the manuscript.'

'We do?' Lang asked.

'No.'

'What are we doing?'

'We're going to figure out who did what to whom.'

'On the spot?'

'Yes,' Carly said.

'Cream or sugar?' William asked, coming into the room unclothed, his fortyish body looking like a thirtyish one.

'Where are you?'

'At a coffee shop.'

'Who's with you?'

'I'm just talking to the barista.'

'You're up and out early,' Lang said.

'The early bird gets the worm.'

'Some people say that,' Lang said.

'No one said the early bird is witty.'

'Are you dressed?'

'Why would you ask a question like that?'

'Because there is no buzz. No sounds of dishes or conversation. It's all too soft, padded, no echo. So you're not in some commercial coffee shop. It's more like you're in bed.'

'And if I were?'

'Then we would talk about what else the early bird was getting . . .'

'The list. Just talk to the list, OK?' She flipped the phone shut. She had to call him back to give him the time and place.

'Does he always get to you that way?' William asked, still naked and smiling, but bringing her the coffee.

'What way?'

'You are flustered a bit,' William said.

'He's difficult sometimes.'

'What are you doing today?' William asked.

'I need to talk to Gratelli, get the folks to Alighieri's tonight, check out some bank statements. All sorts of things. You can stay here if you need to. If you go out on the balcony, please put some clothes on. Don't want to give Mr Nakamura a heart attack.'

'A proper lady,' William said.

'A proper lady,' she repeated. For some reason that description made her sad. Yet, no matter how many nights like last night she might have, the description seemed apt. 'You'll be there tonight,' she said matter-of-factly. It was a statement, not a question or even a request.

'Maybe,' he said, sitting on the bed, sipping his coffee. 'There's nothing wrong with being a proper lady. Learn to love yourself a little,' William said.

*        *        *

Lang, while shaving, briefly discussed plans for the day with Buddha. It was doubtful the cat cared even the slightest about the words. Instead, attention was paid to the strokes of the razor and the peeling of the shaving cream. Buddha was interested in how things worked. He, for example, watched intently a few months ago when Lang set up the video and sound system. He always watched Lang cook or make coffee. He usually watched him dress and was all too curious about the human urination process for Lang.

'I don't watch you,' Lang told him once before shutting the door.

This morning, like most mornings, Lang dressed and went down the street to Central Brewing – a coffee shop on the corner of Fell and Central – for a morning cup of coffee and a muffin, usually blueberry.

It was a cool, sunny morning. It had every indication of warming up and becoming the kind of day that lucky tourists seem to think is the norm. It was not at all a time Lang expected surprises.

Sitting at a table in front of the coffee shop was Inspector Stern, overflowing his suit much like a muffin top. After a sip from the large paper cup, he gave Lang the smile: I know you are not happy to see me and that makes me very happy.

Lang went in, asked for his non-latte, non-foamy, not steamy, normal, everyday coffee and got it in seconds. He decided to skip the now unappetizing muffin. He stepped out and pulled a chair up to the table where Stern presided.

'You are so predictable,' Stern said. 'Every day the same routine.'

'Home away from home. I didn't know you cared. But I'm honored to have my very own stalker. I had hoped for a pretty woman, but . . .'

'I don't like you.'

'I'm shocked,' Lang said, smiling. 'I am deeply shocked.'

Stern gave him the smile again.

'Where's your keeper?'

'Errands,' Stern said, unrattled. 'Nice day, don't you think?'

'Was. Yes.'

'Do you know why I don't like you?' Stern asked.

'Because you think I'm shady, sleazy, and way too lucky.'

'Oh,' Stern said. 'You do know.'

'Was that what you wanted?' Lang asked. 'I'm going to be late for homeroom.'

'The Chinese woman,' Stern said.

'I didn't do it, Stern.'

'Women die when you're around. Remember the woman at the pier?'

'That was almost fifteen years ago.'

'The Russian guy's wife?'

'Yeah, I remember.'

'Now the Chinese woman.'

'I didn't kill anyone. I've never killed a woman.'

Stern smiled.

'I don't see the point of this conversation,' Lang said.

'It's a small matter, really. I just don't want you to think that you're going to skate through all of this. Time isn't on your side.'

'Time isn't on anybody's side.'

'I'm watching you,' Stern said.

'You're not my favorite person either, Stern, but I'd wish you a better life than that. This makes me sad.'

'Oh, I'm enjoying every moment of it.'

'That makes me sadder. I think I'll get a muffin after all. See you tonight.'

Stern raised his coffee cup in a mock toast.


Lang would have walked down to the park and had his muffin amidst the morning dog walkers, baby strollers, homeless sleepers, and purposeful bicyclists, but Stern turned him against further public appearance. No rest for the stalked. Instead he took his coffee and plump muffin back to his place, where Buddha turned down, as he always did, a bite of Lang's breakfast.

Lang put on some 'cool jazz', took his coffee, muffin and cellphone out to the back. He began making calls to the people on his list, inviting them to Alighieri's for free drinks and a special reading from the late Mr Whitney Warfield's last book.

No one expressed surprise. Ms DeWitt graciously accepted the invitation. Marlene Berensen, who had her wits about her, indicated in a gravelly, bored voice that she'd 'think about it'. Sumaoang said he'd be there anyway and might check things out. When it was suggested that he was not only in the book but in the X-rated exhibition, he laughed and said he couldn't possibly miss it. Elena Warfield was noncommittal, and Ralph Chiu thanked Lang for the invitation but gave no indication he would be there. Hawkes feigned disinterest.

'And I understand,' Lang told the painter, 'you'll be there in the nude whether you show up or not.'

'There's an exhibition?'

'Of the photographs. You are naked but not dead, I'm told. Unlike Warfield who is both.'

'How literary of you,' Hawkes said. 'I don't approve. Perhaps I'll have it shut down.'

They would all be there, Lang was sure.

If the great 'legend in his own mind' Whitney Warfield had his eternal soul's send-off at the magnificent cathedral of Saints Peter and Paul in North Beach, it was fitting that Frank Wiley, a lesser personage, would have his farewell at the smaller, no less beautiful but less grandiose, St Francis of Assisi.

Those were Noah Lang's thoughts as he entered the understated little jewel of a church. North Beach was a Roman Catholic neighborhood to be sure – two of their top brand name houses of the Lord separated by a couple of blocks of roasted garlic, fresh oregano and basil, Tuscan wine and strong espresso. Inside organ music filled the spare, open space, but the services had not yet begun. Some people were seated, but others lingered, chatting. Some toured the space, taking in the beautiful murals and stained-glass windows.

Lang, who came after the affair was to begin, saw the players who would make the evening a genuine event. He hoped so, at least. It was up to Carly and her strategy. Elena Warfield was in the front pew. Across the aisle in the first pew was Marlene Berensen. Malone was there with his wife, as were Sumaoang and his girlfriend. Bart Brozynski sat in a pew near the rear, also near the exit. Samuel McFarland stood, talking with Ralph Chiu at the end of one of the pews. Whatever would a board supervisor and a developer have to talk about? The lovely and delicate Agnes DeWitt was also paired. Marshall Hawkes, wearing some sort of black mourning cape, sat beside her. The two of them chatted, hands over mouths, conspiratorially, it seemed.

Gratelli stood with Carly off to the side. The two were engaged in conversation. Gratelli handed her some papers. Lang moved toward them, then looked back. Over the entrance to the church was the choir loft. It was from there that the haunting organ music emanated. There were a number of gold pipes in a small balcony. In front of the pipes, looking over the gathering, was a duo – Rose and Stern, scanning the nave.

Wiley was there too. In an ornate box in the front. Of all the deaths, for Lang, this one made the least sense. Lang looked around at the gathering. Wiley may not have been a shining star in the same way that Warfield was, but he had many friends. Even so, with what would follow after the service, this seemed to be some sort of perverse, darkly humorous pre-party.

Who was missing besides the dead? Only one. Lang looked around for William Blake. No sign of him.

'You have these only because I asked you to consult with the police department,' Gratelli said. 'These are not for public consumption.'

Behind him was Saint Rita of Cascia, Carly noticed. Schooled in these sorts of things she thought this might be more than a coincidence. She blushed as she considered the chaste saint while lusty images of last night wafted through her brain in some sort of divine, smartass justice. Catholic guilt. No matter how old you get, how removed from religion you think you are, there it is.

Carly shuffled through the papers in the manila folder. Bank statements for each of the folks on the list. She hoped her hunch was right. She also found phone bills for each.

'Phone bills too?' she asked.

Gratelli grinned. 'Your partner requested those. You didn't know?'

'You see how complementary our actions are. I call that backup,' she said, knowing full well she wasn't fooling him at all.

'Calls around the time of Whitney's death,' Gratelli continued. 'I added some other dates as well. I also added Scotty Markham and Angel LeGard, or Angel Chang as she is sometimes called. I have the originals. Some interesting relationships, I think.' He shrugged. 'We'll see what you can make of it.'

'I appreciate this.'

'Tonight's the night.'

'It has to be.'

Lang left the services early and walked over to Grant Avenue, up a few blocks and then over toward Alighieri's. It was that awkward time on Grant. The businesses counting on day business were closed and the businesses that came alive at night were just now starting to perk up. A few folks were on the sidewalk on this narrow one-way street. He stopped in at Golden Boy and got a thick slice of pizza and a glass of red wine.

The bar area at Alighieri's was busy – the stools at the bar were full and the booths on the other side of the walkway were inhabited – no doubt because the back room was off limits. There was a sign on an easel in front of the entrance to the area: 'Private Party'.

'Party?' Lang said to himself. He glanced over, saw the bartender looking at him, poker-faced, but definitely looking. The devil posters seemed in keeping with the theme of the evening.

Inside the back room, he saw a dozen easels with each photograph covered by gray drapery. The tables were being moved about by a dark-haired, slender woman who, in her crisp pantsuit, managed to blend a sense of art with serious business. She looked up, smiled, introduced herself.

'I'm Nadia, Carly's friend.'

'I'm Noah Lang.'

'I would have guessed.' She smiled. Her eyes flirted.

'Looks like you have things under control,' Lang said.

'I do this sort of thing – well, nearly this sort of thing – professionally. I'm not usually part of a murder investigation.'

'It's an unusual approach for all of us.'

'You know who did it?' she asked, as Noah helped slide a table in position. The plan was to make sure those sitting at the tables would have a good view of the photographs as they were exposed, the operative word being 'exposed'.

'This is Carly's show,' Lang said. 'I'm here to help.'

'Does she know?' Nadia asked, grinning. It wasn't really a question. She knew the answer. She wanted to know if Lang did. He knew the Nadias of the world very well. Life was a game. If you liked games, you'd like Nadia. And at one time, he would have enjoyed a good game. And Nadia.

Lang shrugged. 'It should be a fun evening,' he said, letting her determine whether the remark was sarcastic or not. 'So, are we drinking?'

'I don't know about you, but I am. And the plan is to make sure everybody drinks this evening. And drinks, and drinks.'

'Reduce the inhibitions.'

'Precisely,' she said.

# Thirty-Three

By the time Carly arrived at Alighieri's, Nadia had the back room ready. Carly was confident that Nadia would set it up right – she had years of experience doing such things – but Nadia had exceeded all expectations.

Sixteen individual spotlights targeted the drapery-veiled photographs. Tables had been arranged so that most chairs faced the line of easels. While the spots cast a silver-white light on the dark gray fabric, the light in the room was red, emanating softly from sconces with red bulbs, suggesting the influence of a 1920s Hades. The leather in the booths which lined the outer walls of the room was red. The floor was a checkerboard of red and black tile.

This was theater. And Nadia knew how to put on a show. She also knew how to promote herself. Among the crowd at the front bar, Carly noted, were a few key members of the media. This would not only ensure that all of this would be in the papers, on television and Twittered about, the buzz would make her formal exhibition of the photographs more popular than King Tut's arrival decades earlier.

Unfortunately for Carly, her performance was what counted. And she was not in the least sure the denouement would match the stage-craft. She pulled Lang from the bar and convinced him to go over to Café Puccini for a cup of coffee. She wanted to work with him on the bank balances and the phone logs. She had much of it together, and one surprise that she was absolutely sure of, but she'd be lying if she didn't admit there were a few missing pieces to the puzzle.

They sat outside at a table on the Columbus Avenue sidewalk. Neon signs blazed. Warm, gold light escaped restaurant windows. Taxis, autos and buses added flashes of headlights and celebratory trails of red tail lights to give Columbus a constant sense of buzzing, flickering electricity.

Carly was in no hurry. The program, such as it was, would be late. Participants, she hoped, would lubricate their boredom with spirits. With the help of a tiny flashlight on her key ring, Carly began to read the papers Gratelli had given her. Lang, always prepared to read in the dark, had a small penlight to do the same.

'You see the pattern?' Carly said, pointing out numbers on the bank statements. 'Time. Amount. Not a coincidence.' Looking at one state-ment meant nothing. Perhaps two. But putting them side by side told a story.

'And here,' Lang said. 'Look who made some late-night calling the night of Whitney's death.'

Lang caught the smile on Carly's face. She had already developed the concept. Before tonight, she had the outlines of the crimes. It was coming together, coming together enough for her to launch into the evening show.

\*      \*      \*

'Stage fright?' he asked as they walked slowly back to Alighieri's. It was well after ten. By this time the participants should have arrived and begun to salve their anxieties with drink.

'A little,' she said. 'It reminds me of what I did at Vogel Security. It's not that much different than presenting a complicated case to our staff or findings to our client. I did that at the old job; I would get people together, question them, push them, challenge them.'

'You know the answer?'

'Answers plural, I think. No, not every piece is in place. You have some of them.'

He did. The two agreed on the major points. Was there enough detail for a jury to convict? Not by a long shot.

Lang could tell by her voice that despite all the seeming frivolity of gathering the suspects together in one room, whatever might emerge this evening, she was aware of the fact that there would be a murderer or murderers in the room – that lives had been snuffed out and that soon lives would be changed forever. There was a little drizzle now and the lights from the neon signs softened and blurred. The little Italian village they walked through was portrayed in a watercolor rather than as a photograph.

At the entry to the block where Alighieri's small blue sign whispered its existence there were TV trucks and police cruisers. The bar was packed and the din loud. The events that would follow were not secret, it seemed.

'Nadia's doing,' Carly tried to say, her lips grazing Lang's ear.

Stern had the door to the back room and smirked an OK to go in. The room itself wasn't that crowded. Tables were full. Lang's eyes took inventory. The suspects on the list who hadn't expired were there. So were Rose and Gratelli.

'Let's get the show on the road,' Sumaoang shouted.

Lang noticed that the painter had been drinking. Was this also Nadia's doing?

'We're getting there,' Carly said. 'C'mon. No cover. The drinks are free. This may be your last day of freedom.'

There was laughter among the grumbling.

'Who is in charge here?'

The question came from McFarland. He'd stood up. He was used to being in public settings.

'I'll talk us through this,' Carly said. 'But we have some others here who will provide you with information. Noah Lang, my partner.

And Inspector Gratelli, who is just about to put an end to the murders and lock up the guilty.' She moved in front of the covered photographs. 'This evening we will talk about jealousy, greed, betrayal and deep, deep embarrassment. Motives for murder. Oh, and art. We'll talk about art.' Carly nodded toward the line of photographs.

'There's nothing keeping us here,' Ralph Chiu said.

'No,' Gratelli said, 'unless we arrest you, you are free to go. Of course, you would then miss out on what is being said. Perhaps about you after you've gone. You know we have a newspaperman here. We can't keep him from writing about all this. Right, Mr Brozynski?'

'You couldn't be righter,' Brozynski replied, grinning. Aside from Ms DeWitt, Brozynski may have been the only one in the room enjoying the party.

'And with your usual passion and viewpoint.'

'Yes, absolutely.'

McFarland stood and went toward the door, but not to leave, merely to shut it.

'I don't know what those of us who have essentially been cleared of the deaths of these individuals are doing here. I don't. I really don't.'

'No one has been cleared of all the crimes in this case,' Gratelli said. 'No one.'

'Why are you letting a sleazy PI agency do all the work, Inspector?' asked Marlene Berensen, her deep voice fitting nicely with the divey atmosphere.

'Paladino and Lang Investigations have been consulting with us for the last few weeks,' Gratelli said. 'They have some thoughts on the case that bear airing. We are here to learn as well.'

'Did you find the manuscript?' Sumaoang asked. 'That's all we care about. Can we cut to the chase?'

'The chase is part of the fun,' Lang said.

'It isn't a foxhunt,' Hawkes said, his voice dripping in condescension.

'More than you think,' Lang said, soft enough to keep the others from hearing. He moved toward Hawkes.

'May I freshen your drink?'

'I'm sure it is fresh enough,' the painter said. 'I believe the devil is in the cocktails, Mr Lang.'

'First,' Carly said, 'I want to introduce Nadia Gravenstein. 'She is an artist, agent, curator and friend and supporter of the arts. It is only appropriate on an evening honoring and memorializing Frank Wiley, that we show you what would likely have been the most important exhibition of his life.'

Carly nodded toward Nadia.

Someone said, 'Oh, Christ.'

'The drinks are still on us,' Nadia said, moving toward the row of easels. 'Frank Wiley loved North Beach. More than most other writers and artists who lived here and took their inspiration from this village, Frank was completely faithful to it. His early work captured the stores and restaurants and banks and most important, its inhabitants, chronicling lovingly its blessedly slow evolution.'

There was a rustling that reflected more impatience than boredom. It wasn't what Nadia intended, but what Carly wanted. More to drink. Growing impatience. Nadia was a perfect catalyst.

'Many North Beach inhabitants – passing through or permanent – have achieved greater glory. There are indeed still living legends. The photographs we are about to see are remarkable in many ways. They are very different from Frank's usual work. They are indeed revealing in ways that perhaps frightened even him. It took him until now to put together an exhibition and book in collaboration with the late Whitney Warfield. We do not yet know if the proximity of their deaths is significant, yet the coincidence cannot go unnoticed.'

Thanh arrived from nowhere, it seemed, to take orders for drinks. Lang noticed William Blake, shadowed in a dark corner. With him was an immense bearded man whom Lang didn't know. Rose had joined Stern at the back room entrance. Stern looked disgruntled and Rose amused. Gratelli had taken a seat beside Agnes DeWitt, who was sipping something that looked like a Manhattan.

'These are portraits of several North Beach artists and poets who allowed themselves to be vulnerable. These are photographs from their younger days, perhaps when the subjects were more hopeful, less judgmental, and certainly more vulnerable.'

Nadia pulled off the first cover. It was a naked bearded man, eyes looking back at the lens with humor and wit and perhaps some flirtation.

'It wasn't necessarily out of fearlessness that artists like Allen Ginsberg would allow themselves to be photographed naked. There may have been a form of exhibitionism involved, but I would like to think of it as transparency, which I propose is the true meaning of freedom. We hide nothing.

'Others,' Nadia said, pulling the cover off another photograph and hearing a gasp, 'may have experienced that feeling at the moment, at the height of the Beat and Hippie movements. It was a lack of hypocrisy then and a desire for acceptance of the exposed, beautiful uniqueness of each member of creation.'

Lili D. Young looked away, then looked back with, as those close to her could see, determination.

Nadia went on, pulling covers off subjects, some of them in the room, some merely from the era and now gone.

When she reached the last photograph, Nadia spoke again. 'Others have been consumed by the times, or the route their lives have taken, regretting, it seems, their openness, their spontaneous honesty.'

However, Nadia did not pull off the last cover.

'I think that Carly wants to begin the discussion of the missing manuscript and the four murders that appear to be connected to Frank Wiley's and Whitney Warfield's work.'

'You forgot to uncover the last photograph,' the newspaper publisher, Brozynski, shouted.

'I didn't forget,' Nadia said. 'It's a surprise. Drink up.'

It was Carly's turn. She could feel the anxiety settling in her stomach. She grabbed a glass of wine. She had held off until now. She replaced Nadia in the front of the room. She saw three uniformed police slip into the room and settle against the back walls, near the door.

There were six cops in the room. It was up to her now.

# Thirty-Four

Lang figured that most had imbibed more than they might during the relatively short time they were there. Thanh kept score and reported to Lang that even the frail and lovely Agnes DeWitt had consumed at least two drinks. Sumaoang, who professed a bottled water discipline, had three Anchor Steams and two glasses of vodka. He had either made this a special occasion or he had fallen off the wagon. Hawkes had consumed three Cosmopolitans, and his tablemate, Brozynski, several double Scotches.

Marlene Berensen sat with Elena Warfield. Marlene, like the newspaper publisher, had more than a couple of Scotches. Elena was content with a glass of red wine. Malone was a Scotch drinker as well. Lili D. Young nursed a glass of white wine and McFarland drank two vodka tonics. There was only one abstaining. Ralph Chiu had a Coke.

Carly looked confident in front of the group. She spoke without notes.

'Here's what happened on the night of the murder of Whitney Warfield. At two thirty a.m., Richard Sumaoang received a call from Mickey Warfield. It lasted for three minutes. Richard Sumaoang immediately called Nathan Malone. What was their conversation about? We'll get to that. Sumaoang, after a short conversation, again called Mickey Warfield.

'Hold on to that thought. Flashback. Three days earlier, Mickey Warfield called Richard Sumaoang, Nathan Malone, Ralph Chiu, Supervisor Samuel McFarland, Lili D. Young, Agnes DeWitt, Frank Wiley, Bart Brozynski and Marshall Hawkes. There were calls to Marlene Berensen too, but they were many and often.

'What was the nature of these calls? Mickey was a busy guy. So, let's move from phone calls to bank withdrawals.

'During the three days between those calls and the early-morning death of Whitney Warfield, each person I mentioned, with the exception of Lili D. Young and Whitney's wife, Elena, withdrew significant money from their accounts, usually $10,000. Deposits totaling nearly $70,000 were deposited in various accounts of Mickey Warfield.

'So what do we make of that?'

Carly waited. She looked at each one of them. She stopped in front of Sumaoang.

'Noah said you always had that phone right there in front of you, where it is now. He said that you were here every night, a real regular. You . . .'

'Who doesn't have a cellphone, lady?'

'The money,' she continued. 'How is it that each of you withdrew a significant amount of money at about the same time? You all agree to pay him to kill his father?'

'I don't have to stay here,' Sumaoang said, standing up. He headed for the door. Stern stood in front of it. 'Finish your drink. It's only polite.'

'How can you keep me here?'

'We can keep you downtown,' Rose said. 'Murder, tsk, tsk.' Rose shook his head.

'I didn't kill anybody. Lana picked me up at the bar right after closing. You know how it is around here. Two o'clock and it's everybody out on the street whether you've finished drinking or not. When was Warfield killed? Later, right?'

'Go back to your seat,' Stern said. 'Not closing time here.'

'I wouldn't have done it, couldn't have done it,' Sumaoang said as he went back to his table.

Carly shrugged. 'What was the money for if it wasn't to hire a hit man . . . or woman?'

'No one wanted to kill him, we . . .' Marlene Berensen tried to say before she was told to shut up by Supervisor McFarland.

'This is ridiculous,' the supervisor said. 'This has gone on long enough. We want a lawyer. I don't know who you think you are . . .'

'You can leave,' Lang said, moving toward McFarland. 'Just give me a second to chat with the reporters at the bar. You can give an interview. You like talking to the press?'

McFarland sat down.

'So,' Carly said, undaunted, 'Sumaoang's first call went to Mickey Warfield. Mickey knew his father's office best. The computer, the manuscript, all the CDs, notes, etc. – where they were and how to get them. The idea was that Mickey was to get all of this while his father was here at Alighieri's. And for that Mickey would get paid the big bucks. And, why shouldn't he? He had been cut out of the will, hadn't he?'

Carly moved closer to Sumaoang.

'You were busy with the phone. Around two thirty, you received a call from young Mickey and you immediately called Nathan Malone. What was that all about?'

'None of your business. You're nobody. I don't have to answer you.'

'Police may ask the same questions later, but for now,' Carly continued, 'let me guess, there was a problem locating all the material. Maybe the manuscript was somewhere else in the house. Whatever it was, I'm guessing Mickey needed more time and he was afraid his father would get home before he could complete his task. How does that sound?'

No answer.

Carly moved toward Nathan Malone.

'You were called in to talk with Whitney,' she said to Malone. 'You had time to get from Hill Street. Thirty minutes until closing and then Whitney argued with William Blake outside the bar for maybe fifteen more minutes. Who else could keep Whitney busy talking for two hours than his old writer-competitor friend? What did you talk about? Did you argue about who history would judge the better writer? The most profound?'

'Because you say it doesn't make it true, Carly,' Malone said in a voice drenched with amusement.'

'What's true? That's a fine question,' Carly said. 'There was a flurry of phone calls to each of you and a number of calls among you that were exceptional – that is to say, calls you would not normally make.

We have a witness connecting a private investigator to Mickey Warfield and to you, Mr Chiu. So far, no conjecture. All facts. We have other homicides. Poor Mickey was killed. The private eye died trying to kill an investigation. A lovely Chinese woman was killed. These are all facts and all related one way or another to a list provided by an outside party who learned that Whitney was planning to expose some deep secret.'

'You forgot Frank Wiley, Ms Paladino,' Nathan Malone said.

'I haven't forgotten. We'll get to that in time. Unless, of course, you have something you want to say.'

'No, not at all. Just wondering why you didn't include him in your list of facts. Many of us just attended his services. You were there too, I believe.'

'In time. Meanwhile, thank you for getting us back to the facts. The facts suggest a conspiracy to commit murder involving everyone who received a phone call and withdrew money. Simple.'

'If you really had anything,' McFarland said, 'the police would be asking the questions. This is a farce. A complete farce.'

Inspector Gratelli walked up, stopping a few feet from Carly.

'Let me remind you that there is a vast difference in the sentencing of a person convicted of a conspiracy to commit theft and a conspiracy to commit murder. Just thought you all might want to think about that.'

'Are you supporting all this?' McFarland asked. 'It's outrageous and I intend to investigate the behavior of the police in this matter, particularly you, Inspector.'

'You withdrew money and almost immediately went on a vacation, getting as far away from the city as fast as you could.' Gratelli stopped, thought a moment. 'As far away as you could.' Gratelli spoke softly as he often did, without drama, dryly. But he made his point. 'I would think you, of all people, might be more appreciative of this relatively private approach. We can certainly do this in a more public way.'

That seemed to settle McFarland's threats. There was silence. Carly allowed it to go on for a while. People were no doubt evaluating their own personal situation and the risk involved. It was what Carly wanted, needed. She had no proof, only a series of suspicious behaviors and speculation.

'No?' Carly finally asked the group. 'Everyone want to stay on the list of murder suspects? OK, let's talk about the hotel business. Mr Chiu, in addition to your other investments — massage parlors, for example — you have a thriving real estate business. You own more of North Beach than you do of Chinatown and you own the land for the hotel that Mr McFarland pretends he doesn't want built here. Is that right?'

'That's right,' Bart Brozynski said, his booming voice echoing in the room. 'But that secret was already out of the bag. We did a story.'

'But Whitney Warfield presented a problem. Not only did he not want the hotel to be built, he was prepared to make a big deal about the highly respected Mr Chiu's financial interest in sex trafficking, which would have presented one more nail in the hotel's coffin. Though scandal rarely keeps a politician from being re-elected in San Francisco, McFarland, already in trouble, didn't need the added baggage.'

Brozynski laughed. 'Breaking news. Damn, I wish we weren't a weekly.'

'None of this is true,' McFarland said. Chiu remained quiet.

'This is why Angel LeGard had to die. Because she could testify about Mr Chiu's involvement and his other businesses.'

'I beg your pardon,' Ralph Chiu said, standing. 'We all know that Miss LeGard was a reluctant false alibi for Mr Mickey Warfield for the night of his father's death, and that she was changing her mind. It had nothing to do with this so-called sex traffic. Isn't that true, Mr Lang?'

Carly moved forward to keep the focus. 'We'll have more to say about that, Mr Chiu. Perhaps you know what's coming.'

She moved toward Lili D. Young.

'You made no withdrawals,' Carly said. 'Are you the only one left out of this cozy little group?'

The artist seemed to implode. She was silent, unreachable.

'You did get a call from Mr Sumaoang, didn't you?'

She didn't answer.

'We've got the records.'

'Be quiet, Lili,' Sumaoang said. 'Let's stop playing this game.'

'He called. I told him there was no way I could lay my hands on that kind of money.'

'Ten thousand dollars?'

'Didn't matter, ten, five, one. I don't have it.'

'Weren't you afraid that your secret would be made public?' Carly asked.

'What could I do? Can't get blood out of a turnip.'

'Richard,' Carly said in not quite a shout. 'The money. We've got you on the money trail.' Carly turned to Marlene Berensen. 'Ms Berensen, you got a call too.'

'I talked with Richard about Mickey needing some money. That's all.

Richard was trying to help him and I agreed to chip in. It was a loan. Richard was being kind.'

'I think it may be too late to paint Richard as a saint,' Carly said. 'Blood out of a turnip and all that.'

Carly walked by Elena and Marshall Hawkes to get to Bart Brozynski.

'You paid?' she said, surprise in her voice.

Brozynski shrugged.

'I thought you said you didn't have any secrets,' Carly asked. 'What would you want to hide? You revel in being controversial.'

Brozynski smiled. He was smart enough to know he wasn't required to answer.

'Corruption of a newspaper devoted to exposing corruption?' Carly continued.

'No. I have reasons. That's all I'll say.'

McFarland stood up. 'If we all just get up and leave, all at once, all of us, what could they do?'

'This isn't going away,' Gratelli said. 'We're just trying to sort out the thieves from the murderers.'

The room went so silent, you could hear the soft music and low grumbling playing out in the bar area.

'I have a feeling there will be a fire sale on the truth very soon,' Thanh said.

Serving drinks was now a distraction. Thanh, with nothing to do, watched in awe as Carly conducted a mass interrogation.

'She's good,' Thanh said to Lang.

'She is.'

Lang had to give her immense credit. Carly Paladino may not have had much experience with the nitty-gritty of the streets, but she knew how to run a meeting. It wasn't all improvisation either. She had already separated the murderers from the thieves, but she knew she couldn't prove it. She needed witnesses and while they were all in this room, could she get enough of them to incriminate each other? It was pretty amazing. This wasn't a couple of cops interrogating a suspect in a small room with a one-way mirror. This was a group interrogation by one person designed to get a few of them to turn on the others.

'Murderer or thief, which are you?' Carly said, looking around the room.

'This is ridiculous,' McFarland said. 'Even if you had something here, none of this would hold up in court.'

'Wanna go to court?' Carly asked the room, then targeted her gaze. 'Marlene, you want to go to court? Agnes?'

Agnes DeWitt laughed. 'Perhaps they can put me away for life.'

'I thought you told me you wished you had something to hide?' Lang asked.

'Oh, it wasn't about me,' she said. 'It was about the whole idea of that nasty book. It not only focused on perhaps brief lapses of judgment in an otherwise creative career of many of these fine folks, but he seemed to want to destroy this wonderful place called North Beach and its rich, culture-changing history. I don't know why Whitney had to do that. It was as if he was destroying himself. He was going to die and he was going to take all the memories and dreams with him.'

'You read the manuscript?' Carly asked.

'No, we talked though. He would come by and we would talk. He said I was too timid.' She laughed. 'Ten thousand to me is a significant amount of money, but it's quite unlikely I'll outlive my modest resources.'

The room seemed to grow calm. A strange perspective had been given, Lang thought. Is it possible to buy off ugliness?

'Ms DeWitt,' Carly said, 'by stealing the manuscript and all its copies, you are only delaying things. The only way to make sure it never sees the light is to destroy its creator as well. Did you see the inevitability?'

'I would if the embattled Mr Warfield was twenty-five. He was not. It took him years to write this. He hadn't time left. He had been given his death sentence.'

'How is that?' Carly asked.

'Cancer, young lady. In the blood, in the brain. He told me so. Even if he had lived many months more, he would not have had the strength, or the clarity probably, to recreate it. His impending death was noted in the book.'

Quiet again.

Carly continued. 'But he didn't die as nature chose. He died because someone else decided that. And the killer has, in fact, confessed.' She waited. She looked around the room, milking it a bit. 'Mr Malone, when you told me you killed a man, you led me to believe that it was someone deep in your past. It wasn't. It was Whitney Warfield. You told him you were going to kill him. That's why he ran. That's why he was stabbed in the back of the neck. He was trying to get away.'

'Go on, Ms Paladino,' Malone said, sipping his Scotch. 'This is quite amusing. I have to hear it.'

'Mr Sumaoang called you from the bar, saying that Warfield was leaving, going home, and that his son, Mickey, needed more time to make sure he got everything. You knew or Sumaoang knew Whitney's routine – and I'll repeat what I said earlier – you arrived and waited for him in Washington Square Park, where he would cut across on his way to his home up Russian Hill. The idea was that you'd engage him in discussion and slow him down until Mickey could complete his task.'

'I was home asleep. I'm not up late. My wife will attest to that.'

'Your wife, Mr Malone, is an alcoholic. She would have been passed out, not at all likely to awaken when you slipped out of the house. You did intercept Whitney. It wasn't difficult to engage him in conversation. He had already been arguing. He was drunk and the two of you were more rivals than friends.'

'We were probably neither,' Malone said.

'Oh, you were. You spent hours telling me how the two of you tried to out-macho each other. And that was it, wasn't it? He somehow impugned your manliness and your ability as a writer to write about the real world. It was Whitney who had killed someone and he lorded it over you as a very special experience yielding a very special under-standing. And, quite symbolically, you killed him with his own pen. Very poetic. Much like your work.'

'Very fanciful, Ms Paladino. I like it. It's almost believable.' Malone smiled. 'And how might I have killed Mr Wiley, the Chinese girl and the private eye? I went on a spree, is that it? After all these years I went on a psychotic spree.' He laughed.

There was a low-level twittering of laughter in the room.

# Thirty-Five

'You ask the right question at the right time,' Carly said. 'You, Mr Malone, killed Whitney Warfield and no one else. You didn't need to kill anyone else. It was only Whitney who threatened you and no one else's death benefited you in any way. You and Whitney were rivals and you won.'

'Why on earth would I tell you I killed someone?' Malone asked.

'You had to tell somebody. What good is having achieved something so important and no one in the world would know it? So, you and Richard Sumaoang conspired to kill Whitney Warfield.'

'I had nothing to do with Whitney's death,' Sumaoang said, standing. 'I just wanted them to talk to give Mickey time to collect the manuscript and any notes. It wasn't even a crime. Whitney was stealing from us. Our lives. Our private moments. We were merely taking back what was rightfully ours.'

'Thank you,' Carly said. 'You can discuss that with the police.'

'You idiot,' Malone said to Sumaoang.

Carly turned to Lang. 'You want to talk about who killed Ms LeGard, Mr Lang?'

'I can,' Lang said, with a mix of surprise and fear. This hadn't been part of the plan. But he did know this part best. And it did involve him . . . deeply.

'Because Mickey's whereabouts were questionable the night his father was killed, he knew he was in trouble. One, he would be a serious suspect because they didn't get along. Two, he had a specific motive because he wasn't in his father's will. Three, and the biggest problem of all, he had no alibi on the night his father was killed. The reason he had no alibi is that he was busy committing his own crime, stealing his father's book. Mickey's girlfriend, Angel LeGard, initially agreed to lie for him, to say that he was with her the entire evening.'

Lang looked around the room. He let his gaze stop at Ralph Chiu who was dutifully fulfilling the stereotype as inscrutable.

'Angel worked for you, didn't she, Mr Chiu.'

'No, I don't believe so. I have so many enterprises that it might be possible, I suppose, but . . .'

'You knew her, didn't you?' Lang asked.

'I have made her acquaintance.'

'For some reason – and I know this because she told me – she changed her mind about testifying for Mickey should he be arrested.'

'So Mickey killed her?' Mr Chiu said. He shrugged.

'Well, I thought so. But she also told me that she was tired of keeping secrets, that she had something more important to tell me.'

'And she told you what?' Mr Chiu asked.

'She died between the knowing and the telling,' Lang said.

'How unfortunate.'

'The point is, what did she know and how did she know it?' Lang asked.

Chiu looked at Lang, but gave no clue about what he was thinking.

'She knew what she knew because of what Mickey told her during the many intimate moments they had together. About your business. Where and how you get your girls and how you keep them.'

'What is it that you have then besides conjecture? Have you told us who killed the lovely Ms LeGard?'

'In a way, it doesn't matter. If it was Mickey, he's dead. If it was Markham, he's dead. I doubt if it was Mr Malone. But he's going down for Warfield's death. Of course, it could be you, couldn't it? If that were the case you would have had it done. We'll just have to wait and see.'

The truth was, Carly wasn't hired in the first place to find out who killed Angel or Mickey – or Markham for that matter.

Mr Chiu shut his eyes slowly and opened them just as slowly. He looked away.

The businessman's arrogance got to Lang.

'A down-and-out private investigator named Scotty Markham came to you after Mickey went missing,' Lang said.

'That's what you say,' Mr Chiu said.

'I have a witness,' Lang said. 'He stormed out of your office. I thought it was Mickey who hired Scotty Markham to run me off. But Scotty was working for you, wasn't he? I don't know if even the police know that Markham was a great deal more deadly than anyone who knew him casually might imagine. He was a Navy Seal, trained in the art of . . .'

'This is all a mishmash,' McFarland said. 'You're throwing crap against the wall just to see what sticks.'

'What sticks is that Angel LeGard, who may have been on your unofficial payroll, Mr Chiu, was killed expertly and coldly. A hand over the mouth and an ice pick directly into a vital organ. After LeGard's death, which you all hoped could be pinned on me, there was a problem with Mickey. He had a naturally loose mouth and it probably really pissed him off that you had his girl killed. Mickey was found with his neck broken in an abandoned building in Dog Patch. Not many people know how to break another man's neck. It would have to be a pro.'

There was quiet in the room, but Lang knew he had, in fact, only thrown suspicion at the wall, as the man said. Chiu was practiced in the art of keeping a significant distance between deed doer and himself. The connection between Markham and Chiu was tenuous at best. Even the notion that a traditional Tong member engaged in questionable activities would use a white guy as an enforcer stretched credulity.

Gratelli cut across the back of the room to talk with Rose and Stern. Lang could see them nodding their understanding.

'Mr McFarland,' Carly said, stepping in. 'You have anything to say about your business partner, Mr Chiu?'

McFarland simmered.

Carly picked up on his anger. 'So, the publisher of the *Fog City Voice* is here, ready to do an investigative piece on Mr Chiu and the murders and the girls and the hotel and your involvement in the hotel, not to mention that you joined a conspiracy to steal a manuscript that was, in fact, involved in another murder – Whitney Warfield's. You're all right with all this?'

'Chiu is going to walk,' Lang whispered to Carly.

'What can we do? We signed on to prove William Blake didn't kill Whitney Warfield.' As she said it, Stern was asking Malone to stand up.

'The rest of you,' Rose said, 'will need to stop down to your friendly Thomas J. Cahill Justice Center on Bryant Street. Your taxpayer money paid for it, it's time you paid it a visit. All of you.'

Carly went to Gratelli.

'We need for Marshall Hawkes to stay behind,' Carly said.

Gratelli gave her a puzzled look.

'We have a photograph to unveil.'

Under the direction of Rose and Stern and with the help of uniformed policemen, the participants were guided to waiting vans. It wasn't easy. There were protests, threats and demands. Cellphones clicked open and there were shouts of 'I can't hear you', presumably to some too soft-talking attorneys. Lang figured Lili D. Young and Elena Warfield would be questioned and released. Those that paid might be asked to appear before a judge on a date yet to be determined. That would be Bart Brozynski, Agnes DeWitt, Marlene Berensen and the outraged Supervisor McFarland. Ralph Chiu might have a tougher time, but beyond the contribution to the conspiracy to commit theft, evidence was thin. Nathan Malone and possibly Richard Sumaoang could be held and arraigned the next day. Whether Sumaoang was part of the murder was something the police and the DA would have to figure out.

Carly talked briefly with Anselmo and William Blake before they slipped out the back door. When the crowd was gone and the back room again closed off, it was only the four of them. They were seated at a table.

Lang and Gratelli sat on one side, their backs against the row of photographs, particularly the one that had yet to be uncovered. Carly and Marshall Hawkes sat on the other side. The place seemed hollow and haunted. A little barroom noise crept in through the cracks in the door.

'Marshall,' Carly said. 'We know you replaced the photograph of you that Frank Wiley had intended to show and put in the book.'

Hawkes looked beyond Lang and Gratelli.

'You found the original?' he asked. He stood, as stiff-backed as before.

'We know,' Carly continued, without directly answering his question. 'Why?'

He closed his eyes, kept them that way. His hand remained folded on the table. Finally his eyes opened and he spoke slowly.

'How could I, after all these years of being who I am? I am not that person. That person, the woman he photographed all those years ago, is someone else. She didn't paint these paintings. She didn't write those articles. She had nothing to do with my work being in the finest private collections or in the best museums. She had nothing to do with any of that.'

'So, you couldn't allow the world to see that you are a woman, so you killed him.'

Hawkes emitted a short, sad laugh.

'I was confused then. I had just arrived in San Francisco. I had cross-dressed most of my adolescent years and people just assumed I was a boy – a slightly effeminate boy, yes, but in New York, San Francisco, this wasn't a problem. Anselmo knew. I used to pose for him in New York, as a young woman, then later as the boy I wanted to become and eventually had to become. I continued to pose for Anselmo because the way he painted, my identity would not be exposed. And one day Wiley came in unannounced. He saw. It was a crisis for me. The three of us talked. We did some drugs. Wiley wanted to photograph me. There was money and ego and perhaps a little blackmail, along with promises that I would be the one to determine when or if the photograph was ever to be released. He was reneging on his agreement.'

'So you killed him,' Gratelli said.

'No. Yes. It wasn't murder. I didn't intend for him to die. I just wanted my photograph back. We argued. We . . . struggled. He held on to the frame. The only thing close was this big, old camera and I grabbed it and swung it at him. It hit him in the head and I left, thinking I had just knocked him out. Apparently,' Hawkes said, head held high, eyebrows arching, a deep frown on his thin lips, 'I killed him and in my haste to exit unencumbered I struck you, Ms Paladino. I am sorry.'

'We're going to have to go now,' Gratelli said, standing.

'With all the inequities in the world, all the lies, especially those we know so little of, how much does this little bit of truth matter?' Hawkes asks. 'How does it look for me?' Hawkes's haughtiness remained, but it was drenched in weariness.

'In the end, that's up to the DA. The problem is that Frank Wiley's death occurred during and as a result of another crime. Instead of involuntary murder, this becomes felony murder.'

'Oh, God,' Hawkes said, emitting a strange laugh. 'I was stealing my own image.' He shook his head and stood slowly. The ordeal made him weak. 'The world is such a strange place.'

As they approached the door, Hawkes seemed to lose what little strength he had. He swooned. Lang caught him.

'Pepe,' Hawkes said.

'Pepe?' Carly asked.

'His dog,' Lang said.

'I have no one to care for him.'

# Thirty-Six

'I really don't care for God,' Brinkman said to Lang when the younger man came into the office the morning after the arrests.

'Why is that?' Lang asked absently.

'He tries to be all things to all people.'

Lang looked up at Brinkman, whose face would do well in a poker game.

'Very droll. I'll remember that in any future dealings with him.'

'Who's that?' Brinkman asked, looking down at the slender, doe-eyed greyhound.

'Pepe. New guard dog for the office.'

Seeing Brinkman, the fawn-colored dog with a white face and chest backed up behind Lang.

'Trying to replace me? Won't work. I'm tougher than the dog.'

'You are scarier. I'll give you that.'

'What happened last night?'

'A number of them will be arrested for conspiracy to commit theft or whatever the police call it. Sumaoang may be in worse trouble. But it looks like Malone did the dirty deed on Warfield.'

'The others?'

'Related to Mr Chiu probably. The police will be investigating that for years. It wasn't exactly ". . . Chinatown, Jake", but the same rules may apply. Things tend to go unsolved there. We didn't help by eliminating Scotty Markham. He was the connection to Chiu.'

'Why did they do in Wiley?' Brinkman asked, reaching down to pet the shy dog.

'Looks as if poor Marshall Hawkes killed Frank Wiley. That's a sad case. In the end though, Carly's client is cleared. That's what we were hired to do.'

Lang went to the window to gather some light to read his watch. It was ten. He looked out to see Thanh parking his motorcycle, taking off his helmet and crossing the street to the office, shaking out his dark hair as he went. For Hawkes, hiding the secret was his undoing, Lang thought. For Thanh it was different. He wore his secret on the outside, reveled in it. He was comfortable with whatever gender he felt he was whenever he felt it.

Carly came to the office, but didn't stay long. She wanted to talk with Gratelli about various aspects of the cases. She also wanted to tell him that, for what it was worth, she wasn't going to press charges against Hawkes. She wanted to tie up what loose ends she could and take a week or so off, go up to Sonoma County. Relax.

'Hawkes's dog?' Carly asked Lang when she saw the greyhound.

'Pepe. His only friend, I think. Probably for both of them.'

'Where's he going to stay?'

'Haven't worked that out yet. Maybe we could keep him here. Rename our agency. Greyhound Investigations.'

'Sounds like we're bus inspectors.'

'OK, I'm working on it,' Lang said, smiling. 'I'd take him home but since he was trained to chase small furry creatures for a living, I'm a little concerned about Buddha.'

'You are looking at me with some expectation on your face.'

'Couldn't you use a room-mate?'

She shrugged. She hadn't thought about it. And it wasn't like her to make sudden, rash decisions, except when it came to such things as careers and relationships.

'Unless, of course, you are already sharing your apartment with someone.'

Her smile said, 'You're getting absolutely nothing out of me.'

'Carly and Pepe. Has a nice sound to it. You could go running together. I'm sure he knows how to run.'

'Give it up, Noah.'

'Just thinking out loud.'

'Believe me, you don't want to do that,' Carly said.

'What's going on in here?' Thanh asked. He was in an androgynous mood, judging by the V-neck cashmere sweater, tight jeans and a diamond in each ear.

'Carly may take Pepe.'

'That's wonderful,' Thanh said before he saw the expression on Carly's face. 'Then again, one person's wonderful is . . .'

'We'll figure something out,' she said.

And Lang knew this was the first step into giving in entirely.

'Who's Pepe?' Thanh asked. The dog peeked around the corner. 'Oh.'

Carly had mixed feelings about meeting William Blake again. This time, though, it was in a public place and Anselmo Ruiz was going to be with him. They met at Café Puccini on Columbus. The day was at the turning point. The sun was nearly gone, but the night hadn't arrived. The neon, the lights inside the stores, the flashing lights of automobiles and buses were faint, without contrast to the dusky evening. There was no hurry.

They sat outside at a table on the sidewalk as pedestrians paraded by with dogs and bags. Some were natives and some of those were local characters. Some were merely on their way home after a day in the financial district, picking up something at Molinari's for dinner. Others, and they were easily identified, were taking in the sights of 'Little Italy', as some visitors erroneously called the Italian enclave of North Beach.

Carly and Anselmo had glasses of the house wine. Blake had an espresso.

'This was Anselmo's idea,' William Blake said, grinning.

'It was,' said the large bearded old painter. 'I wanted to thank you for going soft on Marshall. Troubled soul. There's only so much of the universe you can control.' He looked out over the streets. 'We want to keep this the same, the way we remember it, or perhaps the way we want to remember it, but it changes. We can only slow it down.'

'Why was Marshall so intent on being male?'

'When Marshall started out, males had it made, didn't they? Women didn't go on the road and write about it. They didn't write challenging poems society thought were obscene or create images that shocked the public. Men were the heroes, not just in comic books, but also in liter-ature, in public figures. Marshall wanted to be one of the boys and yet this troubled soul could not relate to anyone or anything. The more you have to control, the smaller your world becomes. No other way to manage it.'

'So sad.'

'Just for you to know,' Anselmo said, 'Mickey was Hawkes's kid too. The lovely Whitney Warfield – in New York – raped her. He regretted it. She refused an abortion, but wanted nothing to do with the child. Whitney brought her out here. I think she decided she'd never be vulnerable again.'

For Carly, it seemed as if the world went silent. In a moment she felt a hand on hers.

'Thank you for helping me out of my predicament,' William said.

'Look at Sweet William,' Anselmo said. 'He grows old, but oh so slowly.'

'It's speeding up. Every minute passes more quickly than the last.'

'It does, it does.' Anselmo laughed. His body shook and Carly wondered if he might not start an earthquake. 'You have it, William. You know. But you are free again.'

'Shame about the deaths.'

'I know. I feel bad we couldn't have brought this thing to a close earlier.' Carly said.

'Being the self-centered Narcissus that I am, at least I have my life back and I won't forget you for that.'

'Perhaps you'll settle down before too much longer,' Anselmo said, looking from William to Carly. Neither returned his glances. 'And perhaps, Carly, you will sit for a painting sometime soon?'

McKinney's was one of those places that offered escape to workingmen wanting to escape domesticity without much risk. No strippers, no gambling. Just listen to some rock 'n' roll and drift back to your youth when the world held some promise. Some would call the place shoddy, some merely unpretentious. What light there was came from a bulb over the pool table, the television at the end of the bar, and the beer signs. There were hundreds of these bars around town – all pretty much the same.

Other than the fact that he wasn't a regular, Lang, in his jeans and sweatshirt and baseball cap, didn't stand out. The bartender, a heavy-set man hovering somewhere between a hard forty and a soft fifty, came up. Though Lang preferred something a little more complex, he ordered a Budweiser. He wanted to be one of the guys.

'Hey, Marty, while you got your hand in the fridge, get me one too,' a guy at the pool table yelled out.

When the guy came back with his beer, Lang told him that he stopped by to pick up Scotty's package. The bartender gave him the 'Who in the hell are you?' look.

'You know our friend is dead, right?'

'Heard that,' the bartender said.

'He gave you a package. He give you instructions about the package?'

The bartender maintained an appraising attitude.

'Maybe not,' Lang said. 'He always puts things off. He probably hadn't got around to it.'

'What's your interest?' the bartender asked.

'Just doing a favor for a friend,' Lang said.

'What's that?'

'I'm supposed to deliver the package to someone. Scotty said that if anything ever happened to him, I should get the box from you.'

'How do you know Scotty?' the bartender asked.

Lang took out his wallet, showed him his PI license.

'Partners in crime,' Lang said.

'He never talked about you.'

'I never talked about him. Maybe I got the wrong guy. You Marty?'

The bartender nodded.

'I think the least we can do is follow Scotty's wishes, don't you, Marty?'

'I don't know,' the bartender said.

'Scotty's dead. Look inside. There's no gold in there. The stuff's no good to anybody but the person I'm supposed to give it to.'

'I don't . . .'

'Man, it's Scotty's wish.'

Pepe followed her, but stayed a few feet back. Carly put down a bowl of water in the kitchen. This would take some getting used to – having another live being hanging around on a regular basis. And it was a far cry from having Sweet William fixing her a Martini after a hard day. But Pepe's reticence was sweet. It was as if he didn't want to intrude.

'It's OK,' Carly told him. 'We'll go running in the morning.'

There was a half moon. It was perfect. Lang had wrapped the plastic container in a trash bag and brought it out to the back, just beyond the little patio where he enjoyed a late-night drink. With just a touch of light he could see what he was doing and that the neighbors wouldn't. He used the old, rusty spade previous tenants had left behind to dig the hole.

What he was doing, he reminded himself, was concealing evidence. But after reading the manuscript he thought only unnecessary harm could be done by its existence. The sins Warfield exposed, if you could call them sins, were far more venial than mortal – with the exception of one. And with that one notation, the world didn't need its pound of flesh. But that one revelation caused Lang to bury the material rather than destroy it. The unnecessary death of Angel LeGard, who was in fact Hui Zhong Chang, could be linked in an unflattering way with Ralph Chiu. And it was her death that remained unsolved. When the time came, facts could be unearthed.

As he patted down the soft earth, Buddha became visible in the scant light. His eyes gave him away. He appeared to criss-cross the burial ground before slipping away again.

'Was that your way of saying goodbye to Pandora?' Lang asked.